ANTHONY GIANGREGORIO

DEAD WATER

DEAD TERMINAL

OTHER BOOKS IN THE DEADWATER SERIES!

Deadwater / Deadwater: Expanded Edition   Dead Rain / Dead City
Dead Wave/ Dead Harvest / Dead Union   /   Dead Valley
Dead Town/Homeward Bound / Dead Grave / Dead Salvation
Dead Army   / Dead Invasion / Dead Incursion

Other Book Series by the Author

The Dead Rage Series
Dead Rage   Book 1
Blood Rage   Book 2

The Warriors of the Apocalypse Series
Warriors of the Apocalypse: Book 1
Warriors of the Apocalypse: Dark Holocaust Book 2

Copyright © 2021 Anthony Giangregorio
Dead Terminal (Dead Water Series: Book 13)

ISBN Softcover ISBN 13: 978-1-61199-102-4
              ISBN 10: 1611991-021

This book was printed in the United States of America.

Cover art by Jay Moores

A Living Dead Press book

DEAD TERMINAL

ANTHONY GIANGREGORIO

MORE WORKS OF FICTION BY THE AUTHOR
Anthologies Edited by the Author
Book of Horror Volumes 1-2 / Headshots: A Zombie Anthology
Dead History: A Zombie Anthology Volumes 1-2   /   Monster Party
Dead Worlds: Undead Stories Volumes 1-6   /   Tales of Bigfoot
Eternal Night: A Vampire Anthology / Book of the Dead Volumes 1-6
Clowns of Terror: An Evil Anthology   / Rat War: A Horror Anthology
Children of the Dead: A Zombie Anthology / The Book of Horror
Night of the Wolf: A Werewolf Anthology   /   Time of Death
Twisted Fish: An Aquatic Anthology / Superheroes vs. Zombies: A Zombie Anthology
End of Days: An Apocalyptic Anthology Volumes 1-5   /   Horror Carnival
Earth's End: An Apocalyptic Anthology / Emails of the Dead: A Zombie Anthology
Love is Dead: A Zombie Anthology   /   The Book of Cannibals Volumes 1-2
Zombie Erotica: An Undead Anthology About Sex
Tales of the Dead: A Zombie Anthology / Zombie Tales (with Vincenzo Bilof)
Zombies and Fairy Tales: A Zombie Anthology   /   Mutant Apocalypse
House of Terrors: An Anthology of Fear / Zombie Buffet: A Zombie Anthology
An Undead Christmas: A Zombie Anthology
A Very Dead Christmas: A Zombie Anthology
Christmas is Dead: A Zombie Anthology / Dead Christmas: A Zombie Anthology
Christmas is Dead…Again: A Zombie Anthology / Just Before Night (w/ Joe Tonzelli)
Gnomes of the Dead: A Zombie Anthology / Creature Feature: A Monster Anthology
Young Adult Anthologies
Ghostly Tales of Terror / Halloween: Tales of Terror
Kids Books and Young Adult
Zombies Are People Too / The Lonely Zombie   /   Children of the Void
Ten Silly Monkeys Jumping on the Bed / Zombies Are Cool   /   The Haunted Theatre
Ten Silly Monkeys Jumping on the Bed: Coloring Book   /   The Junkyard
The Zombie in the Basement / Only the Young Survive: An Apocalyptic Tale
Novels by the Author
Victory of the Dead: A Zombie Novel / Revolution of the Dead: A Zombie Novel
Deadfreeze: A Zombie Novel / Dead End: A Zombie Novel
Adventures of the Cowl: A Superhero Novel   /   The Monster Under the Bed
Comedy of the Dead: A Zombie Novel / Clan of the Bigfoot /   The Dark
Dead Mourning: A Zombie Novel / Souleater / Road Kill: A Zombie Novel
Rise of the Dead: A Zombie Novel   /   Last Stop   /   Dead Fall: A Zombie Novel
Curse of the Beetle (with Richard Marsh)   /   Kingdom of the Dead: A Zombie Novel
Sunset of the Dead: A Zombie Novel (Sequel to Day of the Dead film)
Visions of the Dead: A Zombie Novel (with Joseph Giangregorio)   / Rats
Human Harvest: Alien Abduction (with Keith Luethke) / The Bottom of the 9th
Short Story Collections by the Author
Dead Tales: Short Stories to Die For / Christmas of the Dead / Dead Things
Dark Places / Dead Offerings: Collected Work (Hardcover)
Editor: Living Dead Press Presents: Spring & Summer Magazines
Opinion
Reviews of the Dead: 25 Zombie Movies to Die For (with Tony Schaab)

Chapter 1

Having made camp for the night, Henry Watson felt a stirring in his sleeping bag, the subtle movement pulling him awake.

His first thought was some kind of animal had gotten in with him, but after the first squeeze of his semi-hard manhood, he knew who it was instantly. He opened his eyes to see nothing but darkness, but as his vision adjusted, a form began to coalesce directly before him.

"Sue," he whispered, the utterance so soft it barely registered within his ears.

She smirked widely, her blonde hair seeming to blow in a wind only she was exposed to. To Henry, the air was still; devoid of any stirrings.

"I thought you were dead," he continued, his tone showing the amazement he was feeling. "I thought I'd lost you forever."

"It was only a dream, silly," she whispered, and leaned forward to kiss him, the familiar smell of her filling Henry's nostrils.

Their lips met, the familiarity of one another enabling the first kiss to flow into the next, until with tongues entwined, they became one.

Lust and passion exploded inside Henry, the need to be close to her chasing any other thoughts of the past from his head. She said her death was a dream, and with her here beside him, he would be damned if he'd waste even a micro-second on debating the issue.

Within moments his clothes were off, the action happening so fast he couldn't recall removing them. Come to think of it, he didn't even remember where he'd bedded down for the night, or where the other people in his group were. Was one of them on watch? Were they laagered down in a safe place?

It all rushed through his head almost instantly, only to be forgotten when Sue reached down and helped him enter her as she sat astride him. The intense feeling of the act sent his head reeling in pleasure, and all other thoughts evaporated.

Before he realized it, their position changed, and suddenly she was below him; he thrust into her repeatedly. Her head was tilted back, her eyes half-closed as she rode the waves of pleasure she was feeling.

As for Henry, he knew he was close to reaching orgasm.

Sensing this, Sue wrapped her legs around him tightly, locking him to her. The rising feeling of pressure became too much, and he exploded inside her, a gritting of his teeth and a single grunt the only giveaway he'd climaxed. He squeezed his eyes closed as he finished, and as a wave of satisfaction came over him, the love he felt for her grew exponentially, until it was as if his heart would explode.

His elbows locked, he remained hovering over her, then he released his arms and settled on top of her, his lips caressing Sue's right ear as he rode the waves of after sex.

Nibbling her ear, Henry lightly bit her earlobe, knowing she always liked that. Only when his teeth gently latched onto it, and gently pulled, instead of getting resistance, the ear peeled off her head as smooth as a ripe banana skin. It hung from his mouth like a sagging wet leaf on a tree in a rainstorm, droplets of blood squirting from the freshly-made hole.

Not understanding, his eyes snapped open. He spit out the ear, the blood from where it had peeled off her head coating his lips bright red. A low moan came from Sue, but Henry had a sinking feeling it was not from pleasure but something else, something terrible.

Pulling backwards, away from her, he gazed down at the woman he loved; only the face he now saw wasn't the one he was used to. Sue's skin was the color of dried parchment, the eyes sunken into the head, the teeth exposed more prominently, the lips pulled back from the mouth. In the corner of one eye, something small and white was wriggling.

She was one of the living dead!

Her milky eyes gazed up at him, her mouth curling into a sneer. "Come on, baby, give me what I need. Come here and kiss me," Sue whispered, then lunged upwards at Henry, her teeth bared, mouth open wide as she lunged for his throat.

Before Henry could react, her teeth sank into his neck, just under his chin. The coldness of her teeth filled him to the bone, but it was only for an instant. She reared her head back, taking a large amount of his throat with her. The hot blood squirted from his neck, saturating the front of his body, while it simultaneously rained down onto Sue's face, who relished the shower with a passion she once showed to Henry when they made love.

Desperate to escape, he tried to push off her, but her legs were still firmly wrapped around his hips, trapping him.

He began to grow weak from blood loss, and though he struggled within her grasp, he was fighting a losing game. Blood filled his mouth, gagging him.

It was just as he began losing consciousness that she pulled him close, her lips touching his right ear, almost caressing the lobe. She said, "Don't fight it, my love. Death is only the beginning."

He didn't understand and there was no time to formulate a reply; to question her curious statement.

Slipping into a dark void, his heart pumped its last, and Henry slumped on top of Sue, not in pleasure after reaching climax, but in the finality of death.

In the small room, deep underground, computer consoles and control banks began to flicker like Christmas lights, their monitors awakening by scrolling unending lines of code across the once-darkened screens. The overhead lights snapped on, bathing the room in white light.

The silence, once formidable, quickly was washed away by the hum of machinery, as the tiny room became alive with activity. At the far end of the room, separate from the computers and what little furniture occupied it, a ten foot round dais began to glow.

Mist began to form on the floor, and within it, sharp flashes of light, similar to lightning bolts, crackled. Inside the mist a miniature storm was brewing, only the dark images of rain clouds missing.

On one of the few desks at the opposite end of the room, stray papers left abandoned began to flutter, some even sliding towards the dais, as if a subtle vacuum had been created.

The hidden machinery within the walls and beneath the floor grew even louder, and on the circular platform the mist became thicker.

The lightning crackled faster, but as this wasn't true lightning, there was no following clap of thunder. The flashing bolts were silent, as if the mist itself muffled it.

Suddenly, an incredibly bright light filled the room, similar to if a small sun had been brought into existence. No sooner did it appear than it was gone, leaving the room once more in only the wash of the overhead fluorescent lights, which now seemed woefully inadequate compared to what had just occurred.

With the disappearance of the flash, so too did the mist die down, most of it seeming to evaporate into the air, though it was actually sucked into the ventilation ducts located on the back wall near the ceiling, which had begun working almost immediately upon the activation of the machinery.

As the mist thinned, to anyone who had been watching, unknowing of the dais' true purpose, there would have been a surprise to see that the platform was no longer empty.

Lying prone and unmoving lay the forms of four adult human beings.

The hidden machinery began winding down until it stopped cycling completely, and when the last wisps of mist were sucked into the vents, that too grew silent.

The computer monitors went dark, the blinking lights slowing down and fading until nothing flickered or moved, with the exception of a few steady lights that remained rhythmic.

All was quiet in the room.

But for one exception.

If anyone had been listening within the small room, and if they concentrated hard enough, they would have detected the slow, steady breathing of the four unconscious humans.

Henry Watson opened his eyes, though he could see nothing.

Like a newborn pup just free of its mother's womb, he was close to blind. But he knew not to panic, hoping and assuming at the same moment, that like the last time he'd experienced the jump through space, it took a few minutes for his body to become accustomed to being whole again. He tried not to think about how his atoms had been torn apart and sent somewhere through the matter transfer system, to then reform someplace new. It was a page out of *Star Trek*, the transporter on the show the best analogy of what he and his friends had experienced.

But to be helpless was a good chance at being dead, and though he could barely see through blurry eyes, he forced himself to sit up, while struggling to clear his vision.

By sheer will alone the darkness began to fade, and shapes became a little clearer. With his Glock drawn, he sat perfectly still, his breathing slow and regular, his ears compensating for what he lacked in vision.

Ever so slowly, the shapes before his eyes became more defined, until he made out the familiar silhouettes of his traveling companions for years lying beside him.

Mary Roberts lay on her side with her eyes closed, her chest rising and falling steadily. There was a puddle of drool near her mouth, signifying just how out of it she was at the moment. But even as he looked at her she began to stir.

Beside Mary was Cindy Jansen, her shoulder-length blonde hair lying limp on her head, as if it could sense its owner was going through some sort of trauma. One eye was already open, the other flickering as she came slowly awake.

Beside Cindy, and directly across from Henry, lay Jimmy Cooper. When Henry locked his gaze on Jimmy's face, he saw that the younger man was also awake.

Jimmy sat up as well, and a sly grin crossed his face, as if to say, "We're alive."

Out of habit, Henry continued his gaze across the dais, as if he expected to see one more companion lying on the floor. But no sooner did he look than he stopped, and as he did so, a familiar ball of grief filled his chest, the wisp of a nightmare tickling the back of his mind. It was only there for a moment, then it was gone, lost in his subconscious. Unknown to Henry, a side effect of the matter transfer was that the people using it would succumb to dreams, sometimes horrible, other times not so much. Unfortunately, Henry had suffered the former.

Still, Henry expected to see Sue Anders, his lover and best friend, sitting there beside Jimmy, her beautiful eyes peering back at him, a generous smile on her lips as always.

But she was gone. Dead. Not even a single finger remained to bury after she was pretty much disintegrated by the explosion of a Russian bomb.

No tears came to his eyes, however, despite his feelings of loss. The reason was simple. He'd shed far too many already when he'd been alone. Whether it was when he was standing guard over the others while they slept, on some lonely hillside in their travels, or back when he'd first lost her, and been showering in the Alaskan redoubt, at the moment, he'd given in to grief as much as he could.

Though there was still a dark pit in his stomach each time he thought of her, he could already feel he was healing. He looked forward to the time that when he thought of her, it would only bring a sense of happiness, as he recalled her smiling face and caring eyes, of the times they'd spent together under the stars talking, or making love, or doing the countless little things a couple would together to pass the time. Things in the relationship they would never have given a moment's thought to, at least not until the other person was gone, and then those tiny things seemed like giants, in wishing that only one more moment in time could be captured by doing them, and sharing with the love of your life.

But those precious moments were over for Henry, but despite his loss, he found that with each passing day he found he was becoming stronger in his resolve to deal with the guilt and grief of his missing partner. Though a week may have seemed like a short time to have recovered so much in the normal world, in a post-apocalyptic world, where death was around each corner, or hiding over a hill, a week could feel like a lifetime, where each day was the potential to be a person's last.

Mary moaned softly, pulling Henry from his grief-stricken reverie and back to reality. His vision now fully focused, he began to study the room with his eyes, wanting to make sure none of them were in danger.

The room was sparse, with only a bank of computers and consoles on one side, a single door on the far end—locked or not was unknown—and another door opposite the other one, also unknown if it was secured or not. There was also another smaller door off to the side as well, which had the look of a broom closet or maybe a supply room.

The room appeared empty of human life, and from his position on the dais, he could see the entire space in full. Only what lay behind the bank of computers was hidden from view. Eyeing the spot warily, and though assuming the room was devoid of anything dangerous, he also knew to assume something without actual facts was a good way to get himself or his friends killed.

Standing on uneasy legs after first getting to a kneeling position, he leaned against the wall for support. Near him, the others were stirring a little more, as they too, came fully awake.

Once more he scanned the room, his hands going to his weapons to ensure they were where they should be. The Glock was in his right hand, a sixteen inch panga on his left hip, a small, hold-out knife in his left boot, and a stainless steel Zippo lighter in his front pocket, filled with precious lighter fluid. The last item had been foraged from the corpse of a dead man, the faded markings on the front cover portraying a pipe fitters' union. Local 546, it said, the number six all about faded to the point it could barely be seen. He was lucky he had fuel for it, the small plastic bottle another scavenged item.

Behind him, as Henry stepped off the dais and into the center of the room, his friends began to chatter softly. The room was warm, and he was still wearing his Anorak. He quickly grew uncomfortable and slid the jacket off, laying it on the floor near the dais.

Out of the corner of his eye Henry saw Jimmy get to his knees, then, after checking his weapons as well, his shotgun, hunting knife and .38 sidearm, Jimmy checked one more piece of equipment, an action that made Mary frown deeply, as she too sat up and scanned her weapons: a matching .38 snub nose similar to Jimmy's and a large hunting knife strapped to her side.

"What are you doing?" Mary asked him, her eyes locked onto him in disproval.

Jimmy looked up, his hand still inside the front of his pants. Slowly, he withdrew it, a sly grin on his face. "Just making sure everything's where it should be."

"Uh-uh," she replied. "What's wrong? Worried it gets smaller each time we use this transfer unit?"

"As if," Jimmy sneered. "If that's true, I haven't gotten any complaints yet." He glanced at Cindy to confirm this. In response, she smiled politely and nodded to Jimmy, who grinned from ear to ear. While Jimmy returned to checking his gear, Cindy turned to Mary so that Jimmy couldn't see her gesture and she used her hand, rocking it back and forth, as if to say, "The sex is okay."

Jimmy was next to step off the dais, and he joined Henry on the main floor. He shrugged out of his heavy jacket, dropping it beside Henry's Anorak, but kept his waterproof windbreaker on, which he'd worn beneath the heavier jacket. "Shit, it's hot in here. You know, old man, I can't say I love the idea of having my atoms sent across the planet like a fucking email."

Mary snickered and couldn't help but say, "If that were true, Jimmy, you'd be Spam mail."

Henry winced when she said it, as did Cindy.

Mary saw their faces and flashed them an apology. "Yes, I know, sorry. The second I said it I knew it wasn't going to be funny."

"Don't give up your day job," Jimmy said wryly. "Whatever that is."

Mary was about to give Jimmy a retort, no doubt a biting one, when Henry cut her off. "All right you two, stop it. All of you shape up and focus. We don't know where we are or if there's gonna be a squad of soldiers about to come charging in here. We need to do a recce and find out what the score is."

Mary stepped off the dais, as did Cindy, both looking fit to fight. Whatever nausea or weakness left over from the jump was fading with each passing second. Both slid out of their heavy jackets and dropped them to the floor.

"We both understand, Henry," Mary said, speaking for Cindy as well. "We're good to go."

Henry nodded, a slight smile creasing his lips. Though the undisputed leader of their little group, he still asked for their input whenever possible, but when the shit hit the fan and there was no time for debates, what he said was law. It had saved their asses more times than not, and even Jimmy, who was willful and argumentative, knew when to shut the hell up and do what he was told.

At the moment, Jimmy was walking around the room, wanting to get the cramps out of his legs. The nausea he'd felt upon waking was all but gone, and the bad headache he had was now only a gentle throbbing, while before it was as if a drum set had been set up behind his eyes with a mad drummer banging away.

Jimmy slowed his pacing to stop before the small door, the one that might lead to a supply room or even a bathroom. Feeling pressure in his bladder, he decided that would be just what the doctor ordered, so with a, "Hey, guys, I wonder what's behind here? A bathroom I hope," he reached for the knob and turned it, pleased to see it was unlocked.

"Wait a second, Jimmy," Henry said quickly, but not fast enough to stop Jimmy from opening the door, as he and the others weren't ready to repel an attack if it was waiting behind the door. "Not yet till we're all set."

But his warning fell on deaf ears as Jimmy pulled open the door simultaneously of Henry's warning.

To Jimmy's disappointment it wasn't a bathroom, or even a janitor's closet, where he could have used a mop bucket for a urinal if nothing else was available. But it wasn't any kind of mundane room at all.

The room was around six feet square, with wires hanging down from the low ceiling, where they were connected to something in the middle of the room. To Jimmy, it looked like some kind of metal canister with wheels on the bottom but with two arms. The entire body was silver, and the first image to come to Jimmy's mind was that of the Tin Man from the Wizard of Oz, only this one had weapons more than limbs for its arms. The left arm looked like a small version of an M-60, while the right arm had some sort of a sci-fi contraption, the tip seeming to glow a soft yellow in the gloom of the room.

Jimmy saw the glowing yellow tip out of the corner of his eye, for his full attention was on the face, or the area where the face should have been.

There was no mouth or nose, merely polished steel, which reflected Jimmy's image back at him. But there were two eyes, or rather, two lenses, which upon first opening the door were dark, but now, as the fluorescent light flicked on overhead, began to glow red.

Jimmy could only stare in amazement as the steel canister slowly rose to a more upright position, the head extending slightly higher, and the center where a waist might be on a human body, which was also jointed, allowed it to swivel back and forth.

Henry and the women couldn't see past Jimmy; he stood in the doorway to the room, his wiry frame more than enough to block the metal droid from view.

"Anything interesting in there?" Cindy asked, walking over to join Jimmy by the doorway.

Jimmy was about to reply when the droid began to emit a loud screeching sound, similar to an alarm. Turning, he began to leap back, not knowing why exactly as the droid hadn't done anything other than screech at him. But something deep down in his gut was telling him that whatever the thing was, it wasn't going to be anything good. Especially not after he'd fought spider sec droids at the last redoubt. Oh no. Nothing good was going to come out of that tin man, and he damn well knew it. As if the droid could read his mind, it rolled out of the room directly behind a retreating Jimmy. Who dropped to the floor and rolled out of the way, as he yelled for the others to look out.

But the others needed no more warning. The instant the alarm went off from the droid, Henry, Mary and Cindy went into action, running for cover, despite not fully understanding what the danger was.

Jimmy was crawling across the floor, his butt in the air, and he didn't stop until he reached a bank of monitors, and much like a human crab, scurried behind them. Slowly peering up and around the monitors, ready to pull his head back if needed, and not wanting to get his face shot off, he looked back at the droid as it emerged from the small room, rolling across the polished tiles on its wheels.

Standing about seven feet tall, its eyes glowing a deep red, the droid took in the room and the four humans within it, scanning the area by using infrared, and seeing the humans as plain as day, despite wherever they were hiding.

"Damn it, Jimmy!" Henry snapped from across the room. "I told you to wait."

The alarm stopped sounding, and in its place, in a loud mechanical voice, the droid said, "Unauthorized personnel. Intruders. Exterminate with extreme prejudice." The yellow light on the tip of its right arm suddenly changed to purple, and before Henry or the others could do more than watch, a brightly-colored beam shot out of the tip and sliced the console Henry was hiding behind in half, the common saying of a hot knife going through butter being apt for this particular situation. The beam missed Henry by mere inches. It struck the wall behind him and seared through the metal plating with a dull hiss, and it was only sheer luck that this had happened. Either that or the droid was playing with him, which seemed unlikely but still a possibility.

Henry could only stare in amazement as the sparking, smoking console, now two pieces, slowly parted before him, hissing with electricity, leaving him completely exposed—not that the console had been any protection to begin with, so it seemed. He shuddered to think what would have happened if he'd been squatting down a few inches to the right a little more.

With his mouth agape, Henry raised himself up, for there was no reason to remain crouched down, and could only stare in horror as the sec droid shifted its aim slightly so that the laser was lined up directly with his chest. It prepared to fire again, this time leaving no room to the chance of missing.

Chapter 2

The tip of the laser seemed to glow even brighter as Henry stared at it, his heart in his throat. There was nowhere to run, nor hide. All he could do was wait to be sliced in half.

He wondered if it would hurt, or if there would be no pain at all. But perhaps as the laser cut him in twain, it would cauterize the wounds, so that he felt everything, remained alive for it all, at least until his brain was sliced like a split melon.

He only had the faintest perception of hearing a shotgun blast, followed by the staccato of an M16, the world around him seeming to stop. Each millisecond he breathed was perhaps his last and he was savoring it all.

But just as suddenly as the world seemed to freeze in time, it began to move again, this time in super-fast motion. The sounds of gunfire snapped him out of his stupor, and he nearly screamed when he felt the air an inch to his left seem to burn, as if the very ozone was cooking.

Both Cindy and Jimmy had fired their weapons simultaneously, their bullets and shotgun pellets doing little to hurt the steel sec droid, but still knocking the machine off-balance, so that its aim was thrown askew, missing Henry by less than the thickness of his thumb.

Henry dropped to the floor and rolled, doing his best to be a moving target as the sec droid began trying to reacquire its target. "Jesus Christ!" he screamed. "What the hell is that thing?"

"Does it matter?" Jimmy snapped as he shot the droid again, then ducked as it fired a fusillade of its armory at him, using its left arm. The heavy rounds stitched across the polished floor, leaving large scars in the finish before finally ending up shooting up another console.

"No, I guess not," Henry muttered as he popped up from behind another console and fired the Glock in a quick double tap. Other than leaving some very small indentations in the droid's armored hull, the 9mm rounds did no damage. "Time to leave, people. Everyone get ready to make a run for the door. I'll keep the bastard distracted."

No one protested. Now wasn't the time for a democracy.

"Get ready," Henry said. "On three." He sucked in a deep breath and let it out, psyching himself up for his next move. "One. Two." He jumped up as he yelled, "Three! Go now!" He began firing his Glock, not caring how many rounds he wasted, only wanting to keep the droid occupied.

Jimmy fired his shotgun while he ran, Cindy and Mary quickly joining him as they raced across the room for the exit.

Henry watched them in his peripheral as he kept firing, yelling all the while. He saw the laser tip glow, and he rolled to the left, a searing beam missing him by inches yet again. He knew his luck was going to run out any second.

"Okay, Henry!" Jimmy yelled from the open door. "Stop fucking around and come on all ready!" To punctuate his words, he began shooting the droid with the shotgun, while Mary put an arm around the doorframe and fired her .38.

Henry didn't need to be told twice, seeing his chance. As the others did their best to distract the droid for him, he turned and dashed for the door. His pack was on the floor, and as he ran past it, he scooped it up without slowing a step. He all but dived head first through the doorway; Jimmy hit the button on the side that sealed off the matter transfer room from the hallway, the sliding door almost catching the heel of Henry's left boot.

Henry used his pack as a cushion as he hit the floor, and was up a moment later, knowing there was no time to lose. Before he could tell the others to move, the center of the door began to glow bright red, starting in a circle that spread out quickly, becoming larger with each tick of the clock. The paint on the door began to crack and peel, the acrid odor of burning paint filling the corridor.

"Shit. It's trying to cut through the fucking door!" Jimmy yelled, declaring the obvious.

Henry only grunted as he turned to look down the corridor, where he could see Cindy taking something off the wall. At her feet was shattered Plexiglass.

"And by the looks of that door, it's probably gonna succeed," Henry said. "That door is thick and metal, it's made for security. It should slow it down for a minute or so."

Mary shifted beside Henry as she ejected the empty shell casings from her .38 and reloaded. "Is that enough time for us to get out of here?"

Henry could only shrug. "I sure hope so."

Suddenly, from within the glowing circle in the center of the door, a slim beam erupted. The laser beam sliced out into the corridor and penetrated the wall across from the door. Immediately, that part of the wall began to smoke and spit flames.

"Time to move," Henry snapped, and began running down the corridor, Mary and Jimmy tight on his heels. Cindy was waiting until they joined her. She held up a large piece of paper, black lines, mostly square-like, covering it.

"Is that what I think it is?" Henry asked.

Cindy nodded. "Sure is. A map of this place."

There was a loud *pop* behind them, and all turned as one to see the hole in the door becoming bigger as molten metal poured onto the floor, to steam and slowly cool.

"Yeah, that's great," Jimmy added, "but where do we go?" He pointed further down the long corridor. "The armory? Motor Pool? Do they even exist here? The exit?"

"Cindy, let me see that," Henry told her, taking the map when she handed it to him. He hated standing there while he searched the map, but to just go off running blindly with no precise destination would be as foolish as staying where they were until the droid escaped its confinement. If they ended up in a dead end, they were quite literally dead.

From the brief skirmish Henry and the others had with the sec droid, it was pretty obvious that conventional weapons wouldn't do it harm. Which made him consider the armory, if this particular redoubt had one. If they could get their hands on some stronger ordinance, such as grenades, frag, HE (high explosive), or even a phosphorous one, they might have a chance of defeating the steel killer.

But if they gained entry into the armory and it didn't have what they needed, they would only end up possibly trapped.

The next option was one that Jimmy suggested. The motor pool. Henry searched the map and quickly found it, along with the armory. Perhaps they could get a vehicle and simply drive away. But once more he had doubts. If there weren't any vehicles in working condition, or if there were vehicles but all were inoperable, then once more they'd be trapped with the droid on their heels.

The exit was the only option. Run like hell for the closest egress from the redoubt and hope they could escape the droid once they were outside. From past experience, he assumed the bunker was underground. But for all he knew they were underwater, similar to the redoubt under a lake in Colorado. Or maybe they were above ground and would come out inside a strip mall. There was no way of knowing where they were at the moment.

Too many choices for sure, but in the end there was truly only one.

They needed to make a dash for the exit and hope they could get outside easily.

"Come on, Henry, make up your damn mind," Jimmy said quickly. "We're running it close to the vest here." The sec droid had burned through most of the door and would be in the hallway in seconds. The odor of burning wires and metal filled the air, tickling the companions' throats and making them want to cough.

Henry hastily folded the map and shoved it into a pocket, and began running for the stairwell. "Outside, it's our best chance of escape," he called over his shoulder while moving. The others didn't need to be prompted and were also on the move, following close behind him.

The corridor grew even thicker with roiling smoke as they sprinted away, the worst of it only coming after they started running. As Henry jogged down the long hallway, memory of studying the map telling him a stairwell was at the end to the right of a dog-eared corner, behind him he heard the heavy clatter as the rest of the door from the matter transfer room collapsed into the corridor.

That meant their metal hunter would be following soon enough.

Henry could only hope there was time to reach the egress three levels up before he and his friends were caught.

Chapter 3

Moving at a fast jog, ever wary of danger from all sides, the four companions made their way through the matter transfer level of the redoubt, before entering a stairwell.

Taking the stairs three at a time, Henry was the first to reach the door leading to the highest floor, where according to the map, would be an egress out of the bunker.

"Okay, I'll go left, you go right," Henry told Jimmy, as he prepared to open the door. There was no time to do a slow recce, speed was all they had at the moment to escape the sec droid.

"What if there's, like, another one of those fuckers waiting for us?" Jimmy offered.

Cindy scoffed from behind the two men as they waited on the stairs. "That's my Jimmy, always the optimist."

"Hey, I'm just stating the obvious. Where there's one killer droid, there's probably more," Jimmy replied.

Brushing off Jimmy, Henry said, "We'll deal with that situation if it happens. It's not like we can change it if it is. All we can do is be as prepared as possible." He locked eyes with Jimmy, so there was no question the younger man was paying attention. "You ready?"

Jimmy nodded in reply, and with an exhaling of breath, Henry pushed open the door and lunged out of the small landing he'd been on, Jimmy right by his side.

Both men rolled and came up in a crouch, Jimmy holding his shotgun, Henry leveling the Glock, his arms out in a classic Weaver stance, one hand supporting the other.

The hallway was empty, a lone security checkpoint standing twelve feet away, looking for all purposes like the security guard had just snuck away for a bathroom break and would return in a minute.

"Clear," Henry called back to the women, who cautiously stepped into the hallway, weapons in hand.

"Looks deserted," Mary said as she studied the hallway and desk.

"Good," Henry said. "Means there's no one to slow us down. Come on, let's find the exit and get the hell out of here."

Off to the right, there was the well-known sound of an elevator chiming its arrival, and a moment later, the door slid open. The bright flash of a laser beam sizzled through the air to strike the wall to the right of the companions.

"Shit!" Jimmy snarled. "The smart fucker took the elevator."

"But how did it find us so fast?" Cindy asked as she began firing her M16 at the droid, while she and the others began running down the corridor in the opposite direction. Bullets ricocheted within the cage of the elevator, the clanging reminding her of the time she'd seen the show *Stomp* when she was a kid, back before the world went to shit. Whether the droid sustained damage from her fire was unknown and she wasn't about to stick around and find out. Her ears rang from the report of the rifle as it bounced off the walls and ceiling. She winced in pain but trudged onward.

Henry glanced upwards at the low, white-painted ceiling. Where the wall met the ceiling, there was a security camera aimed directly at him and the others, its red light flashing repeatedly, signifying it was on. It swiveled slightly as it readjusted, following the group's progress as they moved down the corridor.

"The droid must be patched into the security monitors," Henry said as he fired one round at the camera, destroying it. "From now on, if you see a camera, take it out."

With Henry leading the way, the group dashed down the hallway, the footfalls of their boots sounding loud in the otherwise silent bunker.

As they ran, closed doors appeared on either side of the corridor, and Henry wondered briefly if it was worth slowing their progress to check a few. The doors could lead to their salvation, but also their doom, and the risk was too high, especially if it was the latter option, so he ignored the doors and continued running.

The corridor dog-legged to the left; he rounded the corner, and slowed his pace slightly to make sure the others were close behind, which they were.

Mary was last in line. She rounded the corner, and Henry moved past her to peer around the corner, wanting to see if they still had a tail.

The blast of Jimmy's shotgun made him jump, but as he peered over his shoulder, he quickly saw the reason from the discharge. High on the wall, the remnants of a security camera was sparking as bits of plastic and metal rained down to the floor.

Turning back to the corner, Henry went to his knees before peering around it and quickly found out it was a damn good thing he had.

Smack dab in the center of the corridor, moving at a good pace, was the sec droid. Its internal motion sensors spotted Henry immediately and it fired at him, the left arm shooting bullets as the right arm glowed bright purple and then shot a thin beam.

But the calibration was slightly off, perhaps from one of the companions' bullets having struck something that mattered, and the rounds hit the corner of the corridor a foot above where Henry's head was. Plaster rained down onto his face as he yanked himself back, falling onto his butt.

Jimmy helped him to his feet. "I was gonna ask you if the coast was clear, but I think I already got my answer."

"Cindy, how far are we from an exit?" Henry asked, not responding to Jimmy, as there was no time or point.

She gestured down the long hallway they were standing in. "That way about a hundred and twenty feet or so."

"Then we should be going that way right now," Mary added anxiously, knowing each second wasted was one they might need.

Henry did some quick calculations, from where the sec droid was when he'd peeked around the corner, to how far it would take them to reach the exit, and he realized they'd never make it before being gunned down. Directly across the corridor was another stairwell. Henry pointed to it. "We don't have time, that thing is right behind us. Back downstairs, now," he ordered.

"To where?" Jimmy asked.

Henry was already moving, knowing the others would follow right behind him. This was one of those times yet again, that though they were a democracy most of the time, where each of their opinions was as valid as his, when it came down to life and death decisions, Henry was the equivocal leader of the group.

Knowing their options were limited, he called over his shoulder to Cindy. "We need to get to the motor pool. Cindy, you lead the way, you have the map."

"Right," she called and picked up speed, moving to the door leading to the stairwell, slamming it open and racing down them two and three at a time. She already knew where the motor pool was, having studied the map since finding it.

Henry was last in line. As he moved through the door and it closed behind him, the sec droid appeared at the corner, weapons poised to fire. When it deduced the corridor was empty, it sent a call to the security center, and all the still-active cameras, to discover where its prey had gone. Then it spun around and returned to the elevator to continue its pursuit.

"What about Darth Vader?" Jimmy called while descending the stairs.

"Who?" Henry asked.

"Darth Vader. The sec droid. You know, 'cause it's got that glowing arm. Like Vader's lightsaber."

Once more Henry didn't respond to Jimmy's analogy. There was no time for banter. Instead, he just said, "That thing is right on our heels. We never would've made it to the exit to the outside before it cut us down. Maybe we'll have better luck if we can get a car or something and drive away from here. Our only advantage seems to be that the thing can't climb stairs."

"That's a lot of wishful thinking there, Henry," Mary said, panting slightly as she ran down the stairs. There had barely been any time to recover from awakening in the transfer station, and now she was running around like she was training for a marathon. She was exhausted; both mentally and physically. Looking around at her friends' faces showed they felt about the same as she did.

"Wishful thinking? Maybe, but if we can pull it off, we can escape from here and be better off once we leave," Henry explained. "Being on foot leaves us at a disadvantage, you know that."

"I suppose." Mary seemed far from convinced. There were too many variables to see their future, and she was uncomfortable being in that kind of position.

It didn't take long to reach the bottom floor once more, and with Cindy still leading the way, the four of them made their way quickly though the mostly bare hallways. Sometimes there were sheets of paper along with manila folders scattered around, and once there was what looked like a dried streak of blood on a wall, next to a door.

"We're here," Cindy stated, stopping before a wide white door with a crossbar in the center.

Above the doorframe was a sign. **MOTOR POOL**.

"Okay," Henry said. "Jimmy, same as before, just you and me. First thing is for us to clear the area of any danger, then we take out any security cameras." He gestured to Cindy and Mary. "You two deal with the cameras."

"Right," Mary said, Cindy only nodding in reply.

"You ready, Jimmy?" he asked, his left hand on the crossbar of the door, his right holding his Glock.

"Fuck yeah, I am. Open the damn door and let's get this party started." His shotgun was at chest level, loaded and ready. All of the group had reloaded while on the run.

Nodding in response, Henry pushed down on the crossbar, the door flying inward as he shoved it with all his weight. The door banged against the gray cinderblock wall behind it, and the two men charged inside the room, guns sweeping for a target.

They stopped seconds later, a few feet from the open door to see nothing dangerous was imminent.

Mary and Cindy charged out a second later, first prepared to offer backup to the men, but seeing nothing threatening, turned their attention to searching for security cameras. They quickly spotted three and took them out with precision, wasting only a few bullets when their aim was slightly off.

"Hopefully that'll buy us some time," Henry stated.

With the destroyed shells of the cameras sparking and smoking, filling the air with the faint odor of burning plastic and wires, the women joined the men in the center of the large room they now found themselves in.

There were four vehicle bays off to the right, each one occupied with a form of transport. The large room was the size of a ten car garage, if they ever made them that big before the world collapsed. At the far end was a ramp large enough for one vehicle at a time to traverse it.

"That must be the way out," Henry said, gesturing to the ramp.

"And if it's not?" Jimmy asked, his tone equal amount wiseass and cordial.

"Then were probably dead," Henry replied flatly. "If that droid corners us down here."

"That's not the answer I wanted, old man."

"Well, it's the only one you're gonna get."

"Henry," Mary said, "Maybe we should forget about trying to get transportation and just go." She pointed to the dark ramp leading away from the motor pool. "The way out is right there. We could leave now and be done with this craziness."

Henry shook his head. "We should have a few minutes before that droid shows up, if it even will. We took out all the cameras in here fast. It might not know where we are." He gestured towards the vehicles sitting silently in their bays. "Hopefully one of those will be our ride out of here, and this way, we leave in style. It's worth the chance."

"Fine," Mary sighed, not pleased but willing to go along with the idea, as the others were agreeing with Henry, who began moving to the vehicles, the others following without being told. She felt Henry was being greedy, wanting not only to escape, but to get away with transportation, too. The risk could put them all in jeopardy. But at the same time she knew he had a point. What good would it do to escape the redoubt, only to find they were in the middle of nowhere; out in the desert or on some high plateau days or weeks from anywhere? With limited resources, such as food and water, they could manage to escape only to then die of starvation, dehydration or exposure.

"Okay, let's see if one of these is useable." As he spoke, he ran over to the farthest vehicle, the other three of the group splitting off and doing the same. The overhead fluorescent lighting, sensing motion, flicked on in that section of the room when Henry approached.

Unlike the fairytale of Goldilocks, he didn't care which vehicle was *just right*. All he cared about was that one of them still worked. In the first bay was a black stretch limousine. It wasn't even an option. All four tires were missing, the vehicle propped up on blocks. The tires were off to the side, leaning against the wall. The hood was open also. Too many variables to know if even the tires were placed back onto the limo, if it would even run.

The second bay held a large National Guard truck, the rear bed enclosed in green canvas. The vehicle had its engine removed, said engine resting on a wooden pallet to the side of the truck.

The third bay held a vehicle that had Henry's breath hitching in his chest in excitement. Jimmy was already running towards it, a skip in his step as well.

The armored APC looked like it was in mint condition, the tires so new they still had little nubs on the sides, and the paint shining under a thin layer of dust.

Jimmy climbed onto the APC and dropped down inside, but when his head popped out of the hatch, his smile had become a frown.

"The dashboard is Swiss cheese," he said. "Looks like it's getting fixed for some kind of electrical issue. There's a manual on the floor still open to the page the mechanic was using."

Cursing, Henry was already moving to the remaining vehicle: a simple Army green jeep. Its tires were all there, but were all flat, though there was an air compressor in the bay, beside it. As he came closer, he also saw there was a trickle charger for the battery snaking under the hood, the charger on the floor beside the driver's side front tire, the power cord plugged into an electrical socket that hung down from the ceiling. That gave him hope. Entering the jeep's bay, with both women standing at the front bumper, waiting, Henry searched for the ignition key after seeing it wasn't in the ignition. He found it a moment later resting on the workbench at the back of the bay, across from the rear bumper.

Hopping into the driver's seat, he slid the key into the ignition. "Cross your fingers," he said and turned the key. The engine sputtered for a moment as the starter engaged, and with a belch of gray smoke, turned over and began to idle. The fuel gauge said the tank was half full.

Henry wasted no time as Jimmy joined them.

"Okay, I think we got a working one. Jimmy, get that compressor and fill up the tires, then let's get the hell out of here."

"Got it." Jimmy quickly turned on the air compressor and moved it into position as it began to pack air in its tank.

Henry waved the women into the jeep, so that as soon as Jimmy was finished, they would leave. The tailpipe continued to spit out a noxious gray smoke, and the engine shook roughly under the hood.

Henry frowned. "I bet the gas is either bad or going bad," he said, knowing it couldn't be helped. He leaned over the front windshield and grabbed the dual wires that trailed under the hood from the battery charger. Yanking them out, he tossed them onto the floor.

Meanwhile, Jimmy was filling the last tire. He wasn't trying to fill them to pressure, only adding enough air so the tires would allow the vehicle to maneuver. The air compressor added its hammer-banging sound as it packed more air as Jimmy used it up, to that of the growling jeep's engine.

Henry gripped the steering wheel tightly, knowing it was getting close to the limit of him pushing his luck. If the droid didn't know where they were, then he was concerned for nothing, but if it had discovered their location, it would be arriving at any moment.

As if on the heel of his thought, over the noises of the rough-idling engine and air compressor, there came the soft sound of an elevator ding. Beside the stairwell from where the companions had entered the motor pool, a set of elevator doors slowly parted.

The security droid exited, its right arm already glowing yellow and changing to purple as it prepared to fire.

"Time's up, Jimmy!" Henry yelled upon seeing the sec droid appear. "We need to go, now!"

Before Jimmy could respond, the laser beam fired, its trajectory going directly to the front of the jeep.

Chapter 4

Henry didn't wait for Jimmy to respond, and instead slammed his foot down onto the gas pedal, the jeep leaping forward. He was thrown back in the seat from the acceleration.

Jimmy was holding onto the side of the jeep and was pulled off his feet, as if he'd been water skiing and the boat had surged forward without warning him first. His feet left the floor and he became horizontal, a scream leaving his lips. The hose for the air compressor was still attached to the remaining tire, but it became separated from the machine, the high whistling sound of released air under pressure filling the room, louder even than the noise of the roaring jeep's engine.

The sec droid, detecting the shrieking compressor and calculating it was an enemy, swiveled and shot at it, it's laser beam slicing into the metal canister. Under pressure with packed air, the air compressor housing exploded outward upon being pierced, a loud boom filling the motor pool. Henry felt the shockwave of the blast on his neck as he drove away from the area. There was no fire, however, once the initial blast subsided.

While Jimmy screamed for help as he held on for dear life, Henry swerved the jeep to the left, just as the laser beam connected with the vehicle. But instead of slicing into the engine, the beam barely clipped the outer casing of the driver's side headlight, then burned through the plastic and metal, before exiting out the front fender.

The steering was sluggish from the low air pressure in the tires. Henry fought the wheel and aimed the front of the jeep up the still-dark ramp. Unknown to him, the still-attached and severed compressor hose was now doing the opposite of its job. Air was leaking out of the hose fast, the tire it was connected to already half of what Jimmy had inflated it to, and still going down with each passing second.

Jimmy's feet touched back down to earth and he jumped into the back of the jeep. Seeing the sec droid, he unslung his shotgun, and began shooting at it, while doing his damndest not to get knocked out of the jeep.

"Forget that!" Henry yelled. "You're wasting ammo we might need later!"

The hose kept flap-flapping each time the tire completed a revolution, a steady staccato that never let up.

With the overhead fluorescents snapping on with the jeep's approach, Henry powered up the ramp, the jeep's exhaust belching so much gray smoke it was like a smokescreen, the sec droid following close behind. Laser beams sizzled overhead of the companions, striking the ceiling and high on the walls, cement dust raining down, but the angle was wrong, the droid continually missing. It looked as if the smoke was screwing up its targeting system.

Henry knew it wouldn't take long for it to recalibrate.

He stopped directly before a large metal blast door wide enough to accommodate a vehicle as large as a semi.

"Cover me!" Henry yelled, jumping out of the driver's seat.

As one trained unit, his fellow travelers turned and began shooting the security droid, while Henry ran over to a small, six inch panel set in the wall about chest height. Opening the panel, he exposed the glowing keyboard beneath.

Hoping the code to open the blast door was the same as the last redoubt, praying the uniformity was constant, he quickly punched in the numerical code from memory.

Over the cacophony of his friends' gunfire, Henry felt more than heard a low rumbling. At first nothing happened, and just as he was about to really worry that something was wrong, the blast door began to retract into the floor. A loud wailing siren began to sound as the door retreated into the ground.

In a moment, daylight began spilling into the area above the ramp, and Henry caught a faint whiff of nature: trees, grass, other plant life, and the odor of the earth, such as loam.

The sec droid had been pushed a few feet back and then stopped cold by the barrage of gunfire being poured into it, but it only renewed its forward momentum as the onslaught it had received slowed due to the companions having to reload their weapons.

Henry watched the blast door slowly retracting, then at how the sec droid was still coming, and made the decision the door wouldn't be open in time for them to escape before they ran out of ammunition.

Going to Mary and Cindy, he patted them each on the shoulder to get their attention. Yelling wasn't an option. His ears were already ringing from the reports of their guns, and he knew the others were in a similar situation. The din bounced off the walls and ceiling, the sound hitting them over and over like a punching bag; a shockwave of intensity that would have them hard of hearing for quite a while afterwards.

The scent of cordite filled the space from the discharging weapons, and the distinct scent of burning ozone as well, that latter from the sec droid's laser when it burned the very air itself.

Henry jumped back behind the wheel of the jeep. "Everyone, get to the door and get over it as soon as possible." The blast door was halfway down and still moving. In a few more seconds it would be low enough for the others to jump over it. The door was over six inches thick, and solid metal. Once they were over the threshold and managed to close the door behind them, and if the sec droid didn't have the code to open the door again, they'd be safe.

"What are you doing?" Mary yelled, seeing Henry inside the jeep again, though she moved to the opening, as did Jimmy and Cindy. All three used the jeep as cover as they did so.

"Distracting and slowing that thing down—I hope," Henry added as he put the jeep into reverse.

"You're doing what?"

He flashed her a quick smile. "Relax, Mary. Trust me. I don't plan on dying today."

"I got your gear, Henry," Jimmy said, before he hopped over the lowering steel door, Cindy following close behind him.

A flash of emotions crossed Mary's face. Was she seeing Henry for the last time? Was this goodbye forever? All the history they'd shared over the past few years. He truly was like a father to her, and she knew she'd have a tough time of it if she lost him. All this rushed through her head in a matter of seconds, until she merely nodded and added, "You better not."

"Good, now go. It's time for me to see how good the factory warranty is on this thing." He was already driving in reverse, and twenty feet away from her. The entire back and forth had happened in the span of a few heartbeats, while the others had hopped over the door to the outside and Henry had begun reversing.

As Henry drove away from her, she spared him one last glance and then, she too, was over the door.

Henry watched her climb over the lowering door, her feet scrabbling on the smooth surface before Jimmy and Cindy pulled her over. Any of them would have been easy targets for the sec droid, if not for Henry providing it with an easier target. So at least he could take comfort in knowing he'd made the correct call.

Emerging out of the dissipating smoke cloud that was sucked into vents near the ceiling, the droid powered up the ramp, and at the approaching jeep. Henry struggled to keep the jeep moving in the direction he wanted. With a bad tire, the steering fought him every inch he moved.

But he didn't need to go far, the droid also closing the gap between them. A few errant laser blasts sizzled over his head, the droid still recalibrating. Henry turned in his seat, his Glock in hand, and began shooting the droid as he closed in on it.

He tried to stay low as well, but quickly realized that was a mute point when a beam sizzled past his left hip. The beam went completely through the jeep's seat, exploding out the left headlight casing. If a beam sliced through the center of the vehicle, the motor would be destroyed in an instant.

Maybe this wasn't such a good idea after all, he thought.

"In for a penny, in for a pound," he muttered, holding his course. His father used to always say that.

With the jeep's exhaust still spewing a noxious cloud of smoke, he didn't realize he had run out of distance between himself and the sec droid until the rear bumper connected with it. His head was thrown backwards from the impact; through the smoke, he saw the droid was shoved back only a few feet, though its two weaponized arms were flailing as it tried to regain motion control.

Apparently, it was heavier than it looked. He'd hoped to send it flying backwards, maybe even topple it.

Knowing it wasn't enough to stop it, he put the tranny into 'drive,' and pressed the gas pedal to the floor, the jeep lunging forward six feet as if it were alive. Henry was pleased with the power. The vehicle had a lot of pep for Government Issue. He slammed the transmission into reverse again and floored the gas pedal.

This time he was braced for the impact and he rode with the motion. The droid, however, did not. The strike was good, sending the sec droid toppling over like a fallen tree. It hit the ramp floor with a loud, bell-like clang, and began to emit a piercing wail like a wounded animal, making Henry wince, despite his damaged hearing from the gunshots.

Seeing the droid prone and struggling, he nodded to himself and prepared to make a run for the door, which was now fully retracted. Mary, Jimmy and Cindy were standing to either side of the frame, watching anxiously and calling out to him to run for it. He couldn't hear them with the wailing of the sec droid, but he could see them waving for him to make his escape.

He was about to oblige them when he glanced over his shoulder before making his mad dash to freedom.

It was a good thing, too, for as he watched, new arms popped out of the torso of the sec droid's canister body, spider-like in appearance. It began using these new, thin appendages to begin righting itself. Meanwhile, the piercing wail continued.

Cursing, Henry realized he wouldn't have enough time to reach the exit before the droid cut him down. His delaying tactic hadn't gone as planned, and though the others were safe, his ass was about to be cooked, metaphorically as well as physically.

He needed one more trick, and it came to him instantly. Wasting no time, he jumped out of the driver's seat after putting the jeep in 'park.' Dropping to the floor, he used the sixteen inch panga on his hip to puncture the fuel tank. He had to strike it three times before getting the desired result. Gas began to squirt out of the puncture and splatter the ramp, some but not all flowing away from the jeep, following the incline of the ramp.

Rising, he moved back to the interior of the jeep, his eyes searching for something, anything to complete his plan. He spotted a First Aid kit. Scooping it up, he opened it, thereby doubling its length, then grunted in acceptance. When opened, it was just large enough for his needs.

The jeep's engine was still running, and still spouting smoke from its exhaust.

Without hesitation, Henry jammed the open metal box between the gas pedal and the driver's seat. When it was still slightly loose, he adjusted the seat so it was as close to the steering wheel as it would go.

The motor surged loudly, even more smoke filling the area around the jeep. The sec droid was almost upright, and only needed a few more seconds.

Leaning over the steering wheel, Henry gripped the gear shift, which was located on the steering column due to the age of the jeep, and yanked it from 'park' into 'reverse.'

Even with the flat tire, the jeep bucked backwards, Henry having to snap his arm away or risk losing it. The vehicle rolled away from him, directly towards the security droid.

Henry began to run up to the opening, and when he hoped was far enough away not to be caught in the blast, turned and shot at the spreading pool of gas on the ramp, the jeep only a few feet from the droid.

Bullets struck the concrete ramp, ricocheting in all directions, then one or more sparked enough on impact to finally set the fumes alight.

The pool of gas erupted instantly, and the trail left by the leaking tank quickly began to burn, the flames following the trail until finally reaching the jeep's fuel tank.

The vehicle was less than four feet from the sec droid when the tank exploded.

Henry didn't see the fireball, as he was running full out for the blast door. But he did feel the shockwave when it hit him; it lifted him off his feet and sent him flying. At least he was headed in the right direction—the thought flashed through his mind while he was going airborne.

As he was soaring like a bird through the air, he saw before him that someone had raised the blast door so that it was four feet up; easy enough to climb over, but still giving the door some closure until Henry was safely on the other side.

He managed to briefly glance over his shoulder while flailing in the air, and he saw multiple things happen at once.

The sec droid was fully upright and had raised both arms to shoot Henry, but a micro-second before it could fire, the fireball of the erupting fuel tank rolled over it, causing it to disappear in a swirling cloud of flames.

From the top of the cloud of fire, a laser stabbed out, striking and scoring the ceiling in a long line, while a few feet over, bullets raked the ceiling as well.

Within the confines of the vehicle-sized corridor, and compared to being outside, the shockwave of the explosion reverberated off the walls and ceiling.

Henry felt like he had been dropped head-first inside a snare drum and the drummer was doing a solo number. He landed on his stomach, and only barely was able to use his hands and arms to brace for the impact. Upon hitting the concrete ramp, the air left him in a rush, and he gasped for air. The fire was sucking up the oxygen within the confines of the ramp quickly, despite the open blast door.

He felt himself slipping into unconsciousness. He did his best to fight it, and even tried to raise himself up off the ramp, to crawl if need be, but it was a losing battle.

He felt rain on his back and head. Almost casually, he wondered why it was raining, then his arms slid out from under him and he slumped to the ground.

Falling into a deep pit of blackness, he could swear he heard voices calling his name.

Chapter 5

Henry returned to consciousness like someone had flipped a switch within his brain. One moment he was out, the next wide awake and trying to sit up.

"Whoa there, old man," Jimmy said, trying to get Henry to pause as he knelt down beside him. "Take it easy."

"What? Where?" Henry mumbled as his eyes darted around, not really seeing anything. He may have been awake and moving, but his brain hadn't yet synced his mental and physical processes together.

Mary was beside his prone form, along with Jimmy, Cindy standing a few feet away, keeping watch.

"How do you feel?" Mary asked.

Henry stopped trying to rise and hesitated, then took stock of himself, listening to his body to feel if he had any aches and pains anywhere. To his detriment, he felt pain all over, but nothing that signified breakage. His ribs felt sore as well but not any kind of shooting pain as he shifted himself around on the ground.

"I feel like I've gone three rounds with a city full of zombies, but nothing seems broken." He touched a hand to his forehead. "I've got a raging migraine, too." He gazed up to see clear blue sky. He was outside. Before him was wilderness.

Craning his head slightly over his shoulder, and not liking how it made him feel, he caught a glimpse of the redoubt's blast door, now closed. He was at the side of it, under a tree, its canopy blocking out the sun and casting him and the others in shade.

He tasted blood and realized he'd bit the inside of his cheek. The nightmare he had before waking in the matter transfer room flickered past his mind, but it was gone as fast as it was there. He barely acknowledged it, as he was still too foggy to fully focus.

Mary handed him a wet cloth. When he brushed it away, she placed it on his forehead herself, her mouth down-turned in worry, while Jimmy handed him a canteen of water. He took the water and drank lightly, ignoring Mary's motherly ministrations.

"I take it we're safe from that damn killer robot." He handed the canteen to Mary.

Jimmy nodded. "Sure are." He gestured to the blast door. "That was a hell of a thing you did. If I hadn't gone in after you, you'd probably be dead by now." He stood up, his shadow blocking the sun and casting Henry in slight shadow. "That thing was about to fry your unconscious ass."

"So you dragged me out of there," Henry deduced. Slowly, with Mary's help, he sat up. "The thing isn't dead?"

Mary shifted slightly and said, "Not that we could see. Jimmy was dragging you back to us and that droid was just coming out of the flames."

"So it's still active?"

"We think so," Jimmy said, taking back the conversation. "It might not have been operational. I didn't actually see it move. I thought I did but it might have just been the flames as they moved around it." He shrugged. "It wasn't like I was gonna hang around and find out. When the sprinklers went off plus the fire, it was almost impossible to see anything. We got you out here, which wasn't easy. We had to drag your limp-ass body over the half open door, then Cindy closed the door once you were on this side." He flashed a cautious glance at the blast door, as if double checking it was still closed. "Since then all's been quiet."

When Henry was more lucid, in the bright light of day he noticed the closed blast door had what appeared to be scorch marks on it. On either side were also scrapes and small dents, as if someone or something had been trying to pry at the seams. It didn't appear the culprits had managed to gain entry. If they had, Henry figured he or his friends would have noticed signs of visitors while inside. Then again, he may have been wrong. After all, running for your life from a killer droid might cause a person to miss this or that.

Henry got to his feet, and walked out onto the road, thanks to Mary's help. He leaned on her for more than a minute, than gently gestured for her to step away, that he was okay. The first thing he did when he knew his legs would support him was to change the clip on his Glock. After doing so he checked the old clip, finding only two rounds remaining. Grunting in annoyance that he'd lost count of how many rounds were used, he shoved the clip in a pocket and stretched. He winced from the pain but managed not to make a sound. Jimmy watched him intently, looking for any sign of weakness he could use to tease him about.

Mary handed Henry the canteen again. He took it without protest and drank more deeply. Wiping his mouth with the back of his hand, he took in the surrounding area. This time with an eye of a warrior, and not a man just coming to after being knocked out.

They were on a paved, single lane road surrounded by forest on all sides. The trees had grown together over the road to become a tunnel; a living canopy that blocked out the sun and cast the road in shadows. The road itself was only half visible. On both sides, the forest had been slowly reclaiming what was once nature.

Dirt was more than an inch thick in places on the cracked pavement, and shrubbery and tall grass that might have been wheat was growing there.

In another few years the road would be completely covered, reclaimed by Mother Nature again.

Where the four companions were standing, before the gray blast door, on both sides of the frame, vegetation was also growing wild. The only reason the door was still visible was because before the world ended, the area near the opening must have been cleared back several dozen feet. But spores and pollen had solved that issue, and the once-barren area was quickly turning green.

Though it would take slightly more years than it would for the road to disappear, eventually, the vines and shrubbery would make the opening invisible to the naked eye. At the base of the door, broken bits of vegetation and weeds of varying sizes could be seen, the vegetation having been destroyed when the door opened. Henry knew soon enough the door would be covered in foliage.

Henry realized Cindy was asking him a question. He pulled himself from his thoughts and turned to face her "What was that?"

She took a step closer to him. "I said, do you think we'll be going back in there." She pointed to the bunker.

Henry cast one last glance at the blast door, and what was beyond. "I doubt it. Not with the chances that droid is still active and us with no way to stop it." He shrugged his shoulders. "The only way I'd think we'd go back inside and risk our luck, is if there's something far worse out here we need to get away from, or if we're driving a tank to kill it once and for all."

"What could be worse than a killer machine with lasers?" Mary asked.

"I don't think we want to find out," Henry added. He picked up his pack and shrugged into it where it was lying against the tree, then walked out onto the road and into the sunshine. It was warm out, the sun strong on his face and neck. Not so hot it was terribly uncomfortable, but warm enough that prolonged exposure would become damaging. He already longed to get under the tree canopy covering the road and the welcoming coolness of the shade it would provide. "If everyone's ready, we can move out."

"Shit, old man, we've been ready forever. We've all been waiting on you to wake up from your nap."

"Well, Jimmy, I'm so sorry I've kept you from your next appointment. But I'm up now, so shall we leave?"

Jimmy scrunched up his face in annoyance, then slowly bowed like a dignitary. "Why, yes, my good sir. We shall. And perhaps later we could have a spot of tea?"

Cindy giggled, Mary smiled and Henry frowned. He should have known it wouldn't be long before Jimmy was back to his old ways.

"Cindy," Henry called. "Seems you're already out front, you wanna take point?"

"Sure, Henry, I can do that."

"Good, then Jimmy, Mary next, and I've got your six," Henry ordered. "Let's find out where we've landed, so to speak."

No one complained, and in less than a minute they were moving away from the blast door and into the gloom of the living tunnel of trees.

When the four companions had been swallowed by the shadows, after making their way down the lone road, the area around the blast door grew quiet once more.

Eventually, about an hour later, when there was no more movement discerned, the blinking light on the security camera hidden at the top of the blast door finally went dark. Motion would activate it again, but not before.

Inside the redoubt, motionless on the ramp, the sec droid, still fully operational, waited silently for the intruders to return.

Chapter 6

The companions traveled for more than half a day without finding signs of civilization. Traveling down a long road without markers, they attempted to discern their location, but so far there had been no hint of it.

Henry was of the feeling they were somewhere in the northeast, as the road rolled up and down over hilly land. He knew the South was mostly flat, but that wasn't a perfect hypothesis. A few farmsteads could be seen in the distance when the curvature of the land allowed, but no one even suggested they investigate. There didn't seem to be a need.

A few desiccated corpses were passed from time to time, the rags that were once clothing stuck to the skeletal frames. They were ignored. The bodies were just another part of the landscape, barely given the attention of a blowing trash bag or soda can lying in the gutter.

By the time the sun began to set, and Henry decided it was time to find a place to make camp, they stumbled, more than anything else, into the outskirts of an abandoned town or small city.

There was no way to know for sure how large the settlement had been before the zombie apocalypse, as every building had been destroyed by fire. The half-collapsed walls on the structures in sight all leaned at precarious angles, as if nothing more than a gentle breeze would knock them down completely. Splintered utility poles lined the street, electrical wires lying everywhere. Rebar jutted out of crumbling cement blocks, the once-white facades scorched black from fire.

The conflagration had been massive, burning everything in sight. A car had sunk into the asphalt, the tar seeming to be coming up to grip it, like a living blob. The plastic had melted into rivulets, to then re-harden once the embers had cooled. Every flat surface was covered in gray ash, washing the entire area of color.

Vegetation thrived, growing from the ash that had been compacted over countless rainstorms, the ash the perfect fertilizer.

It was a bleak landscape that the companions traversed in silence, a pall coming over them as they walked. The group kept to the center of the street. Though everything in view was mostly demolished, there were still many places that an ambush could come from, and many piles of detritus. At the base of many a façade, a pile of fallen bricks and cement dust had gathered as the wall slowly decayed further.

The street continued off into the distance, destroyed, colorless structures lining both sides.

Some kind of used car place or perhaps a rental car company was passed. Or maybe it had been a park-and-ride. There was nothing on the one-story structure to indicate its purpose, no signs, only the dozens of cars, each lined up in neat rows. Most of the vehicles were damaged, windshields shattered, pieces missing, possibly stripped for salvage. A few seemed to only have a layer of dirt on them, and with the exception of the tires either being flat or almost flat, the cars looked like they were ready to be washed and used.

It wasn't worth checking. The cars with possibilities of fixing were trapped within others that would never be used again. There would be no way to get the ones worth checking out of the metal trap of derelicts. Unless they had access to a tow truck or bulldozer, which was ridiculous. If they had that kind of vehicle they wouldn't need to bother with the cars.

They covered about another half mile when a red-brick building rose out of the rubble on their left. It was intact, though the two-story structure was severely scorched on all sides that could be seen. Moving closer, it was clear that all the lower windows had been boarded up, and the front egress off the street had also been barricaded—the barricade and wood on the windows all had scorch marks, signifying they had been put there long before the companions had arrived.

It would be the perfect place to conduct an ambush to anyone traveling down the street.

"Stay sharp," Henry said, though he knew he didn't need to. All three of his friends were as battle-hardened as him. Through years of battling not only the living dead but other human beings, they had become a close-knit fighting team.

Mary sniffed from behind Henry, as her eyes played over the rubble. "Maybe we'll find something here that will tell us where we are." So far there had been nothing to tell them what state they were in, and the foliage was too common to decipher their location. Henry once more considered that they were in the northeast, but where exactly was still unknown.

He was about to respond to Mary and tell her this, when a shot rang out and he felt something buzz by his head so close he almost lost an ear. "Get down!"

Everyone went into action instantly, Jimmy and Cindy darting to the left, to hunker down behind a derelict automobile. Henry and Mary did the same, dashing to the opposite side of the street, to take cover behind a faded green transfer mailbox. The green ones were used by postal employees only to drop and pick up extra mail while they did their walking routes.

The lower half of the box was ajar, the door having been pried open. There was still mail inside, and though Henry wasn't fully looking, his eyes did glance across a few of the faded addresses. He saw that the state for most—either addressed to or the return address—was Maryland, and even as he hunkered down behind the metal box, a part of his mind filed that information for later.

He now had a pretty good idea where he and his friends had ended up.

In the gloom of the fading sun it was easy to spot the flash of the gun shooting at them.

"Jimmy!" Henry called out after spotting the flash.

"Yeah, old man, I see it, too." Jimmy quickly made sure Cindy spotted the sniper as well, as did Henry with Mary.

"On three, the girls will give us covering fire, while you and me get over there and take out the threat. Okay, everyone?"

Cindy called out in agreement, Jimmy as well.

"Okay, Jimmy, get ready; right to that building and around the back."

Henry began the countdown, and on two, with Mary beside Henry, and Cindy across the street, began returning fire, Henry yelling the word, "Three!"

As bullets pockmarked the side of the building around the window where muzzle flashes were spotted, the older and younger man made a dash for it, zigzagging their way quickly to the building, then after pressing their backs against its scorched façade, began to make their way along it until they had to turn the corner at the end. Henry felt the hard brick under his shirt and realized the reason this lone building was still standing was because it was built completely of brick and cement, not partially of wood also.

It would have once been an alley they entered, but now it was exposed on all sides but one, that being the still standing structure. There wasn't much room to walk, the alley filled with fallen debris from nearby buildings along with trash. A few body parts, long rotted to bare skeletons, were mixed in with the detriment.

"Blocked," Jimmy stated as they reached the rear entry of the building. The once glass door had been fortified with thick planks of wood, each extending to the sides, where the ends were then secured to the brick with metal bolts. Unless they had tools and the time to use them, or a grenade, they weren't getting through that barricade anytime soon. And time was of the essence.

Cindy and Mary were still shooting back, but had slowed their fire. Now, they were simply keeping the sniper busy.

Henry took a step back to take in the building better. Even with the light fading and shadows growing, he could still make out the features. All the windows were covered with wooden boards, but as he studied the ones on the ground floor, he noticed a gap in one farthest from the door.

"Hey, Jimmy, come here," he said and went to the window. "Little help?"

Jimmy knew what he wanted from the way Henry was looking at him. Frowning deeply, as Henry was larger than himself, Jimmy laced his fingers together so he could cup Henry's boot in them. Henry jumped up as well, and working in tandem, managed to grab the plywood covering the window by the gap and yank it off.

The covering went flying across the alley and Henry almost fell on his ass, but Jimmy managed to stop that from happening.

Henry grabbed the sill and pulled himself inside, then reached out for Jimmy, who jumped up, caught Henry's hand and was pulled into the building, his boot soles scrabbling at the brick the entire time. He landed with a crunch on shattered glass, the shards covering the floor near the window. His shotgun dug into his ribs when he landed but nothing was damaged on him or the firearm.

"No nails were holding that piece," Henry said, gesturing at the window.

"Yeah, I kinda figured. Either that or you'd become Superman overnight."

"Not likely. That wood was just propped there, probably by the same person who's shooting at us."

Jimmy hefted his shotgun. "Then let's go do something about that right now."

Henry only nodded and the two men made their way deeper into the building.

Stairs were found that led to the upper floor, and the men quickly ascended, each using the wall as support, and not trusting the railing. There were signs of fire damage within the building as well, but not enough to destroy the interior, only mar its surfaces. Smoke damage seemed the most prevalent.

The reports of a firearm made it easy to track the sniper, and within moments the two men were standing outside a closed door. On the frame of the door was a plastic holder where folders, memos or mail could be placed, signifying the room had once been some kind of office.

Henry glanced at Jimmy, who nodded in reply: both men were ready.

Henry took a step so that he was standing directly in front of the door, and raising his right foot, he slammed the sole of his boot into the door directly below the doorknob. The door was made of a flimsy material, and Henry used way too much force for the cheap material.

The door didn't just swing open; it was nearly forced off its hinges. It bounced off the wall and hung by the upper hinge only, leaning like a drunkard after last call.

Jimmy was through the doorway first, Henry directly on his heels.

The two men didn't need to discuss beforehand what they would do. They'd been together for years, fighting, and winning. Jimmy knew to go left and low, Henry to the right, slightly higher, but only a little.

Henry took the interior of the room in instantly.

A desk, oak or something similar, turned on its side and against the far wall. Two chairs with wheels also lying on their sides. Paper, lots of paper, littered the floor like cheap carpeting. There was dried blood on the wall near the desk, the splatter now a dark brown.

There was a shelf to the right and slightly behind Henry. Though he only saw it for a moment, he realized the shelf was pristine, each memento and souvenir that had been placed there years ago in the exact same place. Only a layer of dust belayed the defiance of passing years, signifying time marched ever onward.

There was one window in the room, directly across from the door, and below the frame, kneeling on the floor, were two people.

Henry took both of the couple's appearances in simultaneously.

The man was in his forties, with a balding pate and a thick beard. He was overweight, not morbidly obese, but damn close. His clothes were patched but seemed clean, and the shoes he wore were made for walking, with strong soles and good leather with well-made stitching.

The woman was wearing a sheepskin jacket and jeans with tennis shoes on her feet. Other than the clothes and jacket being dirty with ash, the material on all of it looked intact. But it was her hair he noticed first; it was blonde, just like…

Then Henry was focusing on the action of the moment, and as he and Jimmy burst into the room, the man by the window shifted his position from aiming a hunting rifle out the window, to swinging it around to shoot at the two invaders of his sanctuary.

Jimmy was already leveling the shotgun at the man, who was the only one armed of the couple, and at the same time, Henry was sizing up the two even further for threats.

Henry's gaze had shifted again to take in the woman by the chubby man's side, and the second he did, he hesitated, for he was confident he was seeing his lost love Sue across the room.

The woman's hair was the same color as his departed lover, as was the way it hung across her shoulders. Even the woman's posture reminded Henry of her.

Deep down, he knew the woman couldn't be Sue, but as he stared at her more, the grief he'd felt came flooding back. Though it went against his warrior's instincts, he reacted before he realized what he was doing.

Just as Jimmy squeezed the trigger on his shotgun to take the fat man out, Henry's arm snapped out and knocked the shotgun's barrel upwards at the ceiling.

The action was barely enough to make Jimmy miss, but miss it did. Instead of connecting with the man's chest, the pellets peppered the wall two feet above and to the side of the man's head, a few pellets shattering the upper window pane, which was still intact.

"What the fuck?" Jimmy snarled, already bringing the shotgun back down and aiming it at the man, who in shock and fear from hearing the blast, yipped loudly and dropped the hunting rifle like a scared cat, his hands jumping up over his head in surrender.

"Don't shoot!" the man yelled. "I surrender. Please don't kill me or Carol." His hands went even higher over his head and he seemed to be trying to touch the ceiling. The woman didn't raise her hands high but she did hold them up before her, showing they were empty. Both had eyes wide with terror they were going to be killed.

Jimmy wasn't about to stop, however. After all, this man had been taking shots at not only himself, but at Cindy, too. Not to mention at Henry and Mary also. He didn't know what had gotten into Henry, but he figured they could sort it out after the threat had been stopped, and the best way to do that was by killing it.

Seeing how the threat the man had been was now neutralized, that the rifle wasn't in the man's hands, and the woman didn't appear to be trying anything, Henry went with his gut, and reached out and grabbed Jimmy's arm, gripping it tightly. "No, wait, don't shoot them. They're harmless."

"Harmless?" Jimmy snapped. "What the fuck, old man, have you gone nuts? This guy was trying to kill us a minute ago!"

"I thought you were cannibals! I thought you were cannibals!" the man yelled quickly.

"What was that?" Henry asked, his Glock still aimed at the man and woman, though his finger was slightly off the trigger. The fat man might have another firearm, even a knife, and he could try for it at any moment. But with his hands high in the air, it seemed pretty unlikely.

"I thought you were part of a gang of cannibals," the man repeated. "Carol and I almost got caught by them about a day ago. But we managed to get away from them."

"How do you know we're not them?" Jimmy demanded, the shotgun still aimed at the couple. But his finger wasn't tense on the trigger, only resting on it. "Shit, we eat you and we got enough food for a month easy." He smirked at his own joke.

"Because we saw how they were dressed," the woman said, speaking for the first time. "They had necklaces made of ears and their clothing was mostly rags. You two have decent clothing and have guns."

"Yes, she's right," the man said. "The cannibals didn't seem to have guns, only knives and axes and bows and the like."

"Tell them about the queen, Mark," Carol said.

The man, Mark, seemed to think for a moment, then he nodded vigorously, and said, "Yes, there was a giant of a woman who led them. They called her their queen. She was in the back of a pickup truck. She's so large I don't think she can walk very well."

"A queen, huh?" Henry said. "Now that's a new one." He gestured for both of them to stand up and face the wall. Upon seeing the fear on their faces, he quickly added, "Relax, we're not going to kill you. If we were gonna do that it'd be done already. We just need to pat you down for weapons." He gestured for Jimmy to do it, while he covered the couple with his Glock.

Sullenly, Jimmy lowered the shotgun and moved over to the couple, picking up the hunting rifle and tossing it to Henry. "No bullshit now, or that 'not killing' thing can be changed," he snarled at the couple.

Mark moved his head vehemently like a bobblehead and Carol only nodded slowly. Now that Henry had a better look at her, he realized she looked nothing like Sue, with the exception of the same hair color and reasonable hair length. The shape of Carol's face was all wrong, as was the woman's body size. Where Sue had been long and lean, Carol was a little plump, though not fat, and was more top heavy than Sue's chest had been. Possibly, before the world had ended with the dead walking, the woman might have been flat out fat, but years of living hand to mouth had caused her to go from obese to only slightly plump.

Jimmy stepped back holding a small pistol. "She only had this on her, the guy's clean." He handed the pistol to Henry, who studied it.

"What kind of firearm is this? I've never seen this kind of grip before."

Carol stood taller as she pointed to the gun, turning slightly to look at Henry, despite orders to face the wall. "That's an Olympic target pistol. 22. caliber with a sculpted wooden grip. It's made to wrap around my hand to steady and brace my wrist."

Henry studied the weapon and then looked over at Carol. "You were in the Olympics?"

Carol shook her head, her blonde tresses moving about her shoulders. "No, but my sister was. That's all I have left to remind me of her."

"Was she killed by the dead?" Henry asked.

"No, a car accident six months before everything…well, you know."

He nodded. "Yeah." He knew only too well. That one word summed up years of fighting, killing and surviving. Countless bodies left in his wake as he struggled to survive. Not to mention the loss of his wife, Emily, and later, his newfound love, Sue. He shook his head slightly, as if to shake the bad memories away. They weren't all bad, he knew, especially those of Sue, but he still needed time to get over the grief and only focus on the good times.

Henry glanced down at the two packs on the floor and pointed at them with the tip of his Glock. "Jimmy, check those, too."

"Sure." It only took a moment to go through them. Other than some spare clothing and a few cans of food, the packs had nothing of interest to anyone but their owners. "They're clear, nothing dangerous."

"We're not dangerous people, I swear," Mark said, his face still aimed at the wall. "We were just protecting ourselves."

Jimmy grunted. "You could have killed us."

"True," Henry said. "But they were only doing what we might have done, given similar circumstances." The couple stood waiting for Henry's decision. Carol was visibly shaking, however she held her head high. Mark was also scared, sweating profusely on his neck and face. But though he showed it more, even he was doing a decent job of maintaining his composure. Given that death might be a second away, he found that admirable of both of them. Finally, he decided the entire situation was a big misunderstanding, perpetrated by two people that were scared. He couldn't blame them too much. Having had run-ins with cannies numerous times, he knew how terrifying they could be.

Dying was one thing, but ending up in a stew pot was just something most humans found abhorrent.

"Okay, you can both turn around," Henry said and lowered his Glock. He didn't holster it. Not yet.

"You're…you're not going to kill us?" Mark asked.

Henry shook his head. "I already said we weren't. Don't see a reason to. Do you?"

Mark shook his head vehemently. "No, sir, I do not."

With a glance at Jimmy, Henry moved to the open window, still keeping out of sight but close enough to call out to Mary and Cindy. "We're okay up here! Hold your fire." He moved to the window slowly so the women could see him. He waved.

Mary and Cindy stood up from their hiding spots.

"You sure, Charlie?" Mary called. "Is Dave okay, too?"

"Both Jimmy and myself are fine, Mary. Stand by, we'll be right down."

Henry turned to look at the couple. They were holding hands. He glanced down and noticed they were wearing matching wedding rings. Whether they were married before the collapse or had become a couple after was irrelevant.

"Come on," he told Jimmy, "let's go join the girls."

"You sure?" Jimmy asked.

He nodded. He gestured to the couple. "Get your packs, you're coming with us. That is, if you want to."

Neither Mark nor Carol had issue with Henry's invitation. It was obvious the two men before them, not to mention whoever was outside, were far more capable of dealing with danger than they were. Plus, traveling in numbers was always a bonus, compared to being alone.

"What about our guns?" Mark asked as the four began to exit the room, Henry in the lead, Jimmy taking up the rear, the couple in the middle.

"Not just yet," was all Henry said.

"Yeah," Jimmy added. "We didn't kill you. One step at a time."

Chapter 7

Mary and Cindy were waiting in the street, remaining behind cover. When they spotted Henry and Jimmy, each carrying their weapons casually, the two women relaxed even more and stepped out into the open. It was dusk, with just a sliver of the moon to illuminate the land. Cloud cover was thick, so when the sun was completely set, without a light source, it would be too dark to see anyone clearly.

"What's all this?" Cindy asked, as she eyed the middle-aged couple warily.

"This is Mark and Carol," Henry introduced. "This has all been a big misunderstanding."

"Misunderstanding?" Mary asked. She noticed the two new weapons Jimmy was carrying, the rifle and the Olympic target pistol, along with his shotgun, figuring where they had come from instantly.

Jimmy went over and kissed a curious Cindy, then wrapped an arm around her thin waist. "Yeah, babe, they thought we were cannies." He answered the question written clearly on her face.

"There are cannies around here?" Mary asked, her head flicking back and forth, as if the mere utterance would ensure the attack of a horde of blood-thirsty cannibals. "Henry, if that's true, we need to get out of here right now."

"Who's Henry?" Mark asked, his face scrunching up in confusion. "I thought you're name is Charlie. I heard one of these ladies call you that earlier."

Henry waved off the question. "I'm Henry Watson, and that's Jimmy Cooper. And these two lovely young women are Mary Roberts and Cindy Jansen."

"His name is Jimmy? But I heard him being called Dave." Mark looked even more confused. Carol said nothing, and just stood quietly.

"It doesn't matter," Henry said, his tone of voice set in a way that said the conversation about names was over. Neither Mark nor Carol needed to be filled in on the code names the companions used in any situation that could mean one or more of them was captured or compromised. Or forced against their will to give up the others' location. If one of them was asked if they were okay, and were using the fake names, and the others, while under duress from the enemy, went along with being called those names, then the signal that the situation was dire would be known. That little heads up could be the difference between living to see the sun come up the next day versus punching a ticket on the last train west. It had served them countless times in the past.

Henry quickly filled Mary and Cindy in on the issue the couple had been having with cannies, Mark having informed Henry on the way out of the building to street level.

"So we need to get out of view of anyone who might come by," Henry finished. He looked at the others' faces in the falling gloom. "We all good?"

There were no complaints and they began moving once more, this time the companions having added two more to their group.

The ash covering everything prevented them from hiding their progress, so Henry had everyone walk in single file, so as to obscure their numbers from anyone who might try to track them. Walking in single file, with Henry on point, then Mary and Cindy, along with Mark and Carol, and Jimmy last, watching their back trail, they quickly moved through the remains of the settlement.

It didn't take them long to leave the rubble behind, as well as the last of the area with ash coating the ground, and it was full dark when Henry decided it was time to make camp. He hoped they were far enough away from being discovered by any cannies in the area.

"We should be far enough from the town by now," Henry stated. "And there are no more tracks behind us that someone could follow." They had walked for about half an hour. He would have preferred more distance covered, but traveling at night was never a good idea, not when things like working streetlights were all but a memory.

But there was another reason, however, why he decided to halt for the night at their exact location. Off to the left, set slightly back from the road, was an old filling station. Two of the four gas pumps were long gone, having been removed for salvage or perhaps they hadn't been there even before the fall of civilization—there was no way to tell.

"This way," Henry ordered, crossing the road and making his way to the one-story building. "If it's safe, we can hole up here for the night."

"This reminds me of the time we found Blackie," Mary said as she approached the gas station. Though the area looked nothing like the one where they found a Black Labrador that became one of their group, it still slightly brought back memories.

"Maybe a little," Henry agreed. His Glock was in his hand as he approached the building. He gestured to Jimmy to move to the side, as he did the opposite, Mary and Cindy hanging back with Mark and Carol.

The two men did a quick recce of the front of the gas station, Henry peering around the left corner to see if there was anything amiss. He saw a few cars rotting into the ground along with the lower half of what appeared to be a propane tank.In the past the tank had exploded, taking off the upper half, leaving the jagged remains of the bottom.

Jimmy did the same to the right side, seeing nothing that could be conceived as a threat. All he saw were shadows but no movement. He relaxed his eyes and turned his head slightly, letting his peripheral vision try and catch movement. After a full ten seconds and nothing happened, the shadows remaining immobile, he nodded to himself and walked over to Henry, who was standing before the main section of the gas station. The two pumps still there stood vigil over the lot, though the hoses were gone.

The main door to the building was intact and closed.

The plate glass window to the right of the door was intact, also, a dark Citgo motor oil sign hanging in the window. The neon OPEN sign was off as well. As if it would be any other way.

Jimmy gestured to the dark sign with the muzzle of his shotgun. "I think they're closed for the night, Henry."

Henry merely grunted in response.

Jimmy stepped up to the door. "I've got this, old man. Wouldn't want you to over exert yourself and break a hip."

"Keep it up, wise guy, and we'll see whose hip gets broke tonight." Henry tried to act annoyed but his heart wasn't in it. He was too tired to banter with Jimmy. It had been a hell of a long day, what with waking up from the matter transfer jump, then being chased by a sec droid, and finally ending up here, at the gas station. He was dead on his feet and couldn't wait to finally lie down for the night.

"I'm right here whenever you're ready," Jimmy quipped, still full of energy, still spoiling for some back and forth sparring. But when Henry didn't respond he quieted down and moved to the door. Bracing his shoulder against it, he shoved hard, but the door didn't so much as budge an inch. "Shit. It's locked." He glanced at the window, figuring he could simply shatter it and climb through, but realized that wouldn't be prudent. The intact window was a deterrent to attack, as well as keeping out flying insects. Being warm and humid out, mosquitoes were already appearing now that the day was finished.

He decided to kick the door in and solve the problem. He waved for Henry to stand back. "I'm gonna break it down to get us inside. That okay with you?"

Henry bowed slightly, in a 'be my guest' gesture, and Jimmy got to work. Henry noticed Mary had stepped away from Cindy and the new couple, and was walking over to the end of the building. She moved around the corner and was gone from sight. He didn't like her exploring alone, but didn't feel there was any immediate threat in the area. Still, he probably should have gone after her, but his attention was focused on Jimmy, who was having a hell of a time with the door.

Jimmy made a run at the door after giving up kicking it. He rebounded off it as if he'd come up against a solid wall.

Henry grinned but said nothing. After the first kick, Henry had seen the way the door took the impact and realized it was made of metal, though the door had been molded to look like it was wooden.

The locking mechanism must have been well made also, the door a formidable barricade. Henry didn't see the reason, not when if someone really wanted to get inside, they could go through the plate glass window, but the gas station was built before the apocalypse, where a thief might try the door, but not want to break a large picture window, in fear of being discovered. In modern times, the station would have been well-lit as well, not lost in shadows as it was now.

Jimmy got to his feet after falling to the ground. With a grunt of anger, he kicked at the door again—to no avail. Disgusted and feeling silly, he unslung his shotgun from over his shoulder and prepared to blow the damn lock off the door.

"Ah, Jimmy, you don't need to do that," Henry said calmly, seeing that his friend was pretty agitated and not wanting to aggravate the younger man's mood. Besides, if he fired the shotgun, the report would alert anyone or anything in the area that the companions were there.

Jimmy turned to face Henry, his face filled with anger and embarrassment. "Why the fuck not?"

Henry couldn't stop the smile that creased his lips, though he did manage not to laugh as he said and pointed to the plate glass window, "Because Mary's already inside."

"What?" He looked around, then focused on the window, and the grinning face of Mary as she looked out at the two men. She waved once, then faded into the shadows as she stepped back. A moment later there was noise at the door as locks were undone. The door opened with falling dust and debris, Mary standing there with an even wider grin than before.

"How the hell did you get in there?" Jimmy demanded.

She shrugged. "There's no back wall. I just walked in that way. You know, we really should recce a place on all sides before we start kicking and punching things."

Henry didn't have an answer for her, knowing she was right. But then, who would have imagined the building would be structurally sound on all sides, minus a rear wall?

Cindy joined them, along with Mark and Carol. "Are we going in or what?" she asked, wanting to rest for the night.

Henry looked at Mary. "It okay in there?"

She nodded. "Nothing dangerous inside that I saw, and the room off this door is separate from the rest of the place, so we should be safe for the night."

"Good, then let's go in, I'm exhausted." He looked at the others. "We'll figure out the watch schedule after we eat."

Everyone agreed, and one by one they entered the gas station, Mary, being last to stand at the door, closing it behind them.

There was no fire burning within the three walls of the gas station, not with the threat of cannies being so prevalent.

Jimmy was on guard duty, and was making his rounds in the immediate vicinity of the building, his orders to stay within a few feet of the old station.

Some ancient and dented oil barrels had been lined up near the interior doorframe to add a measure of protection, but with an entire wall missing, there was only so much that could be done.

After a quick meal of MRE's, canned goods, and bottled water, along with a few vitamins to replenish much-needed nutrients not being taken in by the companions, due to their lack of a healthy diet, everyone was sitting quietly, talking.

Cindy and Carol had hit it off quickly and were chatting softly together, while Mary leaned back against the doorframe leading into the interior of the station and listened. She thought Carol was a nice person as well, but wasn't as taken with the older woman as Cindy was.

Mary considered that perhaps she was slightly jealous of Carol. Mary and Cindy had been traveling together for years and in that time had become more than friends. Sisters would be a better description. But now there was another female vying for Cindy's attention, and subconsciously Mary wondered if she resented it.

Mark and Henry chatted together as well, a few feet from the women.

"Have Carol and I joined your group?" Mark asked hopefully. He had willingly shared what little food he had with the others in the hopes of being accepted by the companions.

Henry said nothing in reply at first, and with his face lost in the shadows of nightfall, Mark couldn't read him.

Finally, after what seemed an intolerable silence, but was in fact only seconds, Henry responded, "Let's just say we're going in the same direction for now."

"Oh, okay," Mark said with disappointment in his voice. "That's fine with me, and thank you." There was an awkward silence between the two men, Henry not volunteering anything. Mark let the silence hang for a moment between them, then asked, "So where are you and your friends from? Have you been together long?"

"Why don't you go first with the wheres and whens," Henry said flatly.

"Oh, uhm, okay, I can do that." Mark smiled friendlily, then realized Henry probably couldn't see him. "We're from San Bernardino. Have you ever been?"

Henry shook his head, not saying anything.

"Oh, well, it's beautiful, or it was before the, well, you know."

"Yeah, I know," Henry said.

When nothing further was offered, Mark realized he should continue. "It's east of L.A. There's a resort town there called Big Bear Lake. That's where I met Carol. She was visiting with her family and we hit it off. A year later and we were married. That was a little over six years ago." He gazed across the small room to look at her, his wife not noticing, as she was engrossed in conversation with Cindy. "I always loved the temperature in Cali. Did you know it rarely gets below 35 or above 104? And no snow, never. Most people know of the city because it lies along RT 66." He stopped talking, realizing he was rambling. He was nervous. Henry made him nervous. And why not? Mark wasn't a killer, nor a fighter, but as he looked at the man before him, sitting silently in the dark, he knew that the man in front of him was. But he also knew there was mercy within Henry, or else he and Carol would have been killed, instead of the present results. Mark decided he needed to voice his thoughts. "Thank you for not killing us. I sure thought we were goners when you first barged into the room and yelled at us."

"You don't know how close you were," Henry stated, leaving it at that. He didn't feel the need to go into his hesitation upon seeing Carol's blonde hair and mistaking the woman for his lost love Sue. Why would he ever go into that with a total stranger?

"I think I did actually, which is why I'm in your debt. We both are." Mark sighed. "Things are so different now. Sometimes I don't know how I've managed to make it this far alive, and with Carol." He shrugged. "I guess you could say I'm the luckiest guy in the world, given all I've been through. And despite it all, I still managed to hold onto my wife."

There was a time a comment like that would have been stinging to Henry, when he thought about his late wife Emily, but time had managed to heal that wound. Sue had filled that hole in his heart, and losing her was still fresh. Emily was gone for years and his time with her felt like another lifetime ago. In truth, it really was another life. He'd come so far, killed so many, survived so much since he'd lost his wife.

What was odd was there was no guilt for barely feeling the loss of Emily anymore.

So much loss.

But he was still here, alive, and he had his friends. Mary, Jimmy and Cindy were his kin, if not in blood, than in reality.

Mark was still talking, but Henry hadn't heard a word, too lost in his thoughts to really care, if he was being completely honest. The fat man was nice enough, but Henry knew not to become invested with a stranger. When they ended up dead there would be less to forget.

Deciding he was done talking for the night, Henry stood up abruptly. "I'm gonna go check on Jimmy, see if he needs a break."

"Oh, uhm, okay, sure. Do you need me to come?" Mark asked.

"No, you're fine here." He glanced over at the women and got Mary's attention. "I'm gonna check on Jimmy."

"Okay, Henry, be careful," Mary said.

He smiled at her. "Always."

Henry scuffed his boots on the ground a few times, then cleared his throat so Jimmy would hear him coming, as he stepped out into the night, away from the building. The wind had died down, leaving the night relatively silent, not even the tree branches swooshing. There were a few stars out, peeking through the low cloud cover. It looked like it might rain, some of the clouds too thick to see through in the distance, but the air smelled clean for the moment, with nothing to suggest it would rain anytime soon.

Jimmy slapped his neck with the palm of his hand, turning at Henry's signal, knowing who it was automatically. "Fucking mosquitoes are eating me alive."

One buzzed by Henry's face and he swatted it away. "Yeah, I can tell." Upon joining the younger man, the two stood silently, looking out onto the road the gas station was set back on. Nothing stirred. "You need me to spell you for a bit?"

Jimmy shook his head. "Nah, I'm good. That dinner we had sucked hard, Henry."

"Yeah, it's never very good when we can't have a fire. But beggars can't be choosers. Your belly's full. Be thankful for that, at least."

"I guess." Jimmy changed the subject, not wanting to dwell on the terrible meal he'd had to consume. "So, we keeping those two now? Is that what we're doing? Taking in strays? They're not worth the effort, and they could get one of us killed if they make a mistake."

Henry assumed Jimmy was talking about Mark and Carol, and he said as much for confirmation.

"Who the fuck else would I be talking about?" Jimmy insisted.

Henry sighed. "What would you prefer we do with them? You want to kill them?"

Jimmy scratched where the mosquito had bit him. "Fuck no, I mean, not in cold blood. Jesus, Henry, that's cold to even say that."

"Exactly. So we're stuck with them for a while. At least 'til we can drop them off somewhere safe. I don't want to leave them on their own. It's pretty obvious they won't last long. It's a damn miracle they're still alive as it is."

"Would you consider taking them with us to the bunker if we go back?" Jimmy asked.

"No, wasn't planning on it."

"So you'll just abandon them then, if not now, later, is that right?"

Henry sighed. "Jesus, Jimmy, I don't really want to have to plan that far ahead. Let's worry about the here and now." He stepped away from Jimmy, his voice carrying over his shoulder, despite his tone being low, close to a whisper. "Besides, that sec droid is still waiting for us. We're not getting back inside there unless we can kill that thing." He began to walk away. "I'll be back in an hour to relieve you."

Jimmy said nothing, watching Henry's retreating silhouette in the darkness. Turning, he began walking again, following the route he had made for his time on guard duty. Cursing softly, he slapped at another mosquito. "Shit, at least something's eating well out here tonight."

Chapter 8

The night passed uneventfully, the rain holding off. Henry relieved Jimmy, and later in the morning, Mary took over. Henry had given her orders not to wander outside the station. After an entire night of no activity, he didn't want her walking around the perimeter exposed. Not to mention, with someone walking around, it would only draw attention.

So Mary sat behind the plate glass window, two feet in, so that she could see out without the window causing her any glare from what wan light filtered down from a cloudy sky.

The false dawn was tough on her, her eyes feeling heavy, but soon enough the actual dawn cracked in the east. As the sky lightened, so did her mood, and she was awake and feeling good, the sluggishness banished like the darkness had been, by the time she began waking the others.

Henry wanted to be moving out as the sun rose, not wanting to waste any more daylight than he had to.

Breakfast was eaten quickly, immediately after everyone rotated to use the bathroom. That was done by finding a corner and simply dropping trou. The gas station had a bathroom but it was disgusting, with dried feces covering the toilet seat. Some was even in the bowl, though dried brown was also on the walls of the four foot square room.

Jimmy was the one who had the misfortune of going in first, and after his description, no one was interested in using it. Jimmy brought up the image more than once that morning, finding it hard to comprehend how someone had taken the time to fill their hand with their shit, then use it to paint the walls brown. Why? What was the end purpose?

But one gem found in the filthy bathroom was an unused roll of toilet paper. Jimmy had practically skipped out of the room to show the others. When things like running water were rare, something as simple as toilet paper was a hell of a find.

An hour after Mary woke Henry and the others, they were setting out on the road again. Henry was on point, followed by Mary and Cindy. Mark and Carol were next, both groggy and barely awake. Jimmy was last. He constantly swept his head left and right and turned around to walk backwards, making sure no one was coming up on them.

Mark complained almost immediately as the group set out. He whined about his feet, about the humid air, and after only an hour began asking Henry for a break.

Henry was quickly growing tired of hearing the large man talk. He couldn't imagine how he'd managed to survive for as long as he had, his wife as well, as she seemed dependent on her husband.

Finally, Henry stopped, turned, and waited for Mark to catch up to him. When the heavy-set man was only three feet away from him, Henry said, "Look, Mark, I've been listening to you complain for over an hour and we just hit the road. If you're suffering now, what's gonna happen five hours from now? Because that's the next time we're gonna rest, when we take a break for lunch."

"I'm awfully, sorry, Henry," Mark said, winded. "It's just that my feet are killing me."

"Mark, I'm gonna be as honest with you as I can be, all right?"

"Oh, sure, Henry, please, go right ahead."

"I don't care if your feet hurt. If you're gonna stay with us, you need to toughen up."

"I know but…"

"But nothing. We're only as strong as our weakest link, and it looks like that's now you, pal." Henry glared at the large man. "So suck it up and do what needs to be done, or else…" He let his warning hang in the air, letting Mark's imagination do the rest.

"He's right, Mark," Carol said. "You can do it, honey. I know you can."

Mark only nodded in reply.

Henry looked at the man for another few seconds, then glanced past him at the others. Jimmy ran his finger across his throat. He already wanted to dump the new dead weight, finding both of them a liability. Neither Mark nor Carol was fighting material. The last two recruits had been Sue and Raven, and both had suffered terrible fates. These two new ones were pathetic in his eyes.

"When can I get my rifle back?" Mark asked.

"When I say so," Henry answered before turning around and continuing onward, the hunting rifle hanging over his shoulder, muzzle pointing down at the ground. The road they were on was two lanes wide on either side, with a guard rail in the center. Retail stores were on both sides, but even from a distance it didn't look as if there was anything worth salvaging. As they walked down the road, weaving amongst the stalled cars rotting on the pavement, they glanced across the hardtop at the storefronts. Every one had shattered glass windows, doors stuck open, or propped in that position. All of them were fire damaged, with collapsed roofs and front walls. Henry wondered if perhaps a gas main had exploded, the flames flowing through the pipes to enter each and every structure. The gas station had been unharmed, as it wasn't connected to the natural gas pipes; he remembered the burst propane tank in the back of the building.

A little before noon the sky grew dark, extinguishing the light and making it feel as if dusk was falling. Minutes later, the clouds opened up, dropping a heavy downpour onto the area and drenching them in seconds. Lightning flashed in the distance, followed by the crack of thunder.

Becoming soaking wet so fast, made Henry decide to just keep moving—it wasn't as if they could become any wetter than they already were, and he wanted to cover a little more ground before stopping, perhaps for the day, if the rain persisted.

"Why don't we just stop now?" Mary asked.

"We need to find a place to light a fire," he explained as they walked through the rain. He told her and the others his summary about them being already wet, and wanting to put more distance from where they'd found Mark and Carol, to avoid the cannies if they were still in the area. Water dropped off his nose to splash his mouth as he talked, and it was hard to see. The rain drops were so thick it was like lines of water were filling the air. He gestured to the buildings on either side of them. "None of these building have roofs from the looks of it. We need to find one relatively intact to light a fire to dry our clothes and packs, and with dry kindling inside it."

"Then let's pick up the pace," Jimmy called from the back, after hearing Henry explain. The rain was loud but he managed to hear most of Henry's explanation.

"I agree," Cindy said. Her hair was pasted flat to her head, making her resemble a wet dog.

"Okay then," Henry said. "Double time it, people. The sooner we find someplace with a roof, the sooner we'll get out of the rain."

Henry began to jog, though it was more like a fast walk. Running burned too much energy compared to walking. But being soaking wet, and knowing the ticket to getting dry was moving on from where he stood, the motivation was there, as was the strength.

Mark groaned as they began to double-time it, but Henry ignored him. It wasn't Henry's fault the man was so overweight, and if he wanted to stay with the group, he needed to keep up with them.

Carol spoke encouraging words to keep her husband moving.

When they'd covered less than half a mile, Henry could hear Mark huffing and puffing, even over the downpour. Glancing over his shoulder, he saw Mark's face was set in a grimace, but he was putting one foot in front of the other, though he looked as if he would fall over at any minute.

Respecting the man's willingness to conform, Henry slowed his pace down slightly, wanting to give the fat man a fighting chance. Carol noticed this after only a few minutes, and the next time Henry glanced over his shoulder, she mouthed the words "Thank you."

Henry smiled in reply, then turned and concentrated on the road ahead.

Lightning flashed across the sky and thunder cracked. The road was covered with a heavy film of water that never seemed to disappear. Their boots splashed in the deep puddles as they jogged down the center of the road, zigging and zagging around vehicles and other obstacles.

Desiccated bodies floated by, mostly nothing but sinew and gristle, the clothes falling apart with the movement of the corpses. But bodies were not new to the companions. They either stepped over, walked around, or even kicked the bodies aside, the cadavers nothing more than floating detritus amongst the branches and rubbish the downpour had dislodged.

The rain continued unabated.

After walking around a sharp curve in the road two hours later, Henry stopped in the middle of the wide street, taking in what was blocking it. The others quickly caught up until everyone was standing in a group.

"It's beautiful," Mary said in awe.

Henry nodded in agreement, as he took in Mother Nature.

The entire road on his side was covered from one end to the other with greenery. Kudzu was rampant, which in itself wasn't very attractive, but mixed in with that foliage was a large mass of flowering azaleas. The rainbow of color was a stark contrast to the gloomy day.

"What the fuck is everyone gawking at?" Jimmy snapped. "It's just bunch of flowers."

Cindy punched Jimmy on the arm. "Don't be so ignorant," she stated. "These only bloom for a few weeks in Spring. We're lucky to find them like this."

Henry couldn't tell how thick the greenery was, nor what might be within it, so he began walking to the guardrail. "We can hop over to the other side and keep going."

"Sounds like a plan," Jimmy said. He wiped water from his eyes and ushered the others before him, then like before, took last in line.

The rain had abated somewhat, and the torrential downpour from earlier in the day had subsided. Now, the rain was steady but not as if someone had turned on a faucet.

Small rivers lined the road, the rushing water seeking an escape.

Half an hour later, Jimmy spotted a highway sign and called up to Henry, pointing. "Check out the sign." It was a sign stating that a Holiday Inn was only two miles down the road. Just take the fifth exit from where they were and take a left at the bottom of the ramp.

Henry read the sign and looked back at the others. "You guys want to see if there are any vacancies?"

Mary nodded. "Sure, I'm game."

"Me too," Cindy added.

"That sounds wonderful," Mark added.

Henry pointed a finger at Mark. "You don't get a vote."

"Oh, sorry." Mark studied his feet.

Henry regretted snapping at him. Mark seemed to be trying his best to get along, and so far he'd shown nothing but appreciation to Henry.

"Forget it. Glad you're on board." Henry gestured to the others. "Come on, maybe they'll let us check in early, even though it's before three."

Unfortunately, the mile or so to the hotel wasn't as simple as they'd hoped.

Less than a quarter mile since seeing the sign, they were blocked from passing by a dozen people.

They seemed to appear out of thin air, popping out from behind stalled cars or debris lining the highway. One moment the highway was clear, the next instant it was crowded with enemies, and there was no doubt they were dealing with foes, not friends.

"Shit," Henry hissed. He dropped down to one knee to make a smaller target, then glanced over his shoulder to make sure the others were fanning out around him, so as to not make a tighter target. Mark and Carol stood gawking in the center of the road, until Cindy grabbed both of them and yanked them to the side, where they crouched down near a Saturn with flat tires and shattered windows.

Mary and Jimmy were opposite them, using another derelict car with no tires and missing front fenders for cover.

Henry was alone in the center of the road, nothing around him. The highway where he stood was devoid of anything useful to use for protection, most of the vehicles on the shoulders.

Figuring if the newcomers were going to shoot at him, as they hadn't done so yet, he was already screwed, he decided to stand back up. He stared back at the dozen men and women, as they in turn did the same.

Fifty paces away, they were spread out completely across the highway, blocking passage. Henry studied them, taking in their attire and weapons at a glance.

Wearing mostly rags that had once been clothing, he didn't see a firearm amongst them, which was probably the reason no bullets had come his way upon their appearance. They did carry an assortment of melee weapons, and a few held crossbows, probably looted from some long dead sporting goods store. More than half brandished honed steel, one or two a large machete equal to Henry's panga, and a few even held makeshift spears. There was a Black man in the back of the group wearing an honest to God business suit, only it was in tatters; he wore no tie. Henry figured it must be casual Friday, today. Ties being optional.

They had a sickly look to them, too. Sores could be seen where skin wasn't hidden by clothing, and their faces were pale, as if they'd just gotten over a bad bout with the flu.

Henry heard scuffing feet behind him to his right and saw Jimmy approaching, his shotgun leveled at the enemy. When the younger man was beside Henry, he leaned in close and gestured with his chin at the man who stood slightly in front of the group.

"You see what the necklace that fucker's wearing?"

Henry had to squint a little due to the rain to get a better look at the man's adornment. "Shit," he hissed again. "Is that…?"

"Yeah, it is. Fucking ear necklace."

Henry knew what that meant and said so. "Goddamn cannies."

"Fuck yeah. These must be some of the bastards Mark told us about."

"I count thirteen." Henry had been off by one person from his initial observation.

So far none of the cannies moved; they just stood staring at Henry and the others.

"No guns in sight, that's why they haven't attacked us…yet," Jimmy whispered. "Let's take them the fuck out. There could be a shitload more coming up behind us. We need to go now."

"I know, but not yet. Just hold tight," Henry said softly. "Maybe we can get out of this without any blood."

"Why? You care about these assholes?"

"No, of course not. I'm talking about us. There's still more of them than there are of us." He shook his head. "Let's not take a chance we might not need to make."

Then the leader, a tall man with thick brown hair and small eyes, along with a beard the color to match his hair, began to laugh, long and loud, as rain cascaded down his face.

The rest of his group began to join him, the laughter sounding strangely threatening, which had to be the reason. Instead of some sort of undulating yell, this guy liked to laugh.

Then they began to bang their weapons together, so that clanging sounded across the highway. The sound was slightly muted by the rain, but it was still quite threatening.

Still, the cannies remained immobile, their feet planted on the ground. Henry didn't like it at all, and he knew he was going to have to decide what to do, and take a chance on where the dice fell, when Jimmy took any decision Henry might have made away from him.

"Fuck this shit," Jimmy spat just before he opened fire with his shotgun, killing the leader instantly.

Henry began to fire as well, the highway filling with the sound of gunshots, the laughter of the cannies quickly dying away as all hell broke loose.

Chapter 9

In less than a heartbeat after Jimmy began to shoot, followed by Henry, the rest of the companions joined in as well. After all, who wanted to just stand there looking stupid, and complaining they hadn't been involved once the lead started flying?

The cannies were caught completely by surprise. Whether it was because they were used to people being too terrified of them to fight, or because they weren't a very good fighting unit, the end result was complete carnage.

The cannies that held crossbows did attempt to use them, but before they managed to so much as raise them, they were gunned down, their bodies riddled with bullets. Falling to the ground, their limbs thrashed around in death, until the movements became nothing but feeble twitches.

Jimmy's shotgun blast nearly cut the leader in half, his intestines spilling out along with a few other choice organs. The man's laughter turned to screams of agony as he flopped onto the ground, his legs kicking wildly, his hands going to his stomach. He attempted to shove the greasy-looking ropes back into his torso, with little luck.

Then Jimmy shot him again, this time in the face, blowing half the head clear off the man's neck. The body stopped squirming and was still, other than a squirting of arterial blood from the neck stump.

Henry shot a Latino cannie standing behind the leader with a quick double tap, followed by one more bullet for good measure. All three 9mm rounds hit the cannie's neck, nearly severing it from the man's shoulders. He did a death dance for a few seconds and then toppled over, his jagged neck wound squirting blood onto the rain-soaked asphalt.

Henry wasn't pleased with his aim, however. He'd been aiming for the man's torso, but with rain in his eyes, he'd been off by over six inches. Though Jimmy had acted impulsively, it hadn't been a complete surprise to Henry. His friend wasn't known for thinking before doing, and this time was no exception.

A Black female cannie to the right of the fallen leader took a few steps backwards, then turned around as if to run. Henry shot her in the lower back, the impacts blowing out her stomach to spill her intestines before her. She continued trying to escape but only managed to trip on her own bowels. She toppled face-first onto the pavement, smashing her nose on impact. Her nostrils gushed crimson; the nose was surely broken. Wailing in pain, she sputtered blood and began to crawl across the pavement.

Mary lined up a shot with a short, balding man in his fifties. Her .38 barked once, and the man went down, heart shot. He didn't even twitch; he was dead in such a short time. Twenty seconds from when he was struck to lying on the ground, eyes open in death, rain hitting his face.

Cindy fired a short burst with her M16, keeping the rifle on semi-auto. In the past she was aware of muzzle climb, and by the fifth round her aim would be too high and off target. She kept the bursts short, so she could control the firearm better. Still, the triple burst she sent at a cannie blew the man off his feet. Before he fell, he bumped into another man with a Mohawk, knocking him off balance. Henry didn't allow Mohawk to regain his feet, and shot him through the right eye. That time he'd planned the shot, and grunted proudly when Mohawk's head snapped back and the body dropped to the ground like a puppet with its strings cut.

When the last cannie was down, over fifty rounds had been fired, utterly destroying the cannie attack party.

All were dead with the exception of the one woman Henry had gut shot from behind. Blubbering and mewling, she was attempting to crawl away. A diluted, watery blood trail showed where she had managed to go from her original position to almost off the highway and onto the shoulder. The blast had severed her spine, leaving her legs useless.

Muttering a curse under his breath, Henry walked over to her as she dragged herself across the road, her legs nothing more than dead weight.

As he watched her for a moment, he thought back to years ago, before the world had gone to hell. Back then, he would have felt pity for this poor, suffering human being.

But time and experience had changed him into a man who, though he could show mercy when it was warranted, also had no problem dealing out a death sentence.

Sliding his panga from its sheath, he pressed his right boot onto her back, his left hand grabbing her by her hair and yanking her head back. Before she could try to fight him off, he brought the panga around and sliced her throat, the razor sharp blade penetrating at least two inches, severing the carotid artery and larynx. Blood shot out of her neck a good three feet. He let her go and stepped away, not wanting to get hit with blood spray.

"Make sure none of the others are playing possum," Henry snapped at Jimmy, as he continued to check on the other prone bodies. "And be careful." He glanced at Mary and Cindy. "You two keep watch. Keep an eye on Mark and Carol."

"Right," Mary replied, Cindy only nodding in acceptance.

"Okay," was all Jimmy said. He pulled his hunting knife from its sheath and began moving amongst the presumed corpses, kicking them in the side to see if it resulted in a moan or groan from said body. Not that he needed to for most of them. By the mortal wounds they'd suffered, it was obvious they weren't faking and were truly dead.

"All set," Henry said after checking the last body.

"Yeah, me too. All dead." Jimmy joined Henry, as the two went to join the others, waiting in the center of the road.

Mark's mouth was hanging open, in shock at the brutality he'd witnessed.

Henry saw the look on his face as well. "What's your problem?"

"That woman," Mark said softly. "She was already down, wounded, and you just…slit her throat."

Henry set his jaw at the remark. "And what did you want me to do with her?"

"Oh, ah, well, I don't know really."

"Exactly." He stepped up so that his nose was only inches from Mark's. "She was the enemy, and we don't take prisoners, and that goes double for no-good cannibals. Even if she was gonna die I wasn't about to leave her behind. If there are any more of her kind around, I don't need her telling them about us, which way we went, or our numbers."

"So you just killed her in cold blood? Why, that's murder."

Jimmy stepped up as well now, angry. "Is this fucking guy serious, Henry?" He poked Mark in the belly with the muzzle of his shotgun. "Maybe next time we'll let them have you and your wife for lunch." He jabbed Mark again. "Way I figure it, if they get a hold of you, they won't need more meat for at least a week."

"Jimmy," Cindy said, a little surprised. "That's not called for."

"Isn't it, babe? Look at this guy. We're runnin' around tryin' to find our next meal, sometimes missing one or more, and this guy looks like he's been doing seconds at the buffet since the deaders started running around and everything went to shit."

"It's not my fault I'm so big, it's a glandular problem," Mark said in defense.

Henry snapped his arm down, as if he was slicing the air with his hand. "Enough of this. It isn't getting us anywhere." He looked down the highway behind him, searching for movement, and relieved when there was none. "We need to get a move on. The gunshots will draw any others to our location. There's no way only those thirteen were a single group. There's got to be more of them."

"You think they were some kind of hunting party?" Mary asked.

"Yeah, had to be." He turned and gazed off into the distance, trying to see ahead of them, but not having much luck thanks to the light rain still falling. "Let's get moving. We'll go to the hotel, and if it's safe to stay, we can wait a while, see if anyone else is following us."

"And if there is?" Jimmy asked, Cindy punching him in the arm for his question. It wasn't needed, and she knew Jimmy was aware of it.

"If there is, we'll deal with it. No more talking, move out." Henry turned and began walking, not waiting to see if the others were behind him. He knew they would be. They'd traveled together long enough, so that if there was going to be serious dissension, he would already know it.

Everyone began walking again, stepping over or around the corpses, until the bodies were behind them.

After only a few minutes of walking, Henry gestured to Mary to join him on point. When she was beside him, he said, "Take over here, I need to have a little discussion with Jimmy about how 'chain-of-command' works."

"Okay, have fun. You know how he is when you try to correct him."

"I know, but it has to be done."

Henry slowed his pace until he was beside Jimmy at the rear of the group, after acknowledging Cindy as he passed her. Mark and Carol he ignored.

Walking side by side with Jimmy, who didn't pay much attention to why Henry was with him, Henry realized Jimmy was playing ignorant, so he patted Jimmy on the arm to get the younger man's attention. He gestured for Jimmy to fall back with him a little more, until they were both out of earshot of the others.

"Yeah?" Jimmy said.

"We need to talk."

"About what?"

Henry lowered his voice so the others wouldn't hear, but his meaning was clear all the same, despite the lack of anger in his tone. "About how the next time you open fire like that without my permission, I'll leave you for the cannies to eat myself. You got me?"

"Ah, come on, Henry, I only did what you were gonna do. I just got the jump on you."

"I'm not gonna argue with you about this, Jimmy. I'm in charge, not you. I make the call on what we do in a situation like that."

"Yeah, but…"

"But nothing. This isn't a goddamn discussion, you hear me?"

"Shit, Henry."

"I asked you a question."

"Yeah, yes. I hear you. Sorry, shit, I didn't think it was such a big deal."

"Well it was."

They walked in silence for a full minute, the tension between them heavy. Finally, with a deep sigh, Henry reached out and rubbed Jimmy's wet hair. "Ah, Jimmy, what am I gonna do with you?" He said it like a father would to a mischievous son.

Jimmy yanked his head away, not wanting it to get messed up, well, more messed up than it already was. His hair was getting long, and if he and the others ever got a chance to stop and take a break where it was moderately safe, Cindy would have to cut it for him.

"I really am sorry, old man," Jimmy said. "I guess I got too excited. I mean, those fuckers looked intimidating, and I didn't want to end up on their dinner menu. Thank God they didn't have any guns."

"I hear you. And you're right about that. We got lucky. If they'd had guns they woulda got the drop on us easy. They were overconfident. Figured their numbers and who they are would be enough to scare us into not fighting. Probably figured we'd try to escape, and then they'd run us down and kill us."

Jimmy fought off a shiver, one that wasn't entirely from being wet. "What makes someone turn to cannibalism?"

"I don't know, but the thing that scares me is how many people are willing to do it." He shrugged. "There used to be a saying about how civilization was only one missed meal away from collapsing. I guess that's true."

"Well, well, aren't you all philosophical and shit."

Henry shoved Jimmy playfully. "Screw you. That's what I get for trying to have a serious conversation with you."

Jimmy flashed Henry his best shit-eating grin. "Hey, you should know better."

Henry snickered, and with a nod moved up the line until he rejoined Mary.

She glanced at him, and then back at Jimmy. "Did you two get everything sorted out?"

"As much as can be expected when it has to do with Jimmy."

Her left eyebrow went up as if she was still asking a question.

"It's fine, Mary. Yes, me and him are good." He walked a little faster so he was passing her, saying, "You fall back with Cindy. I'm on point again."

"Okay." She leaned over as he passed her and kissed him on the cheek.

"What was that for?"

"Nothing, just showing my appreciation." She dropped back, leaving Henry with a wide smile. Little did Mary know, he'd needed that from her. With a slight pickup to his steps, he led the companions down the highway.

Half a mile further down, the highway shrunk into a two lane road with a single yellow line in its center. The burned out area of storefronts progressed to homes on both sides of the road. The houses were mostly two and three families, with a few single ones mixed in.

Some still had parked cars in their driveways, as if the owners were home for the day, their vehicles waiting patiently until needed. Of course, the cars were in disrepair after sitting for years. Most had flat tires, and were covered with soot and grime.

Leaves had collected on the lower half of the windshield, where the hood was. One car was almost completely flattened, buried under a fallen tree that must have come down in a storm years ago.

The rain had tapered off, with only a heavy mist remaining. The sun was just beginning to peek out through the fading cloud cover. It was humid and warm out, and Henry was once again glad he'd left his heavy arctic jacket back at the redoubt.

Long-dead bodies were scattered everywhere. On porches, lying in gutters, on overgrown lawns.

It was obvious from their looks that these corpses had been the living dead, that is until all the walking dead had simply collapsed, whatever force having animating them ceasing, as if a light switch had been turned off.

Some corpses were in pieces, and scattered here and there were body parts, shiny bits of white bone peeking out amongst the weeds.

Animals had been at them, tearing apart the skeletons to get at whatever meat might have remained.

Sometimes a severed skull glared back at them, its piecemeal body a dozen feet away.

The homes had the typical look Henry had become accustom to.

Weeds grew thick in the gutters of the roofs, sticking out of drainpipes, windows shattered, front doors hanging open.

A few homes looked untouched, with dirty, hazy but intact windows, all the doors closed, and no signs of damage.

"Hey, Henry, some of these houses look like they've never been messed with," Jimmy stated from the rear of the group. "We should check 'em out. Might be some good shit inside we could use."

Henry shook his head no. "Not a good idea right now."

"Why the fuck not?"

He turned around and began walking backwards so he could make eye contact with Jimmy.

"If that hunting party is found by the rest of their people, they'll be more on our heels."

Jimmy checked his six for the hundredth time, as if by Henry saying the words, it would become true. But nothing was following them for as far as he could see down the road behind him. "Sure, that makes sense." But he still looked at the homes longingly as he passed them.

"Maybe we can check them out later."

Jimmy looked like a toddler who had his ice cream taken away. "Yeah, I guess."

Cindy slowed until she was beside Jimmy, then rubbed his back. "I wouldn't mind seeing what's inside some of them either."

"Thanks, babe," Jimmy said.

On the last half mile stretch to the hotel, the residential neighborhood changed over to a street with a row of stores on both sides.

"This must be Main Street," Mary said.

There was a sign ahead for the National Aquarium in Baltimore. Mary was the one to point it out.

"Hey, look, we're on the outskirts of Baltimore. According to that sign, we're only a few miles from it," she said. "I was there once when I was a little girl. I was with my family on vacation. My dad took us and my mom..." She trailed off, suddenly overwhelmed with grief for the loss of her family. It may have been years ago when she assumed they had died when the dead began to walk, but it still hurt to think about them. She missed her family terribly.

"You okay?" Cindy asked.

Mary shook herself back to the present. "Yes, I'm okay. It's just that reminiscing made me think of my parents, that's all."

"Emily wanted to go to the Bahamas on a cruise one time," Henry explained from the front of the group. "But I didn't want to spend the money. Between airplane tickets, hotel, and the price to go, it was all too much to me." He sighed. "Looking back, I wish I'd gone. Saving for the future made sense back then, but now it all seemed pretty redundant."

"You lost your chance, old man," Jimmy said. "I doubt many ships are sailing anymore."

"Nothing I'd want to go on, anyway." His eyes roamed across the new row of storefronts, searching for signs of life. So far Henry had seen nothing to indicate danger, but he'd traveled far and wide enough to know better. "Look alive, people. Lots of places for someone to hide."

"Henry," Mary called, though she kept her voice low.

"Yeah?"

"Have you noticed there are no bodies anywhere? I mean, there's nothing."

"No, not until you mentioned it, but now that you have. Yeah, there's nothing at all." He frowned. "That doesn't make sense. Place like this, all these stores. The dead would have been all over this place. When they all collapsed, they'd still be around."

"Like back in that neighborhood behind us," Jimmy added.

Cindy spoke up. "So someone cleaned them up."

"Must have." Henry stopped walking for a moment, his eyes taking in the dark interior of the stores. There was a little bit of everything. From a dry cleaners to an ice cream shop. A Mexican restaurant and a cell phone store. Near the end, with a shattered front glass window, a Realtor office could be seen. In between was the typical smattering of pizza, sub shops and convenience stores. Even from where Henry stood—the ones closest to him—he could see those places were completely gutted, not so much as a pencil or pen remaining.

"Look over there, Henry, is that a gun store?" Jimmy called with a hint of excitement in his voice.

Henry followed where Jimmy was pointing and saw what the younger man was talking about. Nestled between an acupuncture/massage store and a Dollar store, the sign clear as day, was an Army/Navy outlet.

"That's worth a few minutes to check out," Henry said. "Come on, double time it. In and out in five minutes or less." He began to jog, the others right behind him. Mark wasn't as nimble as the others due to his weight and he quickly fell behind. Carol outdistanced him, but when she realized he wasn't with her, she slowed to help him.

Jimmy caught up to Henry, shaking his head as he ran. "Fat ass back there is gonna get one of us killed, you know that, don't you?"

Henry glanced over his shoulder to see the large man huffing and puffing, doing his best to keep up. Mary and Cindy were right behind Henry, jogging easily. The four companions were all fit and healthy, years of traversing a ravaged world transforming them into a tight fighting unit. "No, he won't. I won't let him. He's not one of us, at least not yet. If he turns into dead weight, I'll be the first one to cut him loose."

"If you don't I will," Jimmy warned.

"Look, Jimmy, I remember a time when I wasn't very athletic. If you recall I had quite a belly on me."

"Yeah, I remember. But even with that beer belly of yours, I don't recall you not being able to run when you had to." He chuckled, thinking back to those days. "Shit, Henry, we did a lot of fucking running back then, too."

Their trip down memory lane ended abruptly upon reaching the storefront. Henry pointed at the girls. "You guys wait here. Anything funny happens, give a shout. Jimmy and I will be right back."

"Okay, good luck," Mary said, hoping there might be something to salvage inside the gun store. The two men stepped through the open glass door to investigate, leaving the women behind.

Mark finally reached Mary and Cindy, and he practically fell over, only Carol preventing him from fully toppling. He dropped down onto an old newspaper kiosk for the local paper, which was lying sideways on the sidewalk. He grabbed his chest and tried to slow his breathing.

Carol looked at Mary and Cindy with what appeared to be either embarrassment, shame or both. "He's not in great shape," was all she said in explanation.

"That's an understatement," Cindy said. "How the hell did he manage to keep away from all the dead when they were everywhere?"

"We spent the first year in a bomb shelter Mark had built for us. It was buried in the backyard."

"No shit?" Cindy said, Mary surprised as well.

"Yes. But eventually we ran low on supplies so we had no choice but to leave it. Then we hooked up with a small group of survivors, and they did a great job of protecting us."

"Really?" Mary asked. "Why?"

"You know, I asked the leader of the group once. See, they were a lot like hippies. You know, Woodstock people?" The two women nodded. "Yes, well, they believed all life was sacred, so apparently, that was enough for them to allow us to be a part of their group. I did work in the preparation of food, in the kitchen, though. So I did work for my food, for both of us."

"Oh, I see," Mary said, then turned away, wanting to keep watch for danger.

There was a torn and faded awning hanging by a few threads over the gun store. A brisk breeze, more of a gust, than anything else, washed over the area, causing the awning to shift slightly. As it did, Mary caught sight of something painted on the wall of the building. Curious, she walked over to the front of the store, grabbed the material, and yanked the awning off its mooring. The material was thin where it still connected to the building and it didn't take much strength to separate it from the wall. With only one pull the awning separated, to fall onto the sidewalk. Due to the rain soaking it, there was no dust when it fell, despite the material being covered in it, most of the debris collecting in gulleys and valleys made from the way it had been hanging.

As soon as the awning was off the building, Mary gasped and spun around, her .38 swinging along with her.

"Mary, what's the matter?" Cindy asked, but then she saw what Mary had seen, and she too, began to study their surroundings more diligently than before. "Better tell the boys," she said quickly.

"I'm on it. You got this?" Mary asked.

Cindy nodded. "Yes, just go."

Mary was already moving. She glanced at the wall one more time, and what was on it, before moving into the gun store.

On the front of the building, in large letters of black paint, with thick drips at the bottom of some of the letters, were the words: *IF YOU'RE READING THIS, YOU'RE ALREADY DEAD!*

Chapter 10

Henry and Jimmy stood in the center of the gun store, surrounded on all sides by empty shelving. Signs covered the walls on three sides, proclaiming SUPPORT THE SECOND AMMENDMENT! BUY A GUN! And CARRY A FIREARM—IT'S YOUR BIRTHRIGHT!

Other posters advertised the new Colt or Beretta, or big bastards like Pythons and Pumas. Hunting rifles from Spain and Czechoslovakia were said to be IN STOCK FOR A LIMITED TIME! BUY NOW BEFORE THEY'RE GONE!

Behind the sales counter was nothing but shattered glass, not even an intact but empty cardboard box that once held ammunition.

"Clean as a baby's ass," Jimmy said. "Not so much as a bullet left." He used his hand as a comb, slicking back his wet hair and wiping off some of the moisture on his face. It felt good to be out of the weather, even if it was only for a few minutes.

Everything on him was wet, even his underwear briefs. He desperately wanted to pull the material out of the crack of his ass, where it had wedged itself, but he didn't want Henry to see him. Moving so that a shelf was blocking him from view, he got to work extricating the offending cotton.

Henry didn't notice, and walked deeper into the store, his eyes roaming across the shelves. "Probably been empty for years. The locals must've cleaned the place out back at the beginning."

"Yeah, fuckers. Coulda left something for someone else."

"Would you have?"

Jimmy shrugged. "No, guess not." He continued wandering around the store. Movement caught his eye, and he swung that way, shotgun leading the way. He saw something dark and large, low to the ground. It jumped from its hiding place and went the opposite way. Yelping in terror, he prepared to squeeze the trigger on the shotgun, but at the very last moment, he paused. It was a cat, a goddamn cat. It was a big one, though, close to the size of a small dog. The cat ignored him, padding onward, giving the human a wide berth. It glanced once over its shoulder to ensure it wasn't being followed. Jimmy saw a mouse in its mouth, which explained why it had showed itself. The feline wasn't about to give up its dinner for anyone, least of all Jimmy.

"You all right?" Henry called.

"Yeah, I'm fine," he replied sheepishly. He felt like an idiot. If Henry hadn't seen the incident, he wasn't about to share. Something like that, Henry would never let him hear the end of it.

On a nearby shelf were a pile of magazines, all with Guns in their titles. Jimmy shuffled them a little, glancing at the covers. His eyes lingered over one cover in particular. A full-breasted blonde was leaning against a WW2 motorcycle with a sidecar, an M60 Maremont cradled in her arms. All she wore was a red string bikini. He studied the picture for a few more seconds, then covered it with some of the other magazines. He sighed. He was horny as hell, something he hoped to rectify very soon with Cindy. That is, if they ever found a place to make camp that they could consider even remotely safe, yet also allow them a little bit of privacy from the others.

There was an old blue towel on the same shelf as the magazines. Jimmy picked it up, shook it off, and used it to dry himself and his shotgun, which had a sheen of moisture on it from the rain. He always carried it under his coat on a day like this one, but even then, it always managed to get a little wet, even if just on the barrel, where it poked out of his jacket. Unlike Henry, who only had a shirt on, Jimmy still wore the lighter jacket he'd worn under his winter one, though he was sweating like a pig in it. But it was waterproof, so he had fared much better than Henry, who was wearing a shirt soaked completely through. When he was finished drying off, he called over to Henry, holding up the towel. "You want? I found it."

"Yeah, thanks." Henry held up a hand to catch it, Jimmy tossing it over.

Henry quickly used it to dry off as well, still moving about the store. Time was short, multitasking was a necessity. He noticed something of interest on the floor before the front counter, where the owner would have been standing behind it, waiting for his customers to come in. At first glance it looked like a tube or pipe, with a thick lanyard for carrying it over a man's shoulder. Henry had become pretty good at identifying ordnance over the past five or so years. Picking up the tube by its strap, he studied it hopefully.

Jimmy saw him pick up the tube and his eyes perked up. "You find something we can use?"

"Maybe," Henry said, only to realize the tube was empty. "Maybe not." He set the tube on the counter, a wistful look on his face. It would have been a hell of a thing to find the piece of weaponry he'd discovered, along with the ammunition that went with it.

Henry saw the quizzical look on Jimmy's face and he replied, "It's empty." He scanned the area around the counter, along with the shelves behind it. All was as empty as the shelves they'd inspected upon entry.

Jimmy moved closer, eyeing the tube. "Shit, that would have been fantastic if it had been loaded."

"Yeah, but it's not." Henry glanced one last time at the tube, then turned and moved to the far side of the store in search of something useful.

The tube wasn't just a tube, but it did look like a simple pipe from first glance; it was painted flat green. It was the firing mechanism used to shoot 66mm armor-piercing rounds at the enemy. The M-72 LAW fired anti-tank rounds.

It would have been a wonderful weapon to have in their possession, whether used for offense or defense against an enemy.

But without the heavy rounds to go with it, the launch tube was beyond useless. It was so lightweight it didn't even have the potential to be used as a bludgeoning tool.

They resumed their search, the two men splitting up in opposite directions. Jimmy went into the back, and a moment later Henry heard the younger man calling out happily. Henry did a quick scamper into the rear of the gun store, where Jimmy was holding up a small orb with a pin sticking out of a lever on the top. A hand grenade by any definition.

"Look what I found!"

"Is that what I think it is?"

Jimmy nodded. "High Explosive by the code on the side."

"Looks like it. Where'd you find it?" Henry moved closer, looking at the code.

"It was under a pile of rags in that corner." Jimmy pointed to the floor, where there was indeed a pile of old camo clothing, the material shredded to the point it wasn't useful as clothing.

"You sure it's real and not a dummy? Check the bottom."

"I already did. Shit, I'm not an idiot. There's no hole there."

In the past while searching for weapons, the companions had come across fake weapons and grenades, souvenirs for military buffs to add to their collection. The grenades were usually purchased as paper weights or mementoes, but could be repainted to look like a live one.

They looked real from first glance, but anyone experienced knew there was nothing inside them, and they had a decent-sized hole in the bottom.

Jimmy's face showed a look that he didn't like the potential of Henry bursting his bubble and spoiling his find. "You want me to pull the pin and see?"

"No, of course not, just double check and make sure it's live ammunition, that's all."

Jimmy did as instructed, studying the orb for any information. If the grenade was inert, it would have tell tale signs. Sometimes people would fill in the hole on the bottom to make it look more real, but from all signs of inspection, the orb appeared genuine.

"Seems like the real thing to me, Henry. We just got lucky, is all."

"That's good, at least it wasn't a complete waste of time to come inside. You never know when that might come in handy." He pointed to the grenade. "Make sure that pin is okay."

"It is. Christ, quit nagging like an old woman. I know my shit," Jimmy sighed.

"Yeah, I know you do." Henry gazed around the rear of the store one last time, seeing nothing of interest. Jimmy had found that one piece of bread, the single crumb in a cupboard, after everything was assumed to be long gone. It was a great find and was incredibly valuable. "Well, I think we've seen all we're gonna see in here," he said, figuring their time was up. "I guess the rest is a bust."

Both men looked over to see Mary come racing into the store. Only a few minutes had passed since they'd entered the gun store, and both were surprised to see Mary approaching with a look of concern on her face.

"Trouble?" Henry asked, assuming there would be no other reason for her arrival.

"Maybe, probably. Yes, I think so," she said, the words coming out one after another, so it was more of a ramble than a reply.

"Well, which is it?" Henry demanded.

"Just come and see for yourself," she said, then turned, and left the gun store, not waiting to see if the two men were following her.

Henry and Jimmy locked eyes for a moment, not saying a word, then spun on their boot heels and exited the building, Henry leading the way.

Back outside, they joined the others, still wondering what had been so important. Scanning the area, and seeing Cindy's posture, it was clear the group wasn't in imminent danger.

"Okay, we're outside. So what was so urgent?" Henry asked.

Mary raised her right hand, pointing at the graffiti on the wall.

Henry followed her gesture and his mouth turned down into a deep frown as he read the words.

"Now, that isn't good," was all he said. He walked over to the wall and touched the letter Y in the second word. It was dry, as he expected it to be. Not even slightly wet. Who knew how long since the artist had drawn it? "This has probably been here for years, Mary, no reason to get so excited."

"He may be right, Mary," Cindy essayed. "After all, that awning was blocking it from view. Who knows how long it could have been there before we spotted it."

Mary didn't respond, her lips pressed tightly together.

Jimmy patted Henry on the shoulder after reading the words. "Hey, there's some more over there."

Henry's gaze followed where Jimmy now pointed, as did the rest of the companions. Two stores over, across the street, on the intact large front picture window of an ice cream store, more scrawled words in black paint could be seen.

Jimmy was curious so he scanned the area quickly, seeing nothing of importance, and walked over to the window, his shotgun held before him, ready for action. The others trailed behind him, not seeing a reason to rush.

Jimmy read the words out loud. ***"ONE MORE STEP & YOU'RE DEAD!"*** He chuckled. "Someone's got big balls, I'll give 'em that."

"Does this mean we're being watched?" Mark asked, his eyes darting back and forth like a scared baby bird.

"I highly doubt it, dear," Carol said. "You heard Henry. That warning was left months ago, years even. We're safe for the moment. This place is empty of life."

Henry pushed past the others until he was side by side with Jimmy. He didn't know why he did it. Perhaps some simple human urge in the need to touch, to have a tactile sensation along with the information he'd received with his eyes. He reached out to the window and touched one of the letters. The words also had deep drips at the bottom, the artist being too heavy with the paint.

The index finger on his left hand pressed into the paint, his right holding the Glock by his side.

When he removed his hand, he stared at his finger in disbelief, the others not understanding what was wrong, and by his expression, something was definitely wrong.

Henry pressed the finger he'd used to touch the letter to his thumb, then separated them. He then held up his hand so the others could see his fingers.

"What the fuck?" Jimmy whispered.

"You're kidding," Cindy said.

"Oh, that isn't good, is it?" Mark asked, not really expecting an answer, the question rhetorical.

Henry looked at each of his traveling companions, his face grim, his entire body taut with tension. "We need to get out of here, right now."

No one argued.

They all knew Henry was entirely correct. He didn't need to say more, everyone able to sum up their situation. Even Mark and Carol understood.

Henry still had his hand up, the others' eyes all locked onto his index finger and thumb. The reason for him wanting to vacate the area was clear. For his fingertips were now smeared in black paint.

The words of the warning spray-painted on the window were still sticky to the touch.

Chapter 11

"Do you think it's some kind of gang around here? Or the cannies?" Mary asked.

"I doubt it's the cannies. They wouldn't be so bold as to advertise their presence," Henry replied as he wiped his fingers on his pants to clean them of paint. Most of it came off, but some still remained. "But whoever wrote this has to be nearby, and there's no way of knowing if there's one of them or two dozen."

"So what do we do?" Mary asked.

"We keep going the way we were headed. Let's get to that Holiday Inn we saw the sign for a ways back. From there we can figure out our next move." He looked around at the surrounding buildings. "But we need to get away from here. Street like this has far too many places someone could take a shot at us from. Someone with a decent rifle could pick us off easily before we could get to cover."

All eyes went to Mark, who smiled wanly. "Hey, I'm on your side, remember?"

Off in the distance, coming from the way the companions had just traveled, was the unmistakable sound of shouting. It was almost too faint to hear, but when no one was speaking, it carried on the wind.

"Shit," Jimmy spit, a chill running down his spine. "I bet whoever that is, they're looking for us."

"You think it's the cannies?" Cindy asked Jimmy as she moved closer to him. Though a warrior in her own right, she was still a woman who was okay with her man protecting her. She was far too confidant of her own attributes to let her pressing into his arms be a deterrent to her showing concern.

"Who else could it be?" Jimmy said while wrapping an arm around her shoulders.

Mary looked back down the lonely road. "We could find a place to hole up here, face them down when they come."

Henry shook his head. "No can do. If they're locals they'll have a tactical advantage over us. They know this place far better than we do. At least the hotel might be out of their territory."

"Then what are we waiting for?" Jimmy demanded. "Let's get the fuck out of here."

The Holiday Inn was a large, sprawling structure; one-story tall, with white paint and gray trim. The paint was chipping and faded on the entire building after years of neglect. Many of the windows of the rooms were shattered, or had thick cracks, and most of the doors that had outside rooms were open, detritus having built up near the frames so that the doors couldn't be closed unless someone got to some serious cleaning of the area.

On the east side of the building, a massive oak tree had fallen, crushing at least six rooms. The roofing had been demolished and water had gotten in, along with local wildlife, making that area of the motel unsafe to enter for fear of the entire thing coming down on anyone foolish enough to enter.

There was a large sign at the end of the parking lot of the hotel. It had seen better days. Countless storms had come and gone, leaving the sign a tattered mess of fiberglass, plastic and wood.

At the bottom of the sign, where there were once words welcoming conventions—Shriners, Kiwanis and Elks, to name a few— now all but two of the adjustable letters were still there, and those two didn't have much longer before they were also blown away in a future storm.

As the group of six walked up the short driveway leading from the street to the lobby, the sound of yelling and shouting was still so faint that only the sharpest of hearing could detect it. Henry was concerned only slightly. The area surrounding the hotel was large. Once fortified inside the building, there would be no way for the cannies to detect the companions' presence, even if the cannies made it all the way to the hotel and were standing in the driveway. The hotel would just be one more abandoned building amongst many.

Once-manicured flower beds lined the horseshoe driveway, now overgrown with weeds and dry leaves. Interspersed with the invasive greenery, the original plantings could be seen. Growing wild, azaleas and bougainvillea were everywhere, covering large swatches of the pavement, along with perennials that continued to bloom each year, despite the world around them collapsing.

Henry was in the lead again, moving quickly, and by doing so, making the others have to keep up or fall behind.

Mark was huffing and puffing like a broken steam engine again, but Carol helped him along. None of the others so much as offered. They wouldn't either, not as long as Mark was just an extra person, an add-on to the group, and not part of their tight-knit family. He would have to earn that position.

If he managed to get that far.

Jimmy was at the rear as usual, keeping an eye on their back trail. So far, all was quiet, only a few stray dogs peeking out from behind rubbish or a derelict car, being the only sign of life. If the companions were being followed, the trackers were being careful not to be seen.

The Holiday Inn was located on a slight rise to the land, so that despite it only being one-story high, once inside the building, the street was slightly below, the building looking down on it.

"Nice hotel, I guess," Henry said as he stood gazing at the building.

"Actually," Mark interjected, "it's not always a hotel, sometimes it's really a motel."

Jimmy had joined the group as they all gathered near the doors leading into the lobby. He'd overhead Mark. "Motel, hotel, what's the fucking difference?"

"Well, the way I always remembered it is this," Mark explained. "If there are doors for each room that are right off the street, from the outside, it's a motel. But if you have to get into your room by being inside the place, it's a hotel."

Jimmy studied the building for a moment. There were some doors that were for rooms located on both sides of the lobby entrance, but only a few. It looked like the rest of the rooms had access to them by entering the building and passing through the lobby. "Huh, I see what you mean. I guess."

"Not going to say something sarcastic?" Cindy asked.

Jimmy shook his head. "No, not this time. That's something I never knew, kind of neat. I used to call them all hotels."

Henry turned and faced Jimmy, as if he was the one who'd instigated the discussion. "Is any of this truly relevant to out predicament?" He looked annoyed.

Jimmy shrugged. "No, not really."

"Good, then let's focus on the issues at hand, all right?" He glared at Jimmy. "You're with me on point, let's go in and see what we can see."

"On it," Jimmy said, joining Henry, the two men pulling open one of the lobby doors.

"The rest of you follow us in, but stay alert," Henry said over his shoulder. With nothing else to discuss, the group entered the first row of glass doors leading into the vestibule.

Despite Mark's interjection with a description, to Henry it was still a simple hotel, as many of the rooms had access from within.

Henry kicked the trash and leaves that had accumulated at the bottom of one of the foyer doors, then gave it a tug. It opened with a dry creak of rusty hinges.

The sun was at their backs as they entered the actual lobby, casting long shadows into the building. Upon stepping inside, Henry and Jimmy paused, studying the large room, the others falling in behind them. Mary was last inside, and she pulled the door closed, sealing them off from the outside world.

The lobby was silent as a tomb.

It was taller than the rest of the building, giving it a look of the White House, with the front being grander in size than the wings. The décor was American Colonial, with central pillars holding up the roof. Its spaciousness made it feel like they were in a museum.

"Okay, everyone spread out and see what's what, but don't go out of sight yet. Stay in the immediate area; for now we're all safer together than apart," Henry ordered. "That goes for you two, as well," he said to Mark and Carol. "Your eyes work as well as ours do."

Everyone moved out, doing a quick recce of the lobby.

The large room was like a cave, with dust-covered chairs and couches scattered about, all done up in earth tones. Cobwebs were everywhere, and years' worth of dead and dried insects were lying below each web. Paintings adorned the walls, most of landscapes, a few of oceans and beaches. The paint on the walls was chipping in a few places, time taking its inevitable toll. There were a few small stains on the high ceiling, where the roof had begun to leak in the past year or so.

Jimmy walked over to the Registration Desk, the rows of empty shelving behind the counter attracting his interest. On either side of the desk, two corridors led deeper into the building. The one on the right led to a restaurant, the sign above the opening stating that Giovannis' Italian Eatery was open from 6 a.m. to 11 p.m., and that rooms 1 through 49 were located.

The corridor on the left had a sign pointing to the pool, gym and rooms with the numbers 50-89.

There was a dried-up corpse hanging half on, half off the Registration Desk, the rest of the body propped up in a swivel chair. Without a glance, Jimmy shoved the corpse out of the way, the head separating with a dull snap. Sweeping his arm across the counter, he rolled the head onto the floor, as if it was nothing more than a piece of trash. "Time to punch out, pal, your shift is finally over."

After using his feet to kick the lower half of the corpse aside, Jimmy stepped up to the counter, and began digging around. There was a note pinned to the wall on a cork board. *Mick Flanagan, call home immediately.* Below that one was another scrawled sentence. *Thomas Sylvester, no show.*

On the floor was a mess of office material, such as pens, pencils, clipboards and room cards. In the corner, where it had rolled, was a clear jar with March of Dimes printed on it. Inside were a few inches of dimes, nickels and pennies, a few quarters here and there as well, though pennies seemed to be the dominant choice left from givers.

He leaned over and picked up the jar. He examined it quickly, before dropping it back onto the floor. It jingled and jangled before it rolled to a stop. Coins were useless nowadays, with the exception of putting them into homemade pipe bombs, which the group had none. Kicking around the debris some more, he spotted a bunch of colorful pamphlets. Grabbing a few, he saw they were for local tourist attractions. Once more he dropped them. Unless he needed to start a fire, he didn't see much use for the glossy paper. The gloss made it unworthy as toilet paper, also.

Getting bored, he stood up fully, and slapped his palm twice on the dusty bell at the end of the counter. The dual-chime filled the room, causing everyone to glance his way.

Jimmy flashed his best grin at them, and said, "Welcome to the Holiday Inn, folks. How long will you be staying with us?"

"Knock it off, Jimmy," Henry snapped, annoyed that the younger man was goofing off. Anything could be inside the building with them. Now was not the time to mess around, at least not until they knew the place was secure.

"Come, come, my good man," he continued, ignoring Henry. "Surely you want to know about all the amenities we can offer you." He caught Cindy's eyes and he winked at her. "Such as the Honeymoon Suite."

She smiled back and blew him a kiss.

Jimmy began looking as if he was waiting on someone, his eyes darting back and forth. "Do you folks have any bags? Now where the fuck is that bellhop?"

"I'm warning you, Jimmy," Henry threatened from across the lobby, where he was peering into a dried-up fountain filled with a spattering of coins. "Don't make me come over there." His tone brooked no argument.

"All right, fine. I'll stop," Jimmy said, then hopped over the counter instead of walking around it.

"Show off," Henry said with a sly grin. He wasn't getting any younger, but Jimmy was as spry as ever.

"You know it," the youth responded, and strolled over to join Cindy.

Henry continued his search of the massive lobby. He licked his lips, the stale air and dust getting sucked into his lungs. It was a familiar sensation, one he was all too familiar with since the collapse of civilization. It was the taste of unuse, of abandonment.

Mary walked over to Henry, and when he glanced her way, she suggested, "Maybe we should split up when we explore the rest of the place. It would be a faster way to search. We could do it in two teams."

Henry considered it for a moment. "I agree. It looks like this place is empty and has been for quite some time. But we won't know for sure until we go completely through it. Why don't you and Carol come with me to the left side wing and Jimmy, Cindy and Mark can go to the right side." He looked at his wristwatch, one of the few items he'd carried from the old world into the new one. It had been a gift from his late wife, a birthday gift on his fortieth. He'd rarely looked at it since it all began, but rather wore it more like jewelry, or just carried it in his pocket. It was a windup so he never had to replace a dead battery, which also made him forgetful to keep winding it. He locked eyes with Jimmy. "Meet back here in an hour, Jimmy. If you're not back, better believe I'm gonna come looking for you."

"Will do," Jimmy said, Cindy joining him while Mark said goodbye to his wife.

"And Jimmy…" Henry called.

"Yeah?"

"Watch your trigger finger as you search. I don't want you shooting me by accident if we cross paths."

"Same goes for you too, old man." He flashed Henry a cheerful smirk and the two teams set out on either side of the Registration Desk. After everyone had left the lobby, the silence of the tomb once more descended on the empty space.

Chapter 12

"Let's check out the restaurant first," Jimmy suggested, as he led Cindy and Mark down the long corridor. "Maybe there's something there that's still edible." He rubbed his stomach. "I'm fucking starving and I am so sick of eating what we got in our packs."

They didn't walk far, despite the corridor being long. Not even halfway down it, an arrow was hanging from the ceiling; it pointed to the right for dining.

Dirty windows lined the large, rectangular room consisting of the restaurant, allowing a suffuse light to seep in. Shadows were in every corner, the gloom a palpable thing, but there was plenty of illumination to see or read by.

The first thing they discovered upon entering Giovannis was a corpse. It sat at the first table, its head lolling on its chest, barely hanging on. One leg had fallen off, a few strands of gristle hanging like string. It was wearing a tuxedo of all things, the black material stained and crusted with dried blood and other viscous liquids. The skin was shriveled and resembled parchment. There was a dried circle of brownish-gray under its chair, where its insides had rotted and turned to soup, before even that had evaporated.

There was nothing to indicate how the man had died, for it was definitively a man. Even in the decayed state it was obvious. Once polished black shoes still adorned the feet. The black pants with piping were visible beneath the table, and as the trio approached closer, the right leg began to twitch. There was no mistaking the movement.

"What the fuck?" Jimmy snapped, his shotgun coming up to blast the corpse and send it back to where it belonged, namely Hell.

"Oh my God," Cindy gasped, raising her M16. "It can't be."

Mark only stared, not truly understanding the significance of what he was witnessing. If the dead were reanimating once more, a fresh set of Hell was about to be revisited onto the Earth.

Jimmy was preparing to squeeze the trigger on his shotgun, his eyes locked on the rippling pant leg, when before he fired, a black nose peeked out of the waistband of the pants. The nose had a set of whiskers framing it, and then two beady eyes appeared, as the full head of a medium-sized rat came into view.

Jimmy paused, his eyes going wide. "It's a fucking rat!" he yelled in relief.

"Damn it," Cindy said softly. "I thought it was…"

"Yeah, me too, babe," he added agreeably. "And it scared the shit outta me."

The rat hopped out of the waistband and darted away, quickly becoming lost in the shadows of the restaurant.

"Big fucker, though," Jimmy commented. He walked over to the table, where a menu lay on one end. Picking it up, he read the specials of the day. "Mmm, roasted chicken, baked potato and corn on the cob, with a garden fresh salad for an appetizer. Sign me up."

Cindy joined him, peering over his shoulder, reading as well. "Not me. I'll take the Maine lobster with drawn butter, mashed potatoes and buttered carrots."

Jimmy dropped the menu onto the table and scooped her up in his arms. "Sure, babe, whatever you want. Hell, get two if you feel like it."

She kissed him and he reciprocated, the two sharing a moment. He began sliding his hands down her lower back, cupping her buttocks, when someone cleared their throat from behind him. The sound was loud in the silent room and it pulled Jimmy from his passion.

"Oh, yeah, sorry, dude, I was getting a little carried away there." He reluctantly separated from Cindy

"It's fine," Mark said. "Just that, well, uh, it was becoming awkward."

"The kitchen is this way, let's go explore."

A set of double doors that swung inward and out separated the kitchen from the main dining room. Immediately upon entering, everyone let out a gasp of happiness.

"Fucking jackpot!" Jimmy exclaimed, his smile so wide it almost fell off his face.

For once, luck was on their side. In an open pantry right off the doors was a supply room with cans of food, mostly condiments, such as mustard and ketchup, but there were a few other items of interest as well. Canned chili was one happy find. One shelf was filled with cloth napkins; salt and pepper, along with other spices, lined another.

This was the room the waitresses would use when they needed to restock tables for each dinner service. Unfortunately, the pantry wasn't fully stocked. It was obvious someone or multiple some ones had already been there, but there was more than enough remaining for the four companions, plus Mark and Carol.

Jimmy grabbed a can of chili, along with some mustard and ketchup packets, and barely flinched when he saw the dead cockroach husks lying behind them. Rats, ants, roaches, all were having a field day since the dead walked. It had been one of the first things Jimmy had become accustomed to seeing.

They left the food on a counter near the double doors for when they were finished searching the kitchen.

"We can come back for more later," he told the others. "But we'll take this with us when we meet back up with Henry."

They began searching once more. Cindy stopped by the freezer and refrigerator doors. "Jimmy," she called. "Want to check in these?"

"Not on your life, babe."

"Why not?" Mark inquired.

"Seriously?" Jimmy shook his head, exasperated. "Jesus, Mark, I'll ask you again. How the fuck have you lasted so long? Do you know what it must be like inside those things? No power, lots of perishable food. Must be like soup in there." He wrinkled his nose. "Must smell like ass, too."

"Ass sitting out in the hot sun for too long," Cindy rebutted, smiling slyly.

"Ha! Yes, I love it. Hot ass!"

Pots and pans were stacked on the stainless steel shelving that lined the counter tops of the same material. It was a standard kitchen. No knives were in the racks however, and all the dried food was gone. No pasta, oats or rice was found either. They did find rat and mouse droppings on the empty shelves, telling them that other life forms had been searching before them.

"I think we've seen enough," Jimmy said. "Let's check out the rooms on our side to make sure they're clear, then meet up with the others."

The three made their way to the double doors, Jimmy leading the way. As he passed the food he'd set near the doors, he called over his shoulder, "Hey, Mark, grab that shit and carry it, will you? Do something useful for a change."

Mark considered arguing, but decided against it.

Sighing, he picked up the canned goods and condiments, juggling everything until he had a decent hold on it all. Jimmy and Cindy were already past the doors and walking through the dining room.

Not wanting to be left behind, Mark used his shoulder to push through the swinging doors to catch up.

Henry and Mary's boot soles, along with Carol's sneakers, barely made any noise as they walked across the commercial grade carpeting lining the hallway.

Seeing a sign for the pool on the wall, Henry pointed and began moving that way, Mary and Carol right behind.

Near the entrance to the pool, Henry found more words in black were scrawled across the wall. When he touched the letters, his finger came back clean. The words had been left there a while ago, but how long was a mystery. Could have been a day or a month. What it told Henry was that whoever had left those warnings found at the storefronts, had been here at one time, too.

The words were foreboding. *IF YOU STAY HERE, YOU'RE DEAD!*

Mary and Carol looked at him, but he only shrugged. What was there to say?

Mary cocked her head to the side, as if to say, "Really?"

He shook his head. "I feel pretty well for a dead man." He turned and walked the few feet to the door leading into the pool area.

He'd detected the odor of old death long before he stepped through the glass doorway leading to the perimeter of the pool area. Unfortunately, he knew the odor well, from years of traveling across a blighted America. After smelling the foul aroma of decomposing human matter for the first time years ago, he'd never forgotten that awful, gut-wrenching stench—ever.

It was an acrid smell, one that punched a man in the face. When it was truly fresh, it was like walking into a wall, one made up of aerosolized purification.

But what Henry discovered in the pool was at least three weeks to a month old.

More than two dozen bodies lay across the almost empty pool. Only the deep end had any water at all, just a few feet of liquid by the looks of it. The corpses in the water were the worst. Even after weeks of decaying they were still bloated, pus-filled sacks of former humanity. The ones in the shallow end were more desiccated and were slowly drying out. The insides had liquefied, burst from the bodies to then seep into the black water at the deep end.

More than three dozen rats and hundreds of cockroaches and other insects were on or around the corpses, nibbling at whatever seemed most tasty. Henry watched a startled rat run across the pool bottom with something that looked like the digit of a hand or foot. It bounded up the shallow side and was lost in the shadows in seconds. The other rats barely gave the humans notice. If the three people weren't there to steal the rodents' food, the rats had nothing to be concerned about.

A miasma so thick it felt solid; it suffused the area surrounding the pool like an invisible fog. Fat flies hovered in the air, the buzzing a steady background noise. Sun chairs were scattered everywhere, along with yellowed towels. The roof was opaque to allow sunlight inside, basically a massive skylight, and though the ceiling glass was filthy and covered with debris from not being cleaned, the dirty, suffuse light was still more than adequate to see by. Too much actually. Henry wouldn't have minded a few more shadows, so that he needn't see everything on display before him. Mary was fairing well, having been used to this sort of tableaux. Other than covering her nose with an arm from the smell, she was barely distracted.

Carol wasn't doing that good. She began dry heaving at first, and then started vomiting, turning her head and spilling her last meal into a corner.

Henry frowned slightly but said nothing. He wasn't about to pass judgment, for none was needed. The disgusting scene in the pool was enough to make even a man with a stomach of lead heave once or twice.

"You should have thrown up into the pool," Mary said to Carol. "It's not like it would have made a difference."

Henry's eyes went wide at hearing this. It wasn't like Mary to take a jab at someone like Carol, especially when the woman was at a time of weakness, but as he looked at Mary and studied her visage, he realized she wasn't teasing at all, and was simply stating a fact.

"When the deaders dropped dead, so to speak, all of these guys must have been in here," Henry surmised.

"Yes, but who put them in here?" Mary asked. She was only a foot from the lip of the pool.

"Careful," Henry told her. "Don't get too close." He grinned. "I wouldn't want you to fall in."

She shivered, imagining such a fate. She couldn't think of anything as grotesque as taking a dip in that pool of horrors.

"Who knows who put them in here? Maybe someone or multiple someones were living here. Maybe they dropped them in the pool instead of destroying them," he wondered.

"Could they still be living here?"

Henry shrugged. "That's what we're trying to find out."

She nodded slightly, but said nothing.

Henry walked to the opposite side of the pool from where he'd entered. Mary went to Carol to check on her. Carol was doing better, though she didn't want to stay. Mary walked her to the glass door, opened it, and told her wait in the hallway. If any danger, all she had to do was step back inside and join Henry and Mary.

Henry kicked some towels out of his path, sidestepped an overturned sun chair, but found nothing of interest. It was humid inside the pool area, more so than in the lobby, the glass ceiling helping to keep the moisture inside. His shirt stuck to him and he felt sticky all over from being soaked by the rain. It was an unpleasant feeling and he didn't want to have to suffer it for any longer than needed.

Deciding he was finished searching, he continued walking forward around the pool, making a full loop, until he joined Mary again.

"Nothing here of value," he said flatly.

"Then can we go?" Mary asked. "Just because I'm not vomiting doesn't mean I don't feel nauseous. It's terrible in here."

"I won't argue with you there." He began moving towards the glass door. "I think we can call this area checked out."

Mary was right on his heels, almost pushing at him to move faster.

Carol opened the door when they approached, Henry passing through the doorway, Mary quickly shoving the door closed after she'd exited. She didn't want any more of that odor to get into the corridor than needed.

The glass door closed with a sucking sound, and she let out a sigh of relief. Even Henry did, but he masked it, not wanting to show his discomfort to the women. It wasn't that he was embarrassed, but as a strong man, he wanted to put up a solid front for the women.

"Okay, so we can rule out a swim after dinner," Henry said, a smirk creasing his lips.

"You think so?" Mary replied; her lips compressed into a tight line of annoyance.

Henry caught Carol's eyes in his. "You okay?"

"Yes, thank you. It's just…it's just that the smell caught me by surprise. It's so…so…fragrant. I've never smelled anything like that bef…"

"Yeah, I know," Henry said, cutting her off. "All right, let's search the rooms, and get back to the lobby and meet up with the others." He checked his watch. "We still have plenty of time."

For some reason, many of the doors to the rooms were open, most having something jammed under the bottom to keep them from closing, as there was a hinged spring on each of them. The darkening drapes in the rooms were always open, allowing what light that entered the room to filter into the corridor. Henry surmised someone had done this so that there would be illumination in the hallway. With all the doors closed and no windows in the corridor, even in the brightest part of the day, it would be close to pitch dark in the hallways twisting throughout the hotel.

They began their search at Room 50, and proceeded to inspect each one thereafter. Most had nothing they could use, not even hospitability toiletries hotels left out. Each room was identical to the last, with the exception the queen or full-sized bed would face the west, and on a room opposite, it faced east.

Some rooms had two beds. Barely half had linen on them. Sometime in the past, the sheets and blankets had been taken for some unknown use.

By the tenth room, and still finding nothing important, nor signs of life—or death for that matter—Henry was getting bored and was preparing to tell Mary and Mark it was time to head back to the lobby, when they turned a corner and Henry stopped cold. Drawing his Glock, he stopped the others from moving further. Mary paused immediately, but Carol walked into Mary, pushing her off balance. She had to slap her hand against the wall of the corridor to prevent from falling into Henry. Mary flashed the blonde woman an angry stare but said nothing.

Mary peered over Henry's shoulder, seeing what had made him halt suddenly.

On the floor, three rooms down, lay five or six prone bodies, all jumbled together. They looked dead, that is 'really' dead, but she knew as well as all the companions to never assume anything.

Assuming got you dead, and fast, if you weren't careful.

"Cover me," Henry told her softly, and began walking towards the bodies. Mary already had her .38 in her hand. She stepped away from Carol, not wanting to get tangled up with her again, then watched silently as Henry made his way closer to the corpses.

Something stirred within the bodies and Henry tensed, the Glock tight in his grip, but then a furry nose with whiskers popped out of a hole in a corpse, followed by a second nose. The black and beady eyes of the two rats glared at Henry before the rodents jumped out of the body and scurried off down the hallway, their skinny tails twitching the entire time.

"Damn things must be everywhere," Henry said under his breath. Moving closer still, he glared at the bodies, but nothing further moved.

There were spaces on the floor between the corpses where Henry could walk, and he stepped around the bodies, until he was standing in front of a hotel room door.

Room 72 was scrawled on the door in chalk, the numbers large. The ones that had once been for the hotel were long gone, though their outline could still be seen. The room across the hall was wide open, allowing sunlight to filter inside the hallway. Henry investigated that room first, wanting to make sure it was clear. Once satisfied, he turned back to the closed door with the chalk numbers.

"Come here, this is different from the rest," Henry explained.

Mary joined him, Carol trailing along behind her. Carol didn't know if she was allowed to come too, so she did it without permission. If Henry cared, he didn't show it.

"Look at this," he said, gesturing with his Glock at the door.

"Someone must have lived here, or still does," Mary surmised.

"Yeah, maybe." Not wanting to get shot in case someone was still inside, he banged on the door, though made sure to step to the side.

Mary too, gently shifted her body off to the side. If someone began blasting, she wasn't about to be an idiot and get shot in the chest or face.

"Housekeeping!" he called out, a grin touching his lips.

Mary smiled, too, finding his comment amusing.

When there was no response, Henry knocked one more time. Looking at Mary, who only shrugged, Henry stepped up before the door, raised his right boot, and slammed the sole into the door, directly to the side of the handle and lock.

The door moved ever-so-slightly inward, separating minutely at the jamb, but didn't fly open. Henry, not deterred, struck the door again, and this time it opened inward a few more inches, the lock giving. There was a deadbolt on the door, but it wasn't strong enough to withstand the force of his dual kicks. The lock itself was of poor quality, more than good enough for normal use, but not strong enough to stop a determined invader.

Henry studied the door, and pushed on it with his hand. The door had separated completely from the frame, but wasn't moving inward.

"Something's blocking it, a barricade of some kind maybe," he mused. "Give me a hand, Mary. Carol, keep your eyes peeled for trouble."

"Okay, Henry, of course," Carol said as Mary joined Henry at the door.

Together, the two of them proceeded to push on the door, Henry shouldering it, Mary pressing her hands against it, leaning her body into it. Her .38 was back in its holster so she had both hands free.

Slowly, with a grinding sound of something heavy on the opposite side, the door shifted, until a good twelve inches of space was exposed. Henry ducked down close to the floor, then carefully slid his head between the door and frame.

He was fairly confident nothing was alive inside the room, but he wasn't about to take more risk than necessary. Peering into the hotel room, he saw nothing amiss. Completely silent, he studied the room for a full thirty seconds before backing his head out. He did glance behind the door as he retreated, seeing there was a desk and padded chair barricaded against it. The legs of the desk had dug deep into the carpet and had torn it when the door was forced open, which explained why it had become so difficult to open. The barricade was really quite feeble in the scheme of things.

Standing, he looked at Mary and Carol. "Looks empty. Nothing's moving anyway. Let's go in."

"Right behind you," Mary said, her .38 in her hand once more.

Shouldering the door by using the doorjamb for leverage, Henry shoved it open another foot, before sliding through the gap, Mary and Carol close on his heels.

Standing silently, he let his eyes take in their surroundings, seeing no reason to move deeper into the room.

The light-darkening shades in the room were open, allowing what sunshine remained to filter inside. The bed was made, looking as if it hadn't been slept in, and some errant clothes were at the foot of it, as if someone had placed them there a few minutes ago and was in the shower.

A nineteen inch TV was across from the bed, two nightstands on either side of the bed as well, one with the TV's remote on it. A padded chair was off to the side, near the window. It was a standard-looking hotel room. A small wastebasket was in the corner by the windows, overflowing with empty food cans and other dry goods once sealed in paper or plastic; all were empty of their contents.

The room was easy to search, not being very large, about the size of a common bedroom. With no nooks and crannies, there was nowhere for an enemy to hide. With the exception of the bathroom.

"Mary," he said to get her attention, and stepped over to the bathroom door, which was closed. Carol walked to the bed, not wanting to be in the immediate vicinity of danger if there was any.

Slowly, Henry reached out with his left hand, his Glock in his right, and grabbed the doorknob. Turning it cautiously, it wasn't locked, and he gently pushed on the door by the knob, so that the lock was away from the jamb. Then he stopped, not moving an inch, straining his hearing to see if there was any sound coming from within the bathroom.

A scrape, a shuffle of a foot, even a growl of an animal, he patiently waited. If anything was inside that bathroom, it wouldn't be able to stop from showing itself. Once he waited a full minute, and when nothing was heard or attacked the door, he gave it a gentle shove. The door swung inward, a slight creaking coming from the dry hinges. He idly thought he should call down to the main desk and have maintenance come up with a bottle of household oil.

The door opened halfway, and stopped. Reaching out, Henry pushed on the door a little more, and it moved slightly. Something was stopping it, but whatever it was, the item wasn't very heavy.

Pushing a little more, the door opened wider still, but stopped a foot from the tub, which was on the left side of the small room. On the right side were a vanity, sink and mirror.

Looking down at the floor, Henry saw what had caused the door not to open fully. The dried-up corpse of a dog lay there.

That wasn't the only once-living thing in the bathroom, either.

The nude body of a woman was in the bathtub, and it didn't take Henry long to figure out how she died. Even in the corpse's decomposed, dried condition, the skin like parchment, it was easy to see the open gashes in her wrists, and the razor blade lying on the floor beside the tub. There was no water in the shower/tub combo, any liquid evaporating over the years, but a thin crust of brown coated the tub all the way around, exactly where the water-line would have been. The bottom of the tub was also stained a brown color, more like rust. When the water had evaporated, the heavier blood suffusing it had stayed behind.

"Oh, how sad," Mary said, peering over Henry's shoulder.

"Yeah," he replied, not having much more to say about the subject. He glanced at himself in the bathroom mirror, not liking his disheveled, unshaven look, then turned away.

The dead woman had long brown hair, past her shoulders, only now there were just a few shreds pasted to the scalp. The rest of it was on the bottom of the tub. Her head was sagging, her chin on her chest, as if she'd simply fallen asleep. If she'd died from blood loss, which seemed the case, that was how she'd gone, simply faded away and passed out, never to awaken.

One arm had been hanging out of the tub, and the hand had detached and was missing. There was a hole on the floor, under the sink, and it was a pretty good chance some rodent had gotten to the corpse at some point.

Near the hole was a book. Henry bent down and picked it up. "It's the Bible." He tossed it onto the vanity. "She must've read a few passages to give her peace, slid into the warm water, and sliced her wrists open, bleeding out."

Each time he moved his feet across the tile floor, they crunched under the hundreds of dead flies that coated it like a second rug, next to the one already there for stepping out of the shower. Cobwebs hung from the ceiling, so thick the ceiling was almost invisible in the dim light of the room. There wasn't a window, and only what sunshine filtered in from the main room allowed Henry to see.

There wasn't much of an odor, the corpse having deteriorated to the point it was more rags and bones than anything once human. Carol had watched everything from the doorway, before ducking back into the main room.

"I'm more curious about the dog, really," he explained. "If this woman wanted to off herself, fine, but why let the dog starve to death like this? It's so cruel."

"I think I might know the answer to that," Carol said as she stood at the doorway again. "There's a large bag of dog food in the alcove where jackets get hung. Nothing left now; ants and the like have had a field day, not to mention rats and mice. The bottom of the bag has many holes torn in it and there's a hole in the wall near the floor as well. There's a plastic bowl near the bed, if you didn't see it before. It was probably full of food at one point."

"So?" Mary said.

"So, I have a feeling the poor dear had no choice. The windows won't open, they're not made to, and if she had tried to let the dog out through the door, the dead would have forced their way inside. She had no choice but to leave some food out, whatever was left, for the dog, and then kill herself when all hope was lost." She paused before continuing. "I bet the dog became locked in the bathroom with her by accident, either before or after she died." She held out a piece of paper. "This was on the nightstand."

Henry read it aloud. " 'No food left, no hope left, dead outside. I'm sorry. God forgive my weakness.' "

Mary sighed as she looked down at the suicide fatality. "She must've had no more food, and only some left for the dog. She knew even if she ate that, sooner or later it was going to run out. Then they would both starve."

"Then why didn't she kill the dog before she did herself?" Henry shook his head. "Or better yet, eat the dog for meat?"

Mary shrugged in reply. "Who knows? Maybe she wasn't that strong, or the dog was a loving pet for years. Maybe she just gave up." Mary grabbed some towels hanging on the wall and opened two, draping them over the naked body. "We don't have enough information to make a true assessment." She draped the last towel over the carcass of the dog.

Henry pushed his way out of the bathroom. "None of it matters anyway. What does is that she's long dead and we're still alive." He spotted a bottle of hand sanitizer on the vanity and snatched it up, sliding it into a pocket. He had a use for it other than keeping clean. "Let's leave her in peace." He checked his wristwatch. "We'll check out a few more rooms and then head back to the lobby."

He led the two women back out into the corridor, and out of the room of death.

Chapter 13

Almost an hour later to the minute, the companions once more were in the lobby, the two teams joining together once more.

Jimmy and Henry shared what they'd found, Jimmy's team bringing a few tubes of toothpaste, some floss, and some odds and ends found in the rooms they'd searched. A few of the items, such as deodorant, were a welcome find. With no more local drugstores or big box stores, something as simple as deodorant before the collapse, was now something to be treasured. No one liked to smell worse than a three week old zombie.

Everything was placed on the Registration Desk so it could be divvied up amongst the group. When Henry saw the cans of food Mark carried, he suggested they all return to the dining room to have a proper feast.

"So you mean I carried these all over the place just to take them back to the restaurant?" Mark asked incredulously.

Jimmy poked Mark in the stomach with the butt of his shotgun. "Oh, quit your whining. Seems to me you can use the exercise."

"Carol, do you hear this? He's been making fun of my weight all day. This isn't the first time."

"What do you want me to do about it, dear?" Carol asked.

"Well, uhm, you could tell him to stop."

Carol glanced at Jimmy, who glared back, as if he was daring Carol to say something. Eventually, she looked away and said, "Well, Mark, maybe he's right. You could stand to lose a few pounds."

Mark looked at her, the betrayal he felt clear in his eyes.

"A few pounds? That's all?" Jimmy laughed, still egging the large man on. He was enjoying himself immensely. Mark was a much easier target to toss jibes at than Henry, who over the years had learned not to take everything Jimmy said so seriously.

"All right, that's enough," Henry said. "Jimmy, give the poor guy a break."

The younger man sighed in defeat. "Fine. Shit, Henry, I was just having some fun."

"Well, fun's over. Come on, let's go eat, I'm starving."

Like a procession of employees, being shown their way around the hotel, Jimmy led the way to the dining room, where everyone took a seat at a large circular table in the center of the room.

"Ignore the guy in front, he's dead tired," Jimmy said, motioning to the tuxedoed corpse at the table his team had found upon entering the first time.

No one acknowledged the corpse anyway, and even Carol didn't seem to care upon first seeing it. If there was no odor of death in the air, they could have cared less that they were dining with a dead body only a few feet away. It wasn't like they were going to take up permanent residence in the hotel. So they sure as hell weren't going to be cleaning it up for such a temporary stay.

Jimmy took the chili back into the kitchen, Cindy with him. It didn't take long before he found an industrial hand cranked can opener mounted to the edge of one of the stainless steel counters.

Cindy took some dishes off a shelf and wiped them with a decent-looking towel she found. There was a pile of them, the top ones covered in dust and cobwebs, but when she went deeper, into the center of the pile, she found one that was close to pristine. The rest below that one were also in pretty good shape.

She also collected some cloth napkins. Some were moldy but many were fine to use. Cindy took on the job of scooping out the chili and placing it onto the dishes. Being cold, it lay on the dishes like oatmeal cooked with too little water, globs of reddish oil congealed on the edges. Some cans of vegetables were also found and she added them to the meal for a side dish.

Using a metal cart, she and Jimmy placed the dishes onto it. Putting on a wide smile, like a good server should, she wheeled the cart out to the dining room, where her hungry customers anxiously awaited.

Henry wasn't idle while waiting for his dinner. He walked around the dining room, exploring. In a waiters' pantry at the back of the large room, on the bottom shelf, tucked all the way in the back, hidden from view, he found an unopened bottle of wine.

Returning to the table, he popped it open and poured everyone a glass, the goblets taken from the pantry as well.

"What's all this?" Jimmy asked as he approached the table along with Cindy.

"I got lucky, that's what," Henry said, and handed Jimmy and Cindy a glass. Cindy took it, and made sure to push the cart close so that others could take the dishes from it. Mary did so, passing each dish to Carol, who continued the process, until everyone had a meal before them.

Silverware had been on their table already, and as soon as the plates were before them, everyone dug in.

For a while, they ate quietly, no one talking. But as the food disappeared, conversation resumed. Jimmy shared with Henry and his team what he'd found when searching his side of the hotel. No bodies had been discovered. Henry did the same, Mary then taking over to tell Jimmy, Cindy and Mark about the corpse in the tub.

After that, conversation stopped and the table grew quiet again, each pondering that lone death.

The bottle of wine was emptied quickly, with each of them taking a second glass. Henry had considered giving a toast, but in the end, decided not to.

Customs such as that were antiquated, more for posterity than for any true reason. There was nothing he could say to them that he needed a glass of wine in his hand. If he wanted to say a blessing or thanks to something, he would, and the wine be damned.

What little sunshine had been filtering through the hotel since their arrival was all but gone, darkness falling quickly. Henry pulled out the bottle of hand sanitizer from a pocket and placed it on the table.

"What's that for?" Jimmy asked. "If you were gonna clean your hands, shouldn't you have done it before we started to eat?"

"That's not what it's for, wise guy," Henry said. He poured some of the sanitizer into a bowl. Pulling out the Zippo he had, he flicked it and set the flame to the bowl. Almost instantly, the hand sanitizer began to burn, surprising everyone else at the table.

"It's got alcohol in it, so it's flammable," Henry explained. "I figured it would come in handy tonight."

With the steady flame burning in the center of the table, the six weary travelers finished their meal, before bedding down for the night.

Henry opened his eyes, for a fraction of a second, unsure where he was. Then reality flooded back and he remembered he was in the lobby of the hotel. His clothes had dried on him eventually, some taken off to dry, like shirts and socks, other items, such as pants, left on in case they were attacked. If any of the companions had extra clothing in their packs, they'd changed out of damp items to let them dry, draping them over chairs or hanging them on the plastic trees scattered around the lobby.

In the far corner of the lobby, was a sitting area with three couches and easy chairs, along with a fat coffee table in the center. Nearby, were three dark computers on desks with plastic partitions, part of the hotel's business center. A fire door was at the rear wall also, in case they needed to exit the building quickly. .

Everyone's sleeping assignments meant that they were scattered amongst the couches, either on or off one. Mary and Cindy were using one of them, the largest piece of furniture, their heads on both ends, their feet side by side. The men were letting the ladies be more comfortable by using the couches, but Carol lay on the floor, Mark on the last couch. He'd cited a bad back for the reason, and Carol had repeatedly stated she was fine with it. Henry, and even Jimmy, hadn't been pleased at the situation.

But if Carol, the man's wife, emphatically said she was all right, who were they to judge the couple's relationship?

They only planned on staying the one night, so dragging mattresses from rooms into the lobby wasn't worth the effort. Jimmy volunteered to grab as much bed linen and pillows as he could find from a few of the empty rooms, to use as either padding for the floor or for coverings. It was warm in the lobby, so protection from the cold wasn't an issue. The rain had stopped, but it was still humid, and inside the hotel was no different.

A thick rug also covered the floor around the sitting area, adding more padding for a body.

Henry was lying on one such nest of bedding. He sat up, his eyes adjusting to the darkness. Thanks to the overhead skylights, some pale moonlight filtered in. Not enough to read by, but more than enough so as not to trip over something while walking around.

Henry's eyes roved over the bodies on the couch and floor, and he was surprised to find both Cindy and Jimmy missing, when only Jimmy should be, as he was on guard duty. Checking his wristwatch, he saw it wasn't Jimmy's shift for another hour, followed by Henry and Mary. Then the sun would be rising.

Despite the hotel feeling relatively secure, Henry knew better than to assume it was. He'd picked the lobby to bed down for the night, as he didn't want to use the rooms. Too many people being in one room, and far too crowded, made that scenario not an option, and spreading the group out to multiple rooms seemed ill-advised as well.

So the lobby was the best option, with its multiple exits on all sides if needed, plus the fire door. Of course, that meant there were multiple avenues of attack by an enemy as well.

But only a wraith could sneak up on them, in the mausoleum silence of the lobby, as long as there was someone on guard duty.

Henry stood up, feeling pressure in his bladder. He walked over to the Registration Desk, where a bucket taken from the kitchen had been placed for urination by the group. Defecating was done in one of the hotel rooms. There was no water in the toilets, but they had over fifty rooms in which to go at least once. Anyone coming into the hotel behind them wouldn't be too pleased, but over time the feces would dry and would be nothing to be concerned about by possible new arrivals.

Finished, he zipped up and walked to the center of the lobby, where he spotted Cindy's silhouette. She'd already heard him, and had watched him cross the lobby silently.

"I thought Jimmy was on right now," he whispered, not wanting to wake the others. The large room caught sound and echoed it like a theater house, the acoustics were that sensitive.

"He is, but he woke me and asked me to cover for him." She spoke softly as well.

"How come?"

She hesitated, before deciding to go on. "That chili gave him the runs. He's off in one of the rooms dealing with it."

"Oh." He took that in, then winced. "Oh, okay, shit, that's a little too much information."

"Yeah, I know."

A clopping of boots soles came from the right, but Cindy didn't so much as flinch. She knew Jimmy's walk when she heard it.

Jimmy joined them, a look of discomfort on his face.

"How you feeling?" Henry asked, his voice low.

"A little better, thanks." He looked down at the floor, a hand on his stomach. "A word of warning, Henry?"

"Yeah?"

"Don't use the toilets in the first six rooms down that hallway. I pretty much destroyed them."

Henry made a face like he'd detected a foul odor. "Nice, good to know. I'll be sure to warn the others when they wake up."

"Yeah, you do that. Just tell them to go to the other side of the hotel if they have to go."

"Sure, Jimmy, will do."

"By the way, Henry," Cindy said softly. "I wanted to ask if in the morning, I could take Mary with me to search a few of the houses nearby. Maybe we can find some new clothing to wear or some feminine products. We're getting really low, and that time of the month is coming any day now." She looked down at her clothing, which was muddy and had some blood splotches from their quick battle with the cannie scouts. "Not to mention I don't want to wear this stuff again if I get wet. I didn't have anything to change into when we got here, and it was so uncomfortable while it was wet. It took forever to dry on me. It'd be nice to have some spare socks and underwear, too. Mary said the same thing when I asked her before she went to sleep."

"There was probably something in that room we found the suicide in," he suggested.

She shook her head. "I don't want to wear a dead woman's clothes, not when she's lying right there. I'm not that desperate. If there's nothing in any of the houses, then I can reconsider."

"Okay, fine, but be careful. Any trouble, fire three spaced shots and we'll all come running to help. And take Mark with you, too. Be good he gets used to foraging, and maybe being with you and Mary will be easier than with me and Jimmy. If he's gonna be with us, he needs to pull his weight more."

"Speaking of weight…" Jimmy began, his voice loud.

"Shhh," Henry snapped.

"Oh, fuck, sorry, I forgot." Jimmy shooed Cindy away. "I'm okay now, babe," he said more softly. "I think I can make it till the end of my shift."

"You sure?"

"Yeah, go lie down, get some rest."

Cindy kissed him on the cheek and padded away.

Jimmy watched her go, admiring, even in the darkness, the way her buttocks swayed back and forth within her jeans. "Shit, I'm a lucky man."

"Jimmy, my boy," Henry said, "you don't know the half of it."

Henry took over guard duty from Jimmy an hour later, after taking some time for himself in one of the bathrooms Jimmy hadn't soiled. He hadn't seen a point in lying back down to sleep for such a short time, nor taking over Jimmy's shift early.

Jimmy went with Cindy to one of the empty rooms for some private time right after Henry had told him to leave. Apparently, Cindy hadn't been prepared to sleep either after waking up to help Jimmy when he'd needed a bathroom break, and as the two rarely got time alone, where they could feel even a little safe, the hotel was perfect.

Henry felt a pang of jealousy as the two lovers went off together. It made him think of Sue, and that hollow feeling in his chest came back with a vengeance.

Wandering around the lobby, ghosts of the past forced their way into his head. With nothing to do but think, he found himself dwelling on his loss, and missing her terribly. He'd never even gotten the chance to say goodbye, so sudden had been her death. Regrets filled his head, making it hard to focus, but he forced it all away, knowing if he let himself succumb to grief, it would only take him down a black hole he wouldn't want to escape from.

He walked over to the lobby doors and peered out into the night. Nothing stirred, even the birds were sleeping. Checking his watch, he saw it was close to dawn, but not that close, unfortunately.

It was slightly lighter near the glass doors, or to be more accurate, less dark, thanks to a mostly cloudless sky. The illumination seeping through the dirty glass panels was paltry at best, but better than nothing. The rain was long gone, the next day looking to be pleasant, which would be a welcome change from the past day. He decided if he didn't become overwhelmed with exhaustion after standing guard for a few hours, he would continue all the way until morning, and let Mary sleep a little bit longer. The way he felt now, he didn't think he would want to close his eyes again.

He plucked a few brochures from where he could find them: on the floor, on a counter near the Registration Desk, where a house phone sat silently, probably forever.

Going back to the lobby doors, he squinted to read the brochures, really just looking at the images on the glossy pages. He wasn't actually trying to read anything; he just wanted something to occupy his mind.

In time, it worked, and the past became just that; the past.

Chapter 14

A little before seven in the morning, Cindy, Mary and Mark left on their foraging expedition, while the others found ways to pass the time. Henry figured to wait until after their midday meal before departing the hotel, wanting to let himself and the others rest up some. But he'd also decided if everyone wanted to, he was okay with the idea of staying one more night.

It wasn't too often they could stop for more than a day or two while on the open road. There always seemed to be something threatening them.

Of course, there was a time not very long ago when the number one danger was the living dead, but after they dropped 'dead' for good weeks ago for some unknown reason, one Henry wondered if he'd ever discover, new threats had popped up, ones that had always been there, but were now much more prevalent.

Cannies, raiders and slavers were the worst of the lot, and Henry and his friends had even had the bad luck of having to deal with invading Russians in Alaska recently.

What could be next? Aliens? Sure, why not? After all, that wasn't too much more farfetched than zombies had been.

Carol had found an old crossword puzzle book, with most of the puzzles already solved. Still, she occupied her mind by trying to finish any that were either partially solved or hadn't been touched.

"I need a four letter word for batrachian," she said. Carol sat on one of the couches, her feet resting on the large table in the center.

"How the fuck would I know what that means?" Jimmy asked, annoyed at the woman. Carol had been doing this all morning and Jimmy was more than a little aggravated. He hated people who would ask for help with crossword puzzles. If someone didn't want to do it, then don't, but don't ask other people to solve it for you, then you take credit.

Carol shrugged. "I dunno. I was hoping you did."

Jimmy frowned from across the table, where he was lying on another couch, his hands behind his head. He was tired from his bout with diarrhea and then his lovemaking with Cindy, both the cause of him not getting much sleep. He was hoping he might be able to catch a nap. "Now how would I know it if you don't? What, you think I'm some kinda scientist or something?"

"I guess," Carol replied, squirming under Jimmy's hatful glare.

Henry was admiring some of the paintings scattered across the lobby. Deciding to have mercy on Carol, he walked over to her. "I think you're looking for the word *frog*, but I might be wrong."

Carol checked the puzzle, seeing how the word fit with the other letters across. She wrote in the word with a battered pencil, barely just a nub and said, "Yes, yes, I do believe that'll work." She looked up at Henry, admiration on her face. "Well done, Henry, well done indeed. How ever did you know that?"

Henry brushed off the praise. "I used to watch a lot of National Geographic."

Jimmy waved a hand at Carol. "Why don't you go check on what food there is in the dining room, pack up what we can take with us," he suggested. "That way I can take a quick nap before Cindy comes back."

Carol looked at Henry, wanting to know what he wanted. She'd figured out quickly that the only one she truly needed to listen to was Henry, as the defacto leader. The others might give her orders, but she could choose to ignore them. Not that she'd defied any of the companions as of yet.

Henry nodded. "That's actually a good idea. Would you mind doing that, Carol? And not because Jimmy needs a nap, but because it's necessary."

She stood up, tossing the crossword book onto the coffee table, but stuffing the small pencil into a pocket. "Sure, I can do it. Do you want me to bring it back here?"

"Yes, thank you." Henry sat down across from Jimmy.

She crossed her arms, annoyed. She felt like the two men were sending her off into the fields while they sat around and relaxed. But she quickly pushed the emotion down. She was new to the team, and knew both she and Mark needed to prove themselves if they wanted to join the group. She and Mark had already discussed it when they had a few moments alone; both had agreed it would be in their best interests. The companions were battle-hardened warriors, a lucky find for the couple, and the fact they appeared to be welcoming the married couple into their group was fortunate.

Forcing a smile on her face, Carol waved sweetly and headed off to the restaurant.

"Finally, some goddamn peace and quiet." Jimmy stretched out like a lazy cat on the couch, sighing happily.

"I'm going for a walk inside the hotel," Henry said and stood up, but Jimmy was already snoring. Leaving his friend to rest, he wandered away, not going far enough to be out of earshot, but far enough to stretch his legs.

Henry strolled through the hotel hallways as if he was a tourist on holiday out for a walk. He passed the pool area again, but didn't go inside, then wandered into the dining room where he chatted with Carol for a few minutes before leaving her to complete her task. He found her pleasant enough. Both she and her husband were nice enough people, and Henry knew he needed to make a decision on whether or not to allow the couple to join up with his group.

He still had doubts about Mark, however. The man's size seemed to be a logistical nightmare. He couldn't run fast, nor climb, and his stamina was practically zero. Henry had learned that the entire team needed to become one cohesive unit. Even one weak link could bring them all down.

He searched a few rooms more thoroughly than he had before, then merely glancing upon his arrival. Finding a few trinkets in some drawers, such as a necklace for Mary, he secreted it all amongst his person, before moving on.

Entering one room, he saw that the window had been shattered by a tree branch. From the watermarks on the carpeting, the breakage had happened quite some time ago. The room looked out onto the rear of the hotel. He could see the rooftops of residential dwellings, and he figured that must be where Cindy had wanted to go scavenging. There was an old animal's nest in the corner of the room, possibly raccoon or possum. It had been vacated a long time ago by the looks of it.

The day was dry but humid, and he quickly grew uncomfortable with the open air on him. He hadn't realized it before but the hotel had insulated the companions from the outside temperature. The stone and steel had become more like a cave, the temperature of the air at least ten degrees cooler within, than outside.

Checking his watch, he saw that the girls and Mark had been gone for more than an hour. The wind blew into the room, a low whistle coming from the shattered panes, where the window frame was still intact. He was lost in contemplation, staring out the window at the swaying tree branches, when a gunshot shattered his thoughts, piercing the silence of the morning.

Then a second shot came, followed by a third. It was Cindy's M16. He'd heard its report many times over the years to know it without challenge.

Shouting and yelling floated into the room, along with the noise of rumbling engines. It was faint, but easy to discern when he focused.

Spinning on his heels, he dashed into the hallway and ran full tilt to the echoing lobby. "Jimmy, Carol, we got trouble! Jimmy!"

He continued calling out as he ran. He was moving so fast he had to use one of the support pillars in the lobby to halt his progress.

Carol had just entered the lobby without hearing Henry, coming from where she'd been in the restaurant, doing quick inventory of what there was for food and packing it. What was salvageable, she'd stuffed in carry bags, so when it was time to leave, it would be ready.

She'd wheeled the bags in on a serving cart once used for room service. She had just stopped near the sitting area when she saw Henry come charging into the lobby, yelling loudly.

"What is it, what's the matter?" she asked, her eyes wide with concern. Since meeting Henry, she'd never seen the man look so scared. He always looked so calm and collected, impassive even in danger, as if no matter what was happening, he had control of the situation.

Jimmy jumped up from the couch, his nap completely over, adrenaline now pumping through his system. When Henry shouted like that, it couldn't be good.

"What's wrong? What's the matter?" Jimmy demanded, his shotgun in his hands.

"Nothing good." Henry motioned for Jimmy to follow him to the lobby doors, where he pushed through them, into the alcove, then opened the outer doors.

As soon as he did, the sound of engines grew slightly louder but still hard to detect if one didn't know to listen for them.

"Shit," Jimmy spit. "You think it's the cannies?"

"Who else could it be?"

"We going or staying here?"

Henry shook his head. "For now we stay. The girls and Mark are out looking for supplies, but I just heard three gunshots. I told Cindy to do that if in danger, so that's gotta mean they're in trouble."

Jimmy's eyes went wider in alarm. "If Cindy's in trouble we need to help her, and Mary, too."

He began to move through the door when Henry grabbed him by his shirt and slammed him against the doorframe.

"Don't you think I know that? But the facts are we don't know where they are and how many of the enemy is out there. If they've been captured we don't know enough to save them, and if they're dead, there's no use going in half-blind just to get ourselves killed, too. You know Cindy and Mary wouldn't want that."

"So, what? We just sit here on our asses while they're either captured or dead?"

"No, of course not, that's not what I mean."

"Then what the fuck *do* you mean, Henry?"

"We wait."

Carol had moved closer to the two arguing men, not liking what she was hearing. Her husband was out there, too. Her hands knotted into fists as she listened, angry, scared and frustrated that there was nothing she could do.

The sound of engines grew louder, along with the reports of more gunfire. Henry was pretty sure he heard Mary's .38 barking, along with Cindy's M16 again. Another weapon sounded as well. Mark's hunting rifle probably, which the man had been allowed to take. There was no other gunfire, signifying the cannies had no firearms, just like their scouting party.

But that only went so far. Superior numbers could still overwhelm a group of defenders, even if there were three of them with firearms.

"There, that's Cindy's rifle. She's still alive!" Jimmy screamed. "We need to go save her."

"No, Jimmy, we can't, its suicide."

"Then I'll go alone." He was still being held against the doorframe, and he shoved Henry away, preparing to leave the hotel.

Henry looked about to physically restrain the younger man again, and Jimmy had the posture of someone who was ready to fight him off. The shotgun was even raised to chest height, as if he was going to use the butt to strike Henry.

The reports of gunfire in the distance had stopped, yelling and shouting now even louder.

It was like a concert was being held a quarter mile away, the ebb and flow of the joined voices echoing softly with the direction of the wind.

"Jimmy, think, goddammit. We don't know what the situation is right now. We go in guns blazing, all we'll end up doing is getting ourselves killed. If there's one thing in this life that's true, it's that if you make a bad choice you die. There are no second chances; this isn't one of those video games you used to play."

"But she and Mary might be dead or dying right now! We need to save them!"

"Don't you think I know that?" Henry shouted, stopping Jimmy dead in his tracks. Spittle flew from Henry's lips as he lost all self-control. "Don't you think I care about Cindy, too? And Mary?"

"No, of course not, Henry, I mean, yeah, I know you do," Jimmy stammered. "It's just, if they're okay but trapped. They could die."

Carol stepped up to the two men, her face devoid of emotion. "We all do eventually."

There were no more gunshots heard, and the next ten minutes was taut with tension as Jimmy, Henry and Carol stood at the lobby doors, one door cracked open, listening.

Eventually, the throaty rumble of engines began to fade away, along with more shouting and yelling.

"We need to decide where we're gonna make our stand if they come here," Henry suggested. "If we pick the right spot, we can deal them a heap of death before they get us. Make it hurt 'em good, pay a steep price for screwing with us."

Jimmy had come back down off his rant, and was more rational. His hands gripped the shotgun so tightly his knuckles were bone white. But other than that he was in control of himself. "You think they're dead, Henry? Or taken captive?"

"Yeah, I'd say the last one. Cannies like their meat fresh. If they were able to take the girls and Mark alive, that's what they'd do. Dead means meat spoils. Alive means it stays fresh." He looked off over the rooftops across the street. "Maybe they'll take what they got and leave, then we can go after them for a rescue. For now, all we can do is wait here and see what happens. I figure if they're not beating down our doors in an hour or less, they're not coming here."

"And if they don't come? Then what?"

Henry's lips went tight, his eyes creased. "Then we go find our people."

Chapter 15

Henry chose a large maintenance shed at the rear of the hotel to make their stand. It was partially connected to the hotel and also gave them the option of slipping out through the back, where they could quickly blend into the residential homes that lined the rear of the shed.

Waiting and listening, guns held tightly in their hands, the group sat silently, for whatever came next.

Carol held her Olympic target pistol in her right hand once more, Henry having returned it to her. All guns would be needed if they had to defend their position. The woman had been accepted into the fold, so to speak, a battle promotion of becoming one of the group officially.

No more gunshots were heard in the distance, and soon the yelling and shouting began to fade as well. The low rumble of engines disappeared, too, until all became peaceful in the surroundings of the hotel.

They stayed in the large shed for a full thirty minutes, no one moving or speaking.

Finally, running out of patience, Jimmy said, "Okay, we need to go see what happened."

"No, not yet," Henry hissed. "Damn you, Jimmy, I know how you feel, but not till I say."

"But…"

"But nothing. Now shut the hell up and don't speak until I tell you to." Henry's eyes were hard, his tone brooking no argument.

Jimmy did as he was told, though not happy about it.

Henry knew he wouldn't be able to stop the younger man for much longer. There would be a time when Jimmy would simply ignore Henry's orders, his concern for Cindy overruling any obedience he had to Henry as their defacto leader.

Time passed slowly. Henry tried not to think about Mary or Cindy, lying somewhere, hurt or possibly dead. He cared for Cindy deeply, but he truly loved Mary. She was the daughter he'd never had. He prayed she was all right.

But common sense fought him every step of the way. It told him that both women, along with Mark, were probably already dead; killed while being taken captive. He knew neither Mary nor Cindy would accept defeat, and would eat a bullet before allowing themselves to be captured.

But there was a slim hope that they had been overrun, and hadn't the opportunity to kill themselves. And if so, that the cannies had taken them as prisoners, to be used as fresh meat later.

It was a slim hope but it was all he had.

The alternative was too much to contemplate.

It was a little past noon according to his watch when Henry decided it was time to go and see what had occurred amongst the homes behind the hotel.

Whether they were going on a rescue mission, or one of vengeance to avenge their dead friends, was unknown.

Henry had everyone return with him to the lobby, where they prepared to move out. They were just about ready to depart when one of the outer glass doors leading into the lobby opened, the second set of doors muffling it slightly, but still making enough noise to startle Henry.

"We got company!" he shouted, but only loud enough for Jimmy and Carol to hear. Carol was caught flat-footed, and she merely stood still, holding her .22 so it was hanging down by her side.

But Jimmy, with razor sharp reflexes, leveled the shotgun at the egress, his finger on the trigger.

Pulling his Glock in a quick draw, Henry swung around, aiming at the doors in a classic weaver stance, when the second set of doors was darkened by a shadow. One door began to open. Slowly at first, but then it was forced inward so hard there was a loud *clang* that almost shattered the tempered glass.

Henry followed the shape with his Glock; when he realized who it was, he lowered his pistol.

Carol was already moving, recognizing the familiar shape of her husband. "Oh my God, Mark, I thought you were dead!" she cried and ran to him, Mark barely able to stop her from knocking him down. If he hadn't had so much weight over her, she would have bowled him over easily.

"I almost was," he said, wrapping an arm around Carol, the other hand leaning against the wall to support him.

Jimmy and Henry went over to him, and helped Mark to a nearby chair. He plopped down into it heavily, gasping for air. He was covered in perspiration, his face flushed. He'd been running, the physical exertion taking a toll on the out-of-shape man.

He dropped his hunting rifle to the floor, barely realizing he'd done so. Henry handed him a canteen of water, letting him take a few seconds to gather his wits, knowing that asking him anything in his present state would be a waste of time. Besides, a few more seconds wouldn't change anything. Once Mark was rested, they could get more information out of him.

Jimmy, however, did no such thing, and immediately began bombarding Mark with questions; about Cindy, Mary and what happened. Rolling his eyes, Henry let his younger friend talk, not seeing a reason to stop him. Besides, Henry was just as eager to know the status of Cindy and Mary as Jimmy was.

Between gulps of water, Mark filled them in, Henry not liking anything he was hearing. Carol was beside Mark, holding him, a look of worry on her face.

"Mary heard them coming first," Mark explained as he sat in the chair, slumping from exhaustion. He wiped his mouth with the back of his sleeve and took another gulp of water. "There were over forty of them, all packed into a bunch of flatbeds and pickup trucks. I think they were watching us long before the main party got there. They knew exactly where we were when they showed up. We went to ground when they came. We were in one of those houses Cindy said she told you about," he told Henry. "We found a few things the women needed, and Cindy and Mary found the female stuff they wanted."

"Then what happened?" Jimmy demanded. "Tell me damn it, what the fuck happened to Cindy and Mary? Are they dead? Captured? What?"

Henry could tell Jimmy wanted to grab Mark and shake him, and only the slightest thread of control was holding the young man back.

"Better get to the point, Mark," Henry said flatly. "Where are the girls?"

"Cindy took the front of the house we were in, Mary went to the back. They told me to stay in the middle where I wouldn't get into trouble. I told them I could help but they wouldn't listen." His eyes glazed over slightly as he thought back. He looked beyond exhausted, at the end of his physical endurance. "The cannibals didn't have guns but they had other projectile weapons. Bows and arrows of all things, crossbows and some carried spears. Most had knives and other bladed weapons." He drank some more.

"They were smart bastards, too," he continued. "You could tell they'd done this before. Some would draw Cindy's fire when others attacked from the opposite direction. There were too many to shoot at once and there were lots of places for them to hide in the street and not get shot. Mary had the same problem, when they tried to outflank Cindy. Mary took down half a dozen easy before they realized it wasn't prudent to keep coming."

"Keep talking," Henry ordered.

"Cindy made a judgment call, and said it was time to bug out. We all headed out the back. But they were waiting for us." He shivered at the remembrance. "They came at us in a massive group. I got separated from Mary and Cindy. I shot five cannibals before I realized it was a trap. I yelled at them to follow me back inside and I turned and went into the house, but when I got inside, I saw that neither of them had followed me. I heard a few more gunshots and then nothing. So I ran to the side of the house, busted out a window and climbed out. Almost cut my stomach open when I did it." He raised his shirt, where there was a clotted line of blood. It was superficial at best. "I made it to the next house and went inside. It was two stories tall so I went up and peaked out a bedroom window, watching what happened next." He paused to drink again.

Jimmy batted the canteen out of his hand with enough force to send the canteen flying across the lobby. "Fuck that, what happened to my Cindy? Tell me!"

Mark glared up at Jimmy, who leered over him. He said nothing at first, the lobby dead silent, then he screamed, "They were taken, all right! I watched them hogtied like cattle and tossed into one of the pickups. There was nothing I could do. There were at least thirty of them still walking around. Even if I started to take shots at them from my position, they would have surrounded the house and eventually got to me, too."

Henry patted Mark's shoulder. "No, that would have been foolhardy, Mark. It's good you stayed quiet. This way we know what happened, and that they're still alive."

"They were when I saw them drive off." He sat up, his hands gripped into fists. "The bastards. The no good bastards."

"There, there, dear, you did your best," Carol soothed as she knelt down and placed her head on his shoulder.

"His best? His best?" Jimmy screamed. "Are you fucking nuts? He ran out on them. Left them to fucking die!" He raised the shotgun. "I should kill you right here, you fat piece of shit!"

The venom in Jimmy's voice was a living thing, and Henry could see the young man was walking a tightrope. He was acutely aware he needed to play this right, or Mark would be a headless corpse in a second.

"Jimmy," Henry said, his voice low, his face impassive. "Calm down, please. I know you're angry but it's not at Mark, though he's an easy target. It's the cannies we need to kill, not him. Hell, if he hadn't come back we'd still be in the dark about what happened." He lowered his voice as soft as he could. "Would you have preferred that?"

Jimmy said nothing, merely glowered at Mark.

"Well, would you?" Henry repeated, not forcing it, allowing common sense to penetrate Jimmy's anger-filled mind.

Mark's hands were gripping the armrests of the chair, knuckles white. He also realized he was in mortal danger. Carol was tearing up but she was wise enough to remain silent, though she hugged Mark tightly. The .22 in her hand wasn't even a consideration to use on Jimmy to protect her husband

Finally, something changed in Jimmy. His arms seemed to relax, and his shoulders drooped ever so slightly. His emotions were no longer driving him, and rationality was slowing seeping into his consciousness.

"No, Henry, fuck no, of course not. You're right, of course. Now we know they're alive and we can go save them." He looked at Henry, his eyes penetrating. "We are going to save them, right?"

"Of course we are. There was never any doubt. They're family; we do what we have to for family."

"But we don't know where they've been taken?" Mark interjected.

Carol squeezed his arm, trying to tell him to shut up but the man wouldn't listen. He stood up on uneasy legs, using a hand to steady himself on the chair.

Jimmy shot daggers at Mark but the large man ignored it.

"If there's a rescue party going to get them, I want to be the first one to volunteer. I might have screwed up before, but I swear to God, Jimmy, I'll make it right."

Jimmy's taut posture lessened a little more as Mark spoke to him. Jimmy was a lot of things that could be considered negatives, but one thing he wasn't, was disloyal. The fact Mark was standing up for himself, and was willing to go into unknown danger to save Jimmy's woman meant a lot to the young man.

"Good, I'm glad to hear it," Jimmy said with the barest hint of a grin. "And yeah, you do have a lot to make up for." He smiled wanly and held out his right hand to Mark. "Sorry about that 'fat piece of shit' remark. I overstepped there."

Mark took the proffered hand and the men shook. "That's all right. I know I should lose a few pounds."

"A few?" Jimmy said, his grin even wider.

Everyone had a little laugh at that. Not that the comment was funny, but it was a way to break the ice on a tense moment.

When everyone was feeling a little better a minute or so later, Henry got everyone's attention. "Okay, the next thing is to come up with a plan of rescue, which is gonna be hard as we don't know where the girls have been taken."

No one said a word, realizing Henry was correct. The women could have been taken anywhere. For all any of them knew, Mary and Cindy were miles away in an unknown direction. Saving them would be next to impossible unless they could figure out a way to find them.

Everyone looked at each other, silent, the shadows of the lobby surrounding them, lost in their own thoughts, when from the gloom-filled corridor that led to and from the pool, a voice said, "I know where you can find your women."

Henry pulled his Glock from his holster in lightning speed for the second time in the past hour. Swiveling on his boot heels, he aimed the barrel of the pistol at the newcomer, prepared to shoot.

But the shadowy figure didn't so much as twitch at the fact that a loaded gun was now aimed directly at him. The posture of the figure was casual, arms crossed across his chest, one shoulder leaning against a stone pillar near the egress.

"If you shoot me, then I can't help you save Mary and Cindy, or you help my people."

Henry was about to open his mouth and ask how the newcomer knew their women's names, but the man responded, "I heard you talking, that's how I know."

That made sense to Henry, so instead he asked, "Who are you and what do you want?"

The man used his shoulder to push off the pillar and stand fully erect, then walked out of the shadows and into the dim light cast from the overhead skylights. "The name's Crow, Thomas Crow, and I think we should all have a little chat."

Chapter 16

Henry and Jimmy said nothing as Thomas Crow walked over to them, a casualness to the man that defied logic. He was Native American, that was easy to tell at first sight, with dark black hair tied in a pony tail and hanging down the center of his shoulders, with a tanned visage that wasn't from the sun. His lips were thin, his nose hawk-like, the eyebrows thick and black to match the hair, the eyes dark as well. His chin was strong, and the all-around characteristics of the face made the man handsome to most people. He looked to be in his late thirties or early forties.

On his hip was a large Bowie knife, the sheath it rode in made of ornately carved leather. A crossbow was hanging from his right shoulder, a quiver of bolts there as well. He was dressed in jeans, a button down plaid shirt and a jeans jacket. Sneakers were on his feet.

"Okay, Thomas Crow, go ahead and talk, we're listening," Henry said.

Crow gestured to Henry's Glock and Jimmy's shotgun, still aimed at him. "You going to lower those?"

Henry remained immobile, as did Jimmy, that in itself a reply.

Crow gave off a slight shrug, then smiled, showing off bright white teeth. Looking away, he reached slowly into his jacket pocket and withdrew a pack of cigarettes. As if he had all the time in the world, he lit the cigarette with a disposable plastic lighter. Slipping the pack of smokes back into his jacket, he looked back at Henry. "Okay, then, if those peashooters make you feel better, keep them up, but you don't need them." He acted as if he wasn't a half ounce of pressure away from death if Henry or Jimmy deemed to do so.

Henry had to admit, he admired the man's courage. Or was it stupidity?

Henry ventured an assumption. "By any chance, you the author of those warnings sprayed around the area and at the pool?"

Crow nodded. "I did some of them, others were done by some of my brothers."

"Brothers?" Henry repeated. "You mean like family members?"

"Nah, man, like brothers from my tribe."

"Your tribe?"

"Sure, I'm Lumbee. My people have been here in Maryland since the early twentieth century."

Jimmy turned to look directly at Henry. "Jesus, Henry, what the fuck are we doing? We need to go get Cindy and Mary, not dick around with Tonto here."

"You think that's an insult, son, but it's not," Crow said, his tone friendly. "I loved the Lone Ranger when I was a kid." Not even a hint of being offended showed on his face.

"I know, Jimmy," Henry said, "but let's take a step back for a moment. This might be the break we needed." He looked Crow in the eyes, the two men locking gazes. "Am I correct on that?"

Crow nodded. "Yes you are, my friend, yes you are. I think we can help each other." He glanced at Jimmy, and the barrel of the shotgun still aimed at his chest. "That is, if your man doesn't decide to kill me for the hell of it."

Henry had a decision to make, one he needed to make quickly, if he was to save Cindy and Mary. This was a time he had to go with gut instinct, and pray what he felt was correct. As he looked on, studying Thomas Crow, seeing how at ease the man acted, as if he wasn't aware of how vulnerable he was at the moment, Henry had a feeling that Crow's confidence wasn't misplaced. Either he knew something Henry didn't, or he was just a damn cocky bastard.

Another added positive was if Crow was a local, he knew the area, so there was a good chance he could help the companions retrieve their women before they suffered certain doom.

Henry lowered his Glock, then reached out gently and placed his hand on the barrel of Jimmy's shotgun, pushing the muzzle down to the floor. "Let's hear the man out. I think he's on the level."

Crow smiled widely and took a hit off his cigarette, blowing smoke straight up. "That's the right choice, Henry." He raised his hand as if to tell Henry to hold on. "Now, don't freak out in a second." He put his right hand to his mouth, and placed two fingers between his lips. He whistled twice, quick and sharp. A heartbeat later, three more men appeared from around the lobby, where they had been hiding, completely unknown to Henry and Jimmy. It was like they'd materialized out of the shadows.

"What the fuck?" Jimmy whispered, as the men walked slowly to join Crow. All three men resembled Crow, their features, hair color, and clothing. All had crossbows and large knives on their hips. No guns were in view.

"These are my friends, Bob, Charlie and Mike," Crow said.

Jimmy had to suppress a chuckle and Crow looked at him in curiously.

"Something funny, son?"

"Well, yeah, a little."

"And what's that?" Crow asked.

"Well, shit, man," Jimmy snickered. "I never heard of Indians called Bob, Charlie and Mike!"

"Sorry to disappoint you, son," Crow explained. "But we're all American citizens here, as much as you are I figure. Or were at one time, when there was a U S of A. So we have names that pretty much mimic that."

Henry gave Jimmy a gentle shove. "Focus, Jimmy. The girls."

Jimmy nodded, the reminder sobering him up.

Crow turned to one of the men with him, Henry had already forgotten who was who, and said something to him in a low voice. The man reached into a pack he carried and pulled out a bottle of whiskey. He held up the bottle so Henry and the others could see it clearly.

"If you've got glasses," Crow began, "we can all be civilized and talk. So let's have a drink and I can fill you in on everything that's been going down around here." He locked his gaze on Jimmy, who found the penetrating stare almost hypnotic. "Then we'll get to saving your women folk."

Gathered around the large table in the sitting area of the lobby, Henry, Jimmy, Mark and Carol sat and listened quietly to Thomas Crow, as the man chatted on about life outside of Baltimore.

Now-empty shot glasses taken from the restaurant sat on the table between them. The bottle of whiskey was missing a good three inches of its liquid. Henry's throat still burned from downing the shot of alcohol in one gulp. Jimmy's face was red, and it had taken all the young man's power not to cough repeatedly. Mark and Carol had sipped the liquor without incident, or they showed none.

Crow told the story of how a small group of cannibals had arrived and taken over the Baltimore port where the cruise ships sailed in and out of.

One cruise ship had been moored to the pier since before the dead walked, and the cannibals had boarded it, and cleaned it of walking dead. Once cleared, they'd made it their base of operations, after towing it off the dock with a tugboat.

They used the tugboat, modified to run on coal, given that they had found a cargo ship filled to the brim with it, to ferry the crew back and forth as needed.

Once secure in their operation, the cannies began raiding the surrounding area for supplies, namely people. But that wasn't the only item on the menu. They raided the surrounding area for canned goods and dried food, too, but as time passed, those items began to dwindle, until the only main menu choice were other humans.

"But how do they keep from getting sick?" Carol asked, her curiosity getting the better of her. "We all need a balanced diet to prevent becoming ill, and even things like scurvy become something to be wary of."

"Carol, don't ask questions, just listen," Henry snapped at her.

"No, Henry, she's right on that subject," Crow agreed. He turned to look at Carol to reply. "They aren't too healthy, at least the ones we've seen. They have sores over a lot of their bodies and from what I've heard from a few deserters was that they get sick all the time."

"Deserters?" Jimmy inquired.

Crow brushed off the question with his hand, which was filled with another cigarette. He wasn't a chain smoker but damn close. "Yes, every now and then one of them tries to back out of the deal they made with the Devil. Any cannibal we find wandering around we capture and interrogate for information, then we kill them."

"You do?" Mark said, speaking up.

"Of course. Once someone's tasted human flesh and has made a habit of it, there's no way I'll ever trust them again. We kill them." Crow saw the horror on Mark's face so he added, "But we do it quick like. No torture or anything."

"How nice of you," Mark added, then remained silent.

"Who leads them?" Henry asked. "Is it a woman?"

"Yeah, it is," Crow said, surprised. "How did you know that?"

Mark was going to reply, but Henry cut him off with, "We heard it from someone, it doesn't matter who."

Crow nodded, not seeing a reason to pursue it. "Well, you're right, their leader is a woman; they call her their queen. No one knows her true name, but they all call her Big Mama."

"Oh yeah? Why's that?" Jimmy asked.

"'Cause she's one big mama, that's why. She's gotta be three hundred and fifty pounds, maybe more. She's so big she can't get around on her own volition, she needs crutches to support her."

Jimmy scoffed. "She doesn't sound like much of a threat."

"Maybe, son, but under all those rolls of fat there's a good amount of muscle. I've heard she can snap a man's neck with her bare hands. 'Course, the trick is she has to get her hands on you."

Crow grew silent for a moment, and concentrated on his cigarette. Henry and the others waited for him to continue. Crow's men said nothing, and just stood behind the couch he sat on, looking ready for a fight at any second.

"How come you haven't taken this den of cannies out already, if they're such a blight on you," Henry asked.

"We can't get to them, that's why," Crow replied. "Out on the water, they can see an attack coming from a mile away, even though they're not that far off the pier. They're about a quarter mile from land, I'd guess. Far enough out to be safe, but still close enough not to have to deal with storm issues when bad weather happens. They dropped anchor out there and damn if that ship is stuck in place." He shrugged. "Besides, there are only about twenty of my people that can actually fight, not including our women. But we all got kids, Henry, so we can't risk the adults on an all out assault. That's why we need help to take out that den of human monsters."

"And you think that's where Mary and Cindy were taken?" Henry asked hopefully.

Crow nodded. "Only place they would end up. If I was a betting man, I'd lay down a bet on it." He smiled. "I figure to save them, you need to take on those bastards, and with my men along with you, we'll finally be able to kill them all and end the scourge that's been hanging over our heads." He locked his gaze on each of the companions, and added, "You all come with us to our settlement, once there we can make a plan on how to take out the queen bee and her followers. From there we're only a few miles from the cruise port."

Henry was silent as he considered everything he'd been told, weighing his options now that he knew more about the situation.

Crow had stopped talking and was waiting for a reply, blowing smoke rings into the air. Jimmy, Carol and Mark looked to Henry, waiting for him to respond.

All eyes were on Henry as he thought about his next move.

Jimmy's face made it clear what he thought. He wanted to get moving, not sit around talking. He was all for joining up with Crow and his people.

Truth was, Henry reasoned, nothing had changed since he'd first met Crow, and his gut instinct had been to trust the man. If Crow meant them harm, he and his three men easily had ample opportunity to do harm to Henry or the others, but he'd done nothing of the kind.

Henry stood up quickly. So fast that Crow's three men reached for their knives, but stopped with hands on hilts. Crow had barely moved, and because he'd shown no reaction to Henry's sudden movement, the three men had held back from doing more than gripping their knives.

Henry held out his right hand in friendship. "To clarify in a lot fewer words. You help us get our women back and we'll help you take out the ship full of cannies when we do. Deal?"

Crow stood up, a wide smile creasing his lips. He took Henry's hand in his and the two men shook. Henry was pleased to see, though the grip was firm, that the man didn't try the squeezing game, which many did. Usually, men who weren't confident in their own abilities would want to try and show dominance over another. It said there was even more about Crow's personality that Henry admired.

"Sounds good to me," Crow said. "We shouldn't waste any more time here. Gather what you're taking and we get moving as soon as possible. Your women should be fine for a few hours, maybe even until tomorrow morning, but because we don't know how the meat eaters are set for food, we don't want to push getting in there."

Jimmy stood up as well, and he took in the scene of the two men. When Crow had released Henry's hand, the man turned and walked a few feet away, where his three guards joined him. He said a few words to them; they quickly moved off to attend to the orders they were given.

"Hey, Crow," Jimmy said, "I take it you're the leader of your people, is that right?"

"Yes, son, that's so. Why do you ask?"

"Oh, no reason, I was just wondering to myself how you got to be in charge."

"Jimmy, shut the hell up, we need these people," Henry hissed low, but not so low Crow didn't hear.

"It's all right, Henry," Crow said lightly. He dropped his spent cigarette onto the lobby floor, stepping on it to crush it out. "I can see this one has a free spirit." He gazed at Jimmy as if the younger man was truly a child, or was his actual hypothetical son. He also replied how a father would to a son, with kindness and patience, knowing the foolishness of youth. "I'm the leader because I've destroyed more of the dead when they still walked, and later when they came, I slaughtered more cannibals than anyone else in my tribe." He lowered his head but raised his eyes as he glared at Jimmy. "Is that acceptable to you, son?"

Jimmy only nodded. "Yeah, sure, it's fine."

"Good, now with that settled, we must leave." There was the sound of an engine from outside, and at first Henry thought the cannies had come to attack, but then one of Crow's men pushed through the glass doors and held one open.

"Good, our ride is here. Can we leave?" Crow asked politely.

Henry nodded. "Five minutes and we're right behind you," Henry said, and began spouting orders to Jimmy and Carol to gather their gear along with any food Carol had found. Mark he left alone, the man looked too shook up to do much more than sit there.

Five minutes to the second, Henry and the others were standing in the center of the lobby, loaded with their gear and ready to depart.

"Good, follow me, please," Crow said, and led everyone out of the hotel to the waiting vehicle.

Around the time Henry was meeting Thomas Crow for the first time, Mary slowly began to regain consciousness. Her cheek was wet with drool, a small puddle under her mouth.

She forced herself not to show it in case anyone was watching. The first thing was to keep her eyes from fluttering, the second was to control her breathing, keeping it slow and steady.

Mary didn't know if she had pulled it off, but she was doing her best, and she slowly felt her mind coming back from the darkness of being knocked out. Not that she remembered much of how that happened. She remembered the cannies charging into the house and she and Cindy shooting them, until eventually becoming overwhelmed. They had fought hand to hand, but briefly, until a blow to the head had knocked her out.

After that she recalled nothing.

Feeling her body by sensing it, she felt nothing hurt, with the exception of a gentle throbbing at the back of her head. When she moved her head a little, the hair pulled on her scalp, as if it was sticking to what she was lying on.

She was on her back, she knew, and horizontal, and as she slowly cracked an eye open, she saw she was in some kind of room, but could fathom no more than that. Her arms and legs were strapped to some kind of table, her legs spread wide, her arms over her head.

She lay as still as she could, straining her hearing to detect if she was alone or not. She waited for a full minute before deciding to risk more than just a peek, after hearing nothing.

Cracking her eyes, bright light from a porthole almost blinded her and she had to close her eyes again. Then, more slowly this time, she opened them again. It didn't take long for her vision to adjust, and she began to look around her, the ceiling being the first place as she was facing the ceiling. There were small spots of dried blood on the ceiling tiles, or she assumed it was. Turning her head side to side, Mary saw she was in a small room, about twenty feet by twenty-five, with only one door she could see in her field of vision.

The porthole was open and the sound of lapping water could be heard, along with the calls of seagulls. From her angle on the table, all she could see through the porthole was blue sky. Still, she took everything she'd seen and deduced she was on a ship of some kind.

There was someone else in the room, situated so that the person was above her, placed at the top of her head. She did her best to turn her head upwards, her chin sticking up high, her neck stretching taut. She could just make out a head with blonde hair, the strands all tangled together. She couldn't tell for sure, but she assumed it was Cindy. The other woman was also strapped to a table in a similar pose. In another corner of the room, were Mary and Cindy's gear, weapons and packs, which had been with them while they'd foraged for supplies.

Mary called out to Cindy but got no response. Hopefully, Cindy wasn't dead, but only unconsciousness as Mary had been. Mary figured when someone had cold-cocked her in the attack, another cannie had also got to Cindy as well.

Sniffing the air, Mary detected the odor of sweat and blood, feces and urine, and the ocean. Quite the cacophony of aromas, actually, all mixed into one.

Craning her neck as far as it would go to the left, she saw that the floor and lower part of the walls were the reason for the smells; they were splashed with bodily fluids, some long dried, some relatively fresh.

There was a long table in the far corner, piled high with an assortment of construction tools, only now they were being used to carve up something other than wood. With the way they were stained red and brown, more of a rust color, really, she had a bad feeling she knew what the tools were used for. The bright red covering some of them told a tale that the tools had been used recently, too.

That wasn't a good sign.

Her heart sank in her chest for what would be coming next.

Chapter 17

Henry's mouth dropped open as he stepped inside the Maryland Science Center in the heart of downtown Baltimore.

The area around the museum had been cleared of any debris, and it looked as if rebuilding was taking place. Crow and his people were working hard to take the world back now that the living dead were gone.

Directly in front of Henry was the dinosaur exhibit. A life-size Brontosaurus was standing before him. It was massive, making him feel like a child again. Overhead, hanging from the ceiling by wires, was the skeleton of a T-Rex, and all around were glass cases filled with dinosaur bones and other artifacts.

There was a large glass wall at the front of the center. Only a few of the panels were broken, replaced by wood. Someone had taken the time to patch them.

"Wow," Jimmy said in awe. "This place is so cool."

"Come on in," Thomas Crow said. "This is home of my people."

"You live in a museum?" Carol asked, Mark standing silently beside her. He hadn't said much since leaving the hotel, still shook up from the attack and his escape from the cannies.

"Yes, it's actually the perfect habitat for us. There are many large rooms with only glass for the roof. Those rooms we've made into greenhouses so we can grow produce and wheat even after summer is over. We've been trying to use fire to heat the rooms as well during the winter, to save on what diesel fuel we have. We vent the smoke in chimneys we've built."

"Has it worked?" Carol asked, intrigued.

"Partially. We haven't figured out a way to maintain an even temperature, but we have people working on it." He smiled, confident in his tribe. "We'll figure it out eventually."

"What about meat?" Henry asked while gazing around the massive room, taking it all in. There was a part of him that wanted to go explore, as the museum had been meticulously maintained, and any damage long corrected. But he knew he was short on time. That night there would need to be a raid on the cruise ship to save his people. Any longer would risk Mary and Cindy's deaths. The chance they were already dead wasn't something he wanted to think about, so he didn't. If he found out later they had perished, at least he could enact revenge on the perpetrators.

"We have a small stable where we raise chickens and rabbits. We don't eat a lot of meat. The grain it takes to raise the animals is better off going to my people directly; we waste nothing. But on special occasions we do eat meat." Crow began leading them deeper into the museum, the three men at the hotel still with him. There were others there now, too. Five men had been waiting when Henry and the others had pulled up in front of the building and climbed out of the pickup truck. All had given the companions wary looks, but Crow told them to relax, that Henry and the others were friends.

Henry found it hard to concentrate on Crow talking as he admired all the exhibits. There was one about space and planets and the solar system, and another room was titled "Your Body: The Inside Story." There were pictures and statues of the human body, of how the human vascular system, veins and arteries all worked in tandem. He wasn't interested in that one. Over the years, he'd seen far too much of the inside of human bodies, after killing what must have been hundreds of zombies, let alone the living beings he'd had to kill after becoming threatened.

There was a large sign on the wall with a list of exhibits, and arrows to point guests in the right direction. Planet Earth, Chesapeake Bay Life, The Kids Room, and the Please Touch Exhibit, plus the cafeteria and where the bathrooms were.

Crow led the companions to a large theater, where more than twenty people were waiting, both men and women, some middle aged, some seniors, all bearing a resemblance to Crow. There was a small stage at the front, and Crow led Henry and Jimmy to it, directing them to step up. Carol and Mark were told to take a seat in the front row.

There were no windows, and oil lamps burned brightly from where they were sporadically spaced around the theater. Flickering shadows were everywhere.

When Crow was standing in the center of the stage, Henry and Jimmy by his side, but a few inches behind him, he raised his hands to show he wanted quiet inside the room, which was a buzz with everyone talking at once. All eyes were on Henry and Jimmy, however, and Henry tried not to look too closely at the guards on both sides of the stage, and at the entrance he'd used to enter. All the guards carried crossbows in their hands, bolts cocked and ready to fire if needed.

"All right, everyone, quiet now! We need to start the meeting. Quiet?" Crow shouted, his voice booming in the room, the acoustics perfect, as the theater was built for sound to carry. Everyone sat down, that is, those that weren't already sitting.

An old woman in her seventies stood up in the crowd. She wore a simple floral dress, her hair tied in a long pony tail. Her once ink black hair was streaked with gray. Even in her later years she was attractive, and Henry wondered what she must have looked like when she was young.

"Black Crow, who are these people?" the old woman asked.

"They're friends, Mother, they're here to help us take down the cannibals," Crow said.

"Who's Black Crow? I thought you said you're first name is Thomas," Jimmy said.

Crow looked at Henry and then Jimmy; out of the side of his mouth he muttered, "That's my tribe name. Not for you guys, only my people can use it."

"Gotcha," Jimmy said with a wink. He wasn't about to be his typical wise ass self. His only concern was to rescue Cindy, and he would make sure he did nothing to mess that up.

Henry stayed quiet, instead studying the people seated in the seats below him. He figured these were the leaders of the tribe, the ones that got a say in how things were run. He reached this con-clusion by the way they were all looking at him, each with an air of authority.

But though they might all get some say in matters of the tribe, it was the old woman Crow had called Mother that appeared to be the one fully in charge.

She was still standing, the only one who was. She looked up at Henry and Jimmy, studying them closely. "We don't need their help."

"Oh, but we do, Mother," Crow said. "Just look at their weap-ons." He took a step forward. "And these men know war, much more than we do. I've talked to them in great length. With their help we can do this. We've been trying to end the cannibals for more than two years now, with no results. Sure, we kill one every now and then when we find one, and even more when they try and attack us when we're out in the city, but we never seem to make a dent in their numbers. I think these two, along with myself and some of our best warriors, can attack tonight and end the threat for good. This is the thing we've been waiting for, this is the time to finally kill them all. Only then can we be truly safe, us and our children."

One of the men stood up, a middle-aged man with short black hair like Crow's, his eyebrows so thick he came close to sporting a unibrow. "We don't need them, guns or no guns."

Henry was growing impatient. He stepped forward so he was beside Crow. "Way I see it, we don't need you either. Just point us in the direction of the port and we'll get our women ourselves. Then we're out of here and you can keep playing war games with the cannies. Who knows? Maybe in a few years you might even win. But it won't be my problem, or my friends'."

There was a murmuring of both agreement and dissent. Some wanted to fight the cannies themselves, others agreed with Crow, and felt the companions' weapons were a valuable asset.

One thing Henry was glad to hear, it was that no one suggested trying to take the companions' guns for themselves, by force if necessary. That wouldn't have gone well for either side.

The man was still standing, and he raised his voice to override the crowd, who were still chattering. "These women you speak of. They important to you?" he asked Henry.

Henry nodded. "Sure are. One is this man's wife," he gestured to Jimmy, "and the other is my daughter."

Jimmy turned to Henry with a quizzical look, but Henry just shook his head subtly. A little exaggeration at a time like this wasn't such a bad thing. And Henry could already tell that one thing the people before him understood, it was family, even more than just traveling companions.

Crow knew the truth, however. Henry looked at him, waiting to see if the man was going to contradict Henry's statements.

Crow said nothing, only agreed with Henry's words. "Family is everything. If we help these men save their family members, we can also help ourselves. Together we can do this. Together we *must* do this. This is our best chance of success!"

Unibrow considered Crow's words for a few heartbeats and then nodded, saying, "I'm with Black Crow. This is the time to do this."

"If we're gonna do this," Henry said loudly, "we need to go tonight, once it's dark!"

Another man stood. "I agree. We do this now, tonight."

Others stood, each agreeing, until Mother raised a hand, the others sitting again, until only she remained standing. She'd never sat down after asking her first question. "It is settled. Tonight we attack the cannibals and destroy them once and for all."

Clapping began, then yelling and shouting, the entire crowd cheering Crow and the companions.

"What's next?" Henry asked Crow, having to almost yell to be heard. Evidently, the group of people in the seats was more than a little excited to finally being able to take the fight to the cannies.

"Next we eat and make plans for tonight," Crow explained. "I can fill you in on some more logistics, and we can decide how we'll do this. I have photographs I can show you as well. A few months ago we took pictures with an old Polaroid that develops the pictures independently of outside chemicals."

"I remember those," Jimmy said. "Funny how old stuff becomes new again, huh?"

"Yes, I agree. We took a lot of pictures, so we have them to plan an attack, only we could never figure out a way to do it successfully." He waited a heartbeat. "Until now."

"Then let's get to work, times a wastin'," Henry said.

*C*lick, *thump, click, thump.*

The noise floated through the only door into the room.
Click, thump, click, thump.

"You hear that?" Cindy asked.

"I do now," Mary had been dozing, trying to rest, in the hopes that if there was a chance to escape, she would be recuperated enough to take advantage of it. Cindy's question had stirred her from a restless sleep. A heartbeat later the door to the room began to creak open.

"Someone's coming in," Cindy said.

"Yes, unfortunately," Mary replied, knowing it couldn't be good. They had remained alone since Cindy also woke up, more than an hour if she had to guess. But how long she'd been unconscious before that was a mystery. Given that it was still day when she'd woken, she figured it hadn't been too long. It also had to be the same day. She believed she would have known if she'd been out for an entire night.

Cindy had woken about an hour earlier, Mary figured, and the two women had exchanged notes. That hadn't taken long as there wasn't much to discuss.

Cindy had inquired about Mark, who Mary had completely forgotten about. She had barely known the man, and being thrust into the situation she was in, he was the last thing she was thinking about.

Both women had agreed the man was probably dead.

Even if he wasn't, they had their own problems at the moment.

The door opened as wide as it would go, a large shape looming in the doorway, darkness in the corridor beyond, so that the figure was lost in shadow.

Heavy breathing, more like panting, floated into the room, along with the stench of a long unwashed body. The body odor was a palpable thing; it got into the sinuses and made the women want to gag.

The figure entered the room, having to push its large bulk though the doorway. Then it was inside, the body odor even stronger. Both Mary and Cindy had to breathe through their mouths to prevent from gagging.

The instant the figure was inside the room, two smaller ones slid in behind, to flank the large one. Once inside, the figure became more apparent, the light from the porthole bathing it, which was the only form of bathing the figure had seen in quite a while by the looks of it.

The woman standing in the room was massive, topping the scales at four hundred pounds. She wore nothing but a filthy muumuu, the material stained a new color than its original one from countless feedings and possibly other things. At one time there had been some kind of butterfly pattern covering it, but the pattern was so faded to be nonexistent.

There was no actual shape to the woman, just a roundish circle. Sores covered her face and arms, the only parts of flesh Mary and Cindy could see. One arm was completely covered in tattoos. There was the picture of a snake on her chest where the muumuu sagged at the neckline. Only the section of the tattoo that reached her neck and face could be seen, and not too much there, as her neck was so short as to be nonexistent. It was like her head simply was perched on her shoulders. The snake art ended on her cheek; the head of a viper. What was visible hinted at something massive drawn on her torso. Her breasts were nonexistent, but were just one more roll of fat on her front. Double chins hung below her mouth, moving like the waddle of a turkey. Two beady eyes were sunk into a chubby face. But though the body was obese, the eyes were bright, showing a high intelligence. Her hair was some sort of dark color, brown or perhaps even dark blonde, but it was so encrusted with filth it was hard to discern under the contaminants.

"Are you okay, Big Mama?" one of the men asked as he stood by the large woman's side.

"Of course I'm okay. Fuck off!" she snapped and waddled deeper into the room. She used a pair of crutches to help support her.

Mary figured with a body so large, either the knees or ankles wouldn't be able to support her, so the crutches were needed to allow her to remain mobile. Even hunched over with the crutches, she still reached six feet in height.

That was the sound they'd heard. The *click, thump, click, thump,* of both feet and crutches working in tandem as the woman made her way down the hallway.

Her hair was thin and short, cut so close to the scalp that skin peeked though in multiple places. It looked like the hair hadn't been washed in months, if not years.

Cindy let out a gasp upon seeing the large woman, and Mary thought she heard a touch of fear in that sound. Not that she blamed Cindy in the slightest. Despite facing countless dangers since the dead first walked, Mary always did her best to keep her head high and heart strong. But there were a few times when she'd felt abject terror.

This was becoming one of those times.

Strapped helplessly to a table with no hope of rescue, it was hard to remain defiant. Fear filled Mary's stomach, a black hole of terror taking over her insides. She did her best to force it down but it was difficult.

Big Mama walked over to Cindy, her breathing heavy as she forced her massive bulk across the room. Upon reaching Cindy, she leaned down so that her face was mere inches from Cindy's.

Mary craned her neck to see what was happening, her peripheral vision allowing her to see only a hint of the two figures.

"Jesus Christ, lady, ever heard of a Tic Tac?" Cindy gagged and turned her face away. The odor of carrion and old cigarette smoke seeped out of the foul-looking mouth, filled with the yellowish teeth Cindy had ever seen.

Big Mama reached out a hand and slapped Cindy across the face, the whip crack so loud Mary winced.

The teeth in Cindy's mouth rattled from the blow, her eyes rolling up into her head. Under all that fat there must have been some muscle, because the blow sure as hell felt like it. Blood began to drip out of Cindy's left nostril, to slide down her cheek and neck to pool under her head.

Big Mama grabbed Cindy's face, her fingers and thumb squeezing into Cindy's cheeks, digging into the skin. Cindy let out a low moan. "You don't speak until I tell you to, slut," she hissed, her voice a grating sound, like two rocks being scraped together.

It reminded Mary of women she'd met in the past who had smoked their entire lives.

"Talk again without permission and I'll have all your teeth ripped out of your mouth." Tears were in Cindy's eyes, the blow had been so bad, but she said nothing.

"Good." Big Mama released Cindy's face. "Your mine to do with as I wish, so why not be a good girl about it?" She leered at Cindy. "You'll live longer that way." Big Mama reached out her hand again, this time squeezing one of Cindy's breasts. "Who knows? You might even enjoy it a little." This time there was no malice in her words, as she caressed the soft globe of flesh. She pulled on Cindy's shirt, hard, but not angrily, so that the shirt buttons popped. She yanked down Cindy's bra to expose her breasts to the air. Once more she began caressing the trapped woman's chest, the fat woman's fingers flicking at the nipples.

"They call me Big Mama, girl. I'm the queen bitch of this here ship you're on. No one fucks with me. If they do, they wind up in next day's stew. There's no way to escape. Even if you manage to get off the ship, we're a quarter mile from shore. You swim that good, girl? Most people don't got the stamina and drown, if they even try. Sometimes we get deserters, decide they don't like eatin' other people no more, try to run. We find the bodies later, floatin' face down, all bloated and pasty like."

Though Cindy was terrified, her nipples became erect, a direct result of the attention given to them, and in no way a sign she was becoming aroused. Big Mama smiled and leaned down, licking one of the nipples with her tongue. Cindy squeezed her eyes closed.

Big Mama bit down hard on the tender nipple, drawing a small droplet of blood, causing Cindy to wince in pain. "Open your eyes, slut. I want you to watch me."

Cindy obeyed, understanding there was no other option.

Big Mama's hand slid down Cindy's body, until it was over her captive's jeans. She ripped the jeans open to get access. As she continued to suck on her prisoner's nipple, her hand went between Cindy's legs, then she began using her index finger to slide in and out of Cindy, the motion making the fat hanging below her arm jiggle.

Cindy could only lay still and suffer the abuse she was receiving. The two cannie guards had their dicks out and were stroking them without a care in the world. Evidently, Big Mama didn't mind an audience.

This went on for five minutes, then Big Mama got bored and yanked Cindy's pants down to her ankles. Panties went as well. Cindy was wearing a new pair, one she'd found in a bedroom drawer in one of the homes she'd been searching earlier that day.

Big Mama used the table for support as she leaned her crutches against the table, then she hobbled down the side so that she was hovering over Cindy's stomach.

Leaning over Cindy's pussy, Big Mama moved close, so that her nose was touching her prisoner's pubic hair. She breathed in deeply, as if she were appreciating the aroma of a delicate flower or a freshly-opened bottle of wine.

"Heavenly," Big Mama whispered, then used a hand to expose Cindy's vagina and leaned in with her mouth. Cindy squeezed her eyes closed despite being ordered not to, but Big Mama was far too busy to notice. There was a slurping sound as the large woman sucked and licked Cindy's pussy, apparently relishing the sexual act so much she reached a hand under her muumuu and began fingering herself. Lost in the folds of fat, Mary could see nothing of the woman's self ministrations, nor would she have wanted to.

Big Mama licked and sucked with gusto, as the two guards masturbated furiously. Finally both men finished, shooting their fluids onto the floor. Spent, they put their dicks away and stood casually, still enjoying the show but now sexually satisfied.

Ten minutes the large woman had her head buried between Cindy's legs, until she began to moan and groan. Her entire body began to shudder. She almost collapsed and had to slap her hands onto the side of the table to prevent herself from going down. Standing up fully, she wiped her mouth with the back of her hand, and stepped back.

"Like ambrosia. I think I'll keep you around for a while, sweetie pie."

She collected her crutches and hobbled over to Mary, who said nothing, merely gazing up at the large woman's face. Her chin and mouth still glistened from being with Cindy. "Unfortunately for you, I don't like brunettes, just blondes, so no such luck for you."

Mary stared, knowing to speak might elicit a slap of her own.

"My boys can have you, though. One of the perks of being my private guard."

"Ah, shit, Big Mama, we just came. We're not in the mood right now."

"Later then, boys, once you got your strength back. Later is fine." She began moving to the door with her crutches. "I'll see you again later, sweetie pie," She told Cindy, a gleam in her eyes. "Next time I'll bring something to fuck you with. Something big and hard. Would you like that?"

"Fuck you, you fat cow!" Cindy screamed, too angry and humiliated to care what would happen to her for talking after being ordered not to.

"Huh, we'll see who fucks who, my darling slut, we will certainly see." Her eyes went cold, the gleam erased. "You're my property now, slut. Displease me and you'll end up roasting on a spit. But make me happy and you might get to live for a very long time." She turned and walked away, saying over her shoulders, "That is, until I find something prettier to replace you with." She left, squeezing back through the door and click-thumping her away down the corridor.

"Her last sex slave committed suicide, you know," one of the men told Cindy before leaving. "We ate her the next day. She tasted sweet. Not as sweet as you'll taste I bet." He looked at Mary, who defiantly returned his gaze. "Me and George are gonna be back for you later, just as soon as we're ready."

"Yeah, Lenny, I'm looking forward to fucking the shit out of her. Hell, my dick's already twitching."

Laughing, the two men exited the room, the door slamming closed with a hope-dropping sound.

Once the door was closed and the two women were alone, Mary called out to Cindy. "Oh my God, I'm so sorry. Are you all right? That bitch. I swear she's gonna pay. I'll cut out her heart myself."

Cindy didn't respond, but Mary could hear her friend sobbing. Deciding there wasn't much to say in consolation, she stayed quiet, letting Cindy weep softly.

Chapter 18

Henry and Jimmy walked through the Science Museum behind Crow, who was giving the two men a more thorough tour; behind them, two guards followed silently. Seen but not heard.

Crow first brought them to one of the makeshift greenhouses, where there were rows of crops, including corn and beans, along with chili peppers, which Crow explained were high in vitamin C, even more than in oranges.

The meal they would have was being prepared for the entire tribe, like every night, and Henry and Jimmy were invited, along with Mark and Carol, who had stayed behind with Mother to learn more about the tribe.

Crow detailed where he was bringing them beforehand, wanting Henry and Jimmy to see his home, how he and the others in the tribe had managed to create a new life in an apocalyptic world. After the greenhouses, he was going to take them to what Crow halfheartedly called the armory. He said it wasn't much, but the tribe had been doing their best to fill it with whatever could be found.

Passing a storage room off one of the growing rooms, Henry stopped and peered inside, seeing white sacks of something, rice perhaps, or some sort of grain. Small granules, like thick sand, were scattered on the floor from where the sacks had sprung leaks due to bad seams. Henry inquired what was inside the room.

"We store our fertilizer in here for our crops," Crow explained. "That's all."

Henry walked into the room, looking down on the fifty-five pound sacks of fertilizer. He read the name on the front of one sack, then more information below what the fertilizer consisted of. "Ammonium Nitrate," he said out loud.

Jimmy stood at the door, anxious to keep moving. He hated waiting, wanting to leave to rescue Cindy and Mary, but he knew it had to wait until dark. Movement was the only thing keeping him sane, as he tried to keep from going crazy with concern for his woman.

"What's the big deal, Henry? It's just some bags of dried cow shit to help their plants grow. Let's keep moving," Jimmy snapped while leaning against the doorframe. From somewhere nearby, he detected the distinct aroma of marijuana. Christ, he could use a few hits, he thought, but it was only wishful thinking. There had been a time when he'd been quite the pot head. But no more. He kept his mind sharp and focused now, knowing at anytime it might mean the difference between life and death.

Henry held up a hand to stop Jimmy from further complaining, his brow creased as he considered something. "Hold up, I'm getting an idea what we can do to stop the cannies for good. And this stuff isn't 'cow shit.' This stuff is chemicals." He leaned over and grabbed a handful of ammonium nitrate from an open bag, and walked over to Jimmy and Crow, who was watching with curiosity. "See? This is a chemical, and if I know my science and history, this can be made into a pretty serious bomb."

Jimmy just stared at Henry, not understanding how a bunch of granules could become an explosive. "That shit? No fucking way."

"Yes, way, and I'll tell you how." Henry looked at Crow, still holding the granules. "Crow, you said you have diesel fuel, am I correct?"

Crow nodded. "Yes, we have a decent supply. We use it in the greenhouses and to run one of our trucks that runs on diesel fuel. Why?"

"Nothing, just thinking," Henry said, a plan beginning to form in his head. But he still needed more to make it complete. First, he needed to see the pictures Crow's people had managed to get of the port, so he could actually see the layout and what he was up against. He said as much to Crow.

"We can go to the 'Intel' room where we have collected everything we have now, if you like. I just thought you would want a few minutes to rest."

Henry shook his head. "There's no time for rest, not until we get my people back. Go on, we're right behind you."

"Actually, Henry," Jimmy said quickly. "I could use a bathroom break first."

Henry looked at his friend and at mention of it, realized so could he. He said as much to Crow who ushered them out of the storeroom and down a hallway, where the restrooms were located.

"We use buckets of sea water we collect to pour into the toilets, you see. No water is running in the pipes but the sewer system still works."

"Yeah, I've heard of that used before," Henry said and he had. It wasn't a new idea Crow shared but it was a practical one.

Henry stopped in front of the Men's room. "As soon as we come out we go to that Intel room, right?"

"Yes, I'll wait here for you."

Jimmy was already pushing past Henry to get into the bathroom. "Outta the way, man, I think that chili is sneaking up on me again!"

Crow watched Jimmy's retreating back, as the younger man rushed into the bathroom, then looked at Henry, an eyebrow raised quizzically.

"Not worth discussing," Henry said, and with trepidation now that Jimmy was in there before him, he too, entered the bathroom.

The sun was just beginning to set, the light diminishing through the single porthole, when George and Lenny, true to their word, returned for some action.

Both men stumbled into the gloom-filled room, slurring their words as they did so. The men had been drinking by the way they acted. Both almost tripped while entering, their feet catching on the raised rim of the doorframe, which was made a lot like a submarine hatch, only wider.

The two men stumbled across the floor until they were standing between Mary and Cindy, still strapped to their prospective tables.

"Do you think I could have a go at Blondie while you take the brunette?" George asked his partner as he swayed on his feet. He rubbed his crotch in expectation before letting out a loud belch.

Lenny shook his head, the action almost making him fall over. "Okay, but I think you're making a hell of a mistake. If Big Mama finds out you touched her new sex toy, she'll have you skinned and thrown in the cook pot." He elicited a huge fart, smiling like a fox that had gotten into the hen house.

George sighed, gazing down at Cindy, who was still exposed from when Big Mama had left her. Her breasts were firm and pale in the dim light of the room, rising and falling subtly as she breathed. Her pubic hair still glistened with moisture from Big Mama's mouth. The V of hair at the junction of her thighs was the same color as her hair.

"But she's still wet from earlier, look at that sweet pussy," George said as he took in Cindy's lithe form, licking his lips with expectation of the delights he might experience. He reached out and cupped a breast, squeezing it roughly.

Cindy winced in pain but said nothing, only glared at him.

"Goddamn, but she's a sweet piece of ass." George slid his hand down and rubbed Cindy between her legs, panting heavily as he did. There was a decent-sized bulge in his pants. "Maybe I could just have her blow me for a bit," he suggested.

Lenny wasn't listening. He was standing over Mary, slowly undoing her shirt, rolling it up so he could expose her breasts. Mary glared at him, her jaw taut. If looks could kill, Lenny would have been writhing on the floor in death spasms.

"Take your fucking hands off me, you piece of shit," Cindy hissed, realizing she did have some power here, if only over George. As she'd laid there and let the man touch her, she thought herself helpless, but when she rolled around what Lenny just said, she came to the conclusion she did have one weapon she could use. "The second Big Mama comes back I'm telling her you fucked me, whether you do it or not."

George immediately stopped what he was doing and looked down at Cindy's face, pulling his attention from her breasts. Though exhausted and scared, she was still beautiful, and the defiance in her eyes gave her a wild look. "Maybe she won't care, did you think of that? Maybe Lenny's full of shit." He tried to act like he believed what he said, but there was doubt in his voice.

"You want to take that chance?" Cindy asked matter-of-factly. "If he's right, you're a dead man, and that fat cow doesn't seem like she shows mercy to someone who crosses her."

George considered her words, and even in his befuddled daze, he came to the conclusion she was right. He stepped away from her.

Relief filled her from head to toe, but a moment later dread replaced it when she saw George step away from her and move the few feet to Mary, joining Lenny in playing with her breasts.

"Shit," Cindy muttered, realizing all she'd done is sent the man over to screw with Mary, something she would have never done willfully.

"Damn nice tits," Lenny said as he pushed up Mary's bra to expose her breasts. He began to squeeze them and roll the nipples in his hands, George caressing Mary's stomach. Mary lay still, her eyes closed, trying to think of something else, anything, so that she wasn't in the room being molested by two men that smelled like compost heaps. The only thing she could do is lie there and take it, so she did her best to blank her mind and not focus on what was happening to her. She winced and let out a small squeak when George opened her pants and slid his hand into her panties, wiggling his fingers a little in her pubic mound before going deeper.

Lenny grinned when he saw her face. "I think she likes that, George, she's smiling."

Mary decided if one of the men was stupid enough to stick his dick in her mouth, she planned on biting it clean off and spitting the detached member back at him. She pulled on the cords holding her arms but there was no movement with the material. She did manage to get her left hand in a better position to pull, but the cord was still too tight to allow her to slip her hand through.

Cindy took a gamble and said, "Hey, assholes, if you don't stop touching her and fix her clothes right now, I'm gonna tell Big Mama you both fucked me."

The men stopped and looked at Cindy. She had their attention.

"What are you talking about?" Lenny slurred. "George isn't bothering you anymore and I never went near you."

"So what? I'll tell Big Mama anyway."

"But it won't be true, she won't believe you." There was worry in Lenny's voice.

"You wanna bet?" Cindy pretended she was talking to Big Mama. " 'They both stuck their dicks in me. One after the other, and they shot their loads inside me. I told them not to, that you'd be mad, but they said you were a fat cow and could go fuck yourself.' "

Both men stopped what they were doing as if they'd been hit by a giant hammer. Thinking about Cindy saying that, and what their queen would do to them, had them quaking in their proverbial boots, as the two men were barefoot. Without hesitation, as if they'd rehearsed earlier, they stepped away from Mary simultaneously, their legs in lockstep with one another.

One looked at the other.

"I think we should leave, don't you?" Lenny said.

George nodded, his head like a bobble head. "Yeah, that's a good idea. Suddenly, I'm not horny anymore."

"Yeah, me neither."

George took a minute to fix Mary's clothing, zipping up her pants and pulling her bra and shirt down. Once he was satisfied she looked the way he found her, both men turned and walked away.

"Wait, fix my clothes, too," Cindy told them.

"No way, lady," George said, the more sober of the two men. "Big Mama left you that way, so that's how you stay."

Before Cindy could threaten the men some more, they were out the door, pulling it closed behind them. The soft sound of a lock being set floated into the room.

The two women were silent for a few minutes, each taking in what had happened, then Mary said, "Thank you."

"No problem, you'd do it for me if our places were reversed."

"In a heartbeat, you know that."

"I do, that's why I did it."

"How did you know it would work with me as well as you?" Mary asked.

"I didn't, but I figured what did I have to lose, or you?"

"Well, your gamble worked out."

"For now."

"You think the boys are looking for us?"

Cindy bent her head upwards so she could try and see Mary. All she managed was to see the top of her friend's head. "Of course they are. I'm sure Henry and Jimmy are hashing out a plan to save us right now."

"But they won't know where we are."

"They'll find a way. They always do."

"There's always a first time they don't."

Cindy tried to see Mary again, but failed. Giving up, she relaxed her head. "Then we're dead, or worse, unless we figure a way to escape."

"I guess we better get to it," Mary said and yanked on the cord securing her left hand again. "Because if I'm right and you're wrong, we're our own best and only chance of getting out of here alive."

Chapter 19

"This is your armory?" Henry asked, disappointed at what was before him.

"What there is of it," Crow said. They stood in a small room, surrounded by a feeble assortment of weapons, mostly crossbows, bows and different kinds of melee weapons and blades.

"Where the fuck are the guns?" Jimmy asked from beside Henry, his eyes roaming over the spears, knives, and even a pitchfork with razor sharp tines.

Crow went to a locker, opened, it, and showed Henry a few pistols, revolvers and an assortment of hunting rifles. Barely ten in all.

"We don't have any ammunition for them, that ran out more than a year ago. The whole area surrounding us has been cleaned out; back before when the dead were still walking around. Unfortunately, none of my people know how to make more."

"But your fucking Indians," Jimmy said, thinking the quiet part out loud. "You're supposed to know how to do shit like that."

Crow turned to face Jimmy, after slamming the locker door closed. "This isn't a damn cowboy movie, son. I told you before, all my people were born here, in Maryland, most of us only a few miles from this spot. We're as American as you are, even if my skin isn't as pale as yours."

"Now, hold on a minute there, Kemosahbee," Jimmy snapped back, speaking before he realized he was doing so.

"Jimmy, shut the hell up. Now." Henry demanded, his tone brooking no argument. "We're guests here, goddammit, fucking act like it."

Jimmy blinked in surprise, taken completely off guard. Henry swore rarely, it was just his way, so for him to use the F word, meant how truly upset he was. "Shit, Henry, I didn't mean anything by it."

"I don't care. Do me a favor and give Crow and me a minute alone, all right?"

"But, Henry…"

"Christ, Jimmy, will you just do what I say one time without giving me any lip." Henry's face was red, and there was a vein bulging on his forehead. He was holding back his anger by a thread.

Jimmy threw up his hands in surrender. "Fine, I'm going. I'll be down the hall in that Space exhibit." He glanced at Crow who locked eyes with him. "Sorry, dude, I didn't mean anything by that Kemosahbee crack."

Crow merely nodded in reply, a silent acceptance to Jimmy's apology.

Jimmy waited another moment for a response, but when none was coming other than a nod, he shrugged, turned and exited the room. He had to push past the two guards, who only grunted in annoyance but let him pass unmolested.

Henry and Crow stood before one another, the silence a palpable thing.

"I'm sorry about that. Jimmy can be a pain in the ass, but he's a good guy at heart."

Crow flashed Henry a grin, his white teeth prominent. "Like I said before, Henry. I could tell he was a free spirit. He's young, too. Hopefully, he'll learn in time, when to speak and when to remain silent."

Henry scratched the back of his head. "Ah, yeah, I hope so, too."

"Besides, it's hard to get offended when a white man can't even get his racial slur correct."

Henry's eyebrows went up in a silent question.

"Well, actually…" Crow reached into a pocket, pulled out a pack of Marlboros, withdrew a cigarette, lit it, returned the pack in one smooth, practiced motion, and exhaled a cloud of smoke into the air. "Kemosahbee was what Tonto called the Lone Ranger, not the other way around."

"I was wondering about something," Jimmy said to Crow as Henry, Crow and Jimmy sat around a small table, an assortment of pictures before them, along with a map of the port. The two guards were standing by the door, looking like two life-size Indian statues carved from wood that once stood outside cigar shops.

"Whats that, son?" Crow asked. There was no malice in his voice. He'd meant what he told Henry. Jimmy was forgiven his slip of the mouth.

"Well, it's just, you and your people."

"Yes?"

"Jimmy," Henry said flatly.

Jimmy held up a hand to stop Henry. "No, I'm cool, I swear. It's just, the cannies have been around for a while, right? Fucking with you all the time, taking some of your people even."

"Yes, sometimes, but not as often as before," Crow agreed. "They know we can defend ourselves and are wary. Only when times are tough for them and they are desperate, do they attack us now."

"Right, so if this is true, why don't you just like, I don't know, move away or something. It's a big city, and an even huger state. Why not go somewhere far away where they can't bother you?"

Crow sat taller, his shoulders stiff. "Because this is our home now, and I'll be damned if myself or my people will run away from it. This discussion has been had in the past with our council, but only a few have voted to leave. They were overruled so they submit to the will of the people."

"Oh. Okay, cool," Jimmy said and grew quiet.

Henry wasn't listening, he was studying the pictures and map. "Crow, this tug was taken off the dock, why is that?"

"The tug boat doesn't stay tied to the dock, Henry. It goes off a little and sets anchor, that way it's safe from attack like the cruise ship. When their raiding parties return, they move to the dock to allow the scouts to load what they've found, or captured." He said the last word with disgust. "Anyone captured by the cannies would end up being killed and eaten." He paused for two heartbeats. "Or sometimes it's said that captives may join the monsters if their numbers are getting low."

"Jimmy," Henry said, "You still have that grenade we found, right?"

Jimmy patted his pocket where he'd stashed the grenade. "Sure do, when we left our packs and gear in that room Crow led us to earlier, I made sure to take it with me, along with this." He patted his shotgun, which hung over his shoulder, his .38 at his side in its holster. He didn't use the revolver much, preferring the larger blast radius of the shotgun. Just point and shoot in the general direction he wanted something dead, and let God take care of the rest.

Henry nodded. "Good, we're gonna need it to make this plan happen."

"So you do have a plan?" Crow asked.

"Yeah, I think so, but there are a lot of moving parts, and it's gonna be tricky to make it all come together."

"Whatever you need, my people will help."

"Good. The first thing you're gonna have to do is get all that fertilizer ready to be moved. Then were gonna need a few barrels of diesel fuel. Once it's all mixed together, it'll need to be loaded onto as many vehicles as it takes to get it over to that port."

"Done," Crow said. He called in one of the guards and spoke quickly to him. The man nodded and ran off; Henry assumed to pass on Crow's instructions.

Crow stood up, looked down on Henry and Jimmy, still seated. "It's about time to eat. You guys want some chow?"

Both men nodded.

"Please follow me to the cafeteria. It's rabbit stew tonight." Crow left the room, not slowing but with purpose, and Both Henry and Jimmy had to jump up and follow.

"You know, Henry," Jimmy commented as they walked down the corridor, flanked by the guards, Crow a few feet ahead of them. "This could be our last meal if things don't go as you planned."

"Yeah, I thought about that, too." He grinned at Jimmy. "Wouldn't be the first time we had that kind of meal."

"Yeah, old man, and I sure as shit hope it won't be our last."

Impatient to leave for the cruise port, Henry was in the main lobby pacing back and forth around the Brontosaurus, when Jimmy appeared.

Mark and Carol were sleeping in a room on a mattress taken from somewhere in the city, just like all the bedding and other home items had been. Henry told them to grab a few hours rest before the rescue party left, or at last make the attempt.

It was only eight o'clock, and the raid was for midnight. Henry was too wired to sleep, and apparently, so was Jimmy. The men were alone, the guards sent away by Crow, who made the decision there was no longer a need to have the two men watched.

"I thought you were grabbing some shuteye," Henry said when Jimmy joined the older man at the large glass window overlooking the wide driveway of the front of the Science Center.

"Nah, man, I can't sleep. You?"

"No, not a wink. I tried, but the second I closed my eyes my mind started racing. I'll be up till it's time to leave."

"Everything ready?"

Henry nodded. "Yes, it's all loaded out back. Crow has men watching the trucks. The fertilizer's been mixed with the diesel fuel." He pulled the HE grenade out of his pocket, taken from Jimmy earlier at dinner. "With this and the barrels, we should be able to make one hell of a distraction, at least a big enough one to find Mary and Cindy and get them out of there."

"Let's hope."

"No hope about it, pal. We'll make this happen."

Jimmy gazed up at the massive dinosaur, most if it lost in the darkness. There were no lights in this part of the Science Center, the large wall of windows too open to outside eyes. When the building had been open to the public, the windows would have been a benefit, which was why they were there. From outside, a person could see within, and the main exhibit waiting for them to explore. But now, with threats a constant thing, anyone passing by would have seen the lights if there had been any, and been drawn to the building. The tribe didn't want that and did their best to be as incognito as possible.

"I hate this fucking waiting. I wish there was something more we could do, like do a recce of the port, you know, to see firsthand what's going on there."

Henry barely let a heartbeat pass before he said, "Then why don't we?"

"What? Go to the port and recce it some?"

"Sure, that's not a bad idea. Let's do a snoop and poop, see with our own eyes what's what. We have a map to get there, not that we need it. The cruise port is right down Route 95."

Jimmy's face lit up with excitement "Earlier, when we were loading the trucks, I saw where they keep the keys to 'em. I could snag a set and we could drive over in style."

"Okay, you do that. Meet me out front in five."

"Okay, I'll see you in a minute." Jimmy ran off, and Henry watched him go. Turning to look up at the Brontosaurus, thinking how long ago the creature had roamed the Earth and was now extinct, he mumbled, "Hope I'm not gonna be joining you tonight."

Henry was waiting outside when the pickup truck pulled up. But Jimmy wasn't driving. Thomas Crow was.

Walking over to the driver's side, Henry looked past Crow to Jimmy, who had a hang-dogged look on his face. It was the look of a kid getting caught filching a cookie before dinner.

Turning his attention to Crow, Henry could see the man wasn't pleased either. He mouth was turned down into a perpetual frown.

"Crow," Henry said nonchalantly, seeing what had happened. Jimmy had gone for the keys and been discovered, and Crow wasn't very pleased with the situation. "I didn't know this was gonna be a threesome."

"Very funny, Henry," Crow replied coldly. "Excuse me if I don't laugh." He gestured to Jimmy. "Your man here told me your intentions, I don't like them."

"Oh really? Why's that?"

Crow put the truck into Park and turned it off. "Why do you want to go over there now, alone? Wait until it's time, when we're together. You have all the Intel you need to make this happen. It's only a few hours to wait. Just stay here, dammit."

"No, Crow, I can't do that. I made my decision and it's happening. If you're worried about some kind of betrayal, Mark and

Carol are still here. I want to see firsthand what's waiting for us." He checked his watch. "Shouldn't take more than two hours, or less. I want to see for myself what the cannies got going on." He shrugged. "Besides, there's still a few more parts of my plan to figure out, and I haven't quite managed to piece it together. Seeing the port up close, I may be able to do that."

"There's no time to change the plan now, Henry, you know that, right? My people are going with or without you now. I have them all riled up and prepared to do what's needed. They're going."

"And we'll be with you. Plans are fine as they are; no reason to change 'em. I just need to add one or two more things."

Crow sat silent for a moment, as he considered Henry's words, his gaze locked on the windshield. He wasn't looking through the glass beyond the truck's hood, but was lost in thought. Then he opened the driver's door, Henry stepping back to let him out. Crow stood before Henry, and for a seconds Henry couldn't read the man, or what he was going to do next. But then Crow stepped aside so Henry could slide behind the steering wheel.

"You know how to get there?" Crow asked finally.

Henry patted his shirt pocket where the map of the area was. "Sure do."

"Then be careful."

Henry flashed Crow a wide smile, the gesture easy to see in the dim glow of the truck's dashboard, which painted Henry's face in a pale light. "Always."

The drive to the cruise port was mostly uneventful. Henry wound his way in and out of the streets of downtown Baltimore, most of it wreathed in darkness. Sometimes they drove under a street lamp that was operational, powered by solar energy. Most were shattered, thanks to some gun nut wasting a round, but a few times the lamps were intact. The pallid glow they sent across the area surrounding each light was eerie, and didn't fit into the way the world was now.

There was a clear sky overhead, which allowed some illumination. Henry drove with the headlights on, despite knowing it would make him a target for anyone around.

Someone fired at them once as they passed an art museum, the bullet going wide of the pickup. He'd simply stepped harder on the gas pedal and quickly drove out of range of the shooter.

A few times animals were caught in the headlights, a few deer, a raccoon and a mother skunk and her babies, not to mention about a thousand rats and mice. With no exterminators working anymore, the rodent population was thriving. Henry had slowed his speed, driving around the animals—even the rats.

"Wow, it's like Mutual of Omaha's Wild Kingdom around here," Henry stated under his breath, but loud enough for Jimmy to hear.

"Huh? What the fuck is that?"

Henry shook his head to wave off the question. "Never mind, before your time."

Jimmy looked over his shoulder out the rear window when they passed the deer. "Wish we could have stopped and killed it. Venison for breakfast would have been a nice way to celebrate getting Cindy and Mary back in one piece."

Henry said nothing, but his thoughts were that Jimmy was far too hopeful they would recover the women alive. He prayed it would be so, but deep down in his gut, there was a gnawing feeling that such an occurrence wouldn't be the case.

He said nothing to Jimmy, keeping his opinion to himself.

Henry pulled over onto the side of the road about a quarter mile from the cruise port, steering the pickup into a thicket of shrubs. Snapping and cracking came from the undercarriage as he rolled into the thicket, until he was satisfied the vehicle was out of view from the highway. He wasn't taking chances tonight. Turning off the engine, he slid the keys under the driver's seat.

Jimmy looked at him curiously when he did it.

"What if I'm carrying the keys and something happens to me? I don't want you stranded."

"Nothing's gonna happen to you, Henry," Jimmy said, and climbed out of the vehicle. He pushed the door closed gently until he heard the latch catch, but not so hard there would be a loud thump.

Henry did the same, the two men moving out of the thicket until they were standing on the side of Route 95. Henry glanced back at the pickup. It was almost completely hidden in the foliage, its faded red paint blending in well due to it being night. The camouflage was more than sufficient for the time it would be there.

They began walking down the highway, staying close to the shoulder in case they needed to retreat into the treeline.

While on the move, Henry checked his weapons, making sure everything was as it should be. He'd already done this before leaving the Science Center, but it was a nervous habit he couldn't quit. His Glock was on his hip, a full clip in it. He had two more seventeen 9mm round magazines in a pocket of his camo pants. One thing he liked about the pants was the voluminous pockets. Crow had given them to him, the new pants replacing the old ones Henry had worn since making the matter transfer jump. His sixteen inch panga rode his left hip, the lower half of the sheath tied to his leg.

Attached to Henry's belt was an eight inch Bowie knife, also given to him by Crow. It was razor sharp on one side and serrated on the other, for maximum damage when penetrating an enemy's body. A carved bone handle completed the work of art.

The walk to the cruise port was quiet, and once at the gate, an empty guard shack on the right, the two men made their way onto enemy territory.

There were many things to hide behind, from old cars and trucks, long headed for the salvage yard, to empty container crates. Hopping from one to another, it wasn't long before they found the dock the cannies used.

There was a large building with multiple windows in front of the pier, painted white, the structure once used for passengers to check in and depart the cruise ships. Signs on walls told passengers which way to go for Baggage Drop-off, or for Taxi Cabs.

Henry and Jimmy watched the darkened cruise terminal, and in a matter of minutes, Henry spotted a flicker of light in one of the upper windows. He pointed to Jimmy, who nodded.

There was a sentry on duty in the building.

Henry pointed to the left, where they could make their way around the building to the water beyond. Jimmy nodded in agreement, and the two began leapfrogging from cover to cover. It was a good thing the sentry wasn't following proper guard duty etiquette, and had lit a smoke without a care for shielding the flame, otherwise, their reconnoiter might have been mighty short.

It took another five minutes to make their way around the terminal to the open pier beyond. No other sentries were spotted. That didn't mean there weren't more, just that none were seen.

Creeping up and hiding behind an old forklift that was lying on its side, they stayed low and watched the dock and what was moored just off it. Henry used a pair of high resolution military binoculars to survey the scene.

It wasn't a wooden dock in the sense of where sailboats would moor themselves to. Rather, it was just an asphalt area, like a parking lot, long and straight, that ended at the water, which was twelve feet below, depending on the tide, where a cruise ship or a tanker ship would once have moored when in port. A two-story or taller walkway would have been connected, for the cruise ships, anyway, a winding ramp that was rolled over to the middle of the ship, where passengers would board or debark.

Openings lower near the waterline would have been opened to allow supplies to be loaded, forklifts placing pallets of food and drink, along with passenger luggage, right inside the ship, where workers would then use hand trucks to wheel the pallets into the bowels of the ship to be sorted.

None of that was there now, the area devoid of vessels or workers. There would probably never be that kind of tableaux ever again.

There were two floating vessels out on the water. One close to shore, the other a quarter of a mile out.

Henry's eyes went to the cruise ship first. It being the larger vessel, he was drawn to it. It was a mid-sized ship in cruising terms, one that would have transported around two thousand plus passengers before the world collapsed.

There wasn't much he could see, due to the distance and the flickering shadows on its high pool deck. There were fifteen levels, so most of the upper decks were hidden by height. There was a promenade that wrapped around the ship, and Henry could see people moving about on it. Even from as far away as the ship was, the sounds of yelling and shouting came to him. The pool deck was lit up with flickering torches, and people could be seen moving around.

In what little light there was reflected off the water, he could see that the once pristine hull was now filthy, with splotches of rust and corrosion everywhere. At the waterline, barnacles were slowly taking over, encrusting the entire lower half of the ship that was below the water.

There was a wide hatch open less than ten feet from the waterline, a light coming from within. This had to be where the tugboat would load and offload people. So climbing up the side somehow to get aboard wasn't needed, which was a good thing. He really hadn't figured out that part, despite considering using climbing gear.

"Maybe there's a party tonight," Jimmy commented. He couldn't make out details with his bare eyes, but could see the ship's lights and hear the faint voices floating across the water.

"Hopefully it's not for Mary and Cindy," Henry said. "It looks like we're not going to need climbing gear to get inside. We should be able to go in through that open hatchway." He pointed, Jimmy squinting to see. "This isn't the movies, it's not like we can climb up the anchor chain like some action hero."

"Crow says he packed climbing gear anyway, just in case, remember? It's in with the stuff loaded onto one of the trucks we're using later."

"Yeah, right, I forgot," Henry said. He shouldn't have, given it was his plan. He was tired, and needed rest. He ignored his fatigue, knowing he wouldn't be able to rest until both Mary and Cindy were safe, or the people that had caused them harm were dead.

He shifted his attention to the tugboat. It was pretty much in the same location Henry had seen when studying the Intel pictures. The tugboat's bridge was lit up, and shadows were moving back and forth. A lantern hung off the stern, illuminating the large boiler for the coal plant. The tugboat, unlike the cruise ship, was close enough to shore for Henry to make out details.

Large truck tires lined the side of the tug in view. It was anchored so that the port side could be seen, the starboard side facing out to sea. He assumed both sides had tires, however, there was no reason not to.

There was a man walking the deck, circling around the wheel-house to the stern, then repeating the circuit. A guard on watch.

"That's gonna be a problem," Henry said as he lowered the binoculars and passed them to Jimmy, who had a look for himself.

"Yeah, I see what you mean. No way to sneak up on them when they're out there in the water."

"We need to figure out a way to get them to the dock."

Jimmy lowered the binoculars. "Any thoughts?"

Henry's mind was already working, as ideas came and went. "Maybe, but before I can commit, I need to have a talk with Carol."

"Carol? Why her?"

"Because for what I have in mind, only a woman can do it." He patted Jimmy on the shoulder. "Come on, let's get back to the others. Crow's probably getting impatient." He glanced one more time over his shoulder, looking out over the dark water to the cruise ship. A floating city, they used to call those ships, and Henry was about to attack it. "If we're real lucky, we just might be able to pull this off."

They returned to the Science Center without incident, joining Crow and his people, who were preparing to leave, on what hopefully, would be a successful raid and rescue.

Chapter 20

Henry watched silently while Crow's people prepared to leave the Science Center. In addition to Jimmy, Henry and Crow, plus Carol and Mark, five more people were coming. Four men and one woman, the latter appearing to have an eye for Jimmy, despite Jimmy's multiple rebukes.

One of the men in the attack party was the man with the unibrow, who had first confronted Henry at the tribal meeting. His name was Sylvester.

It was a quarter to midnight when the three-vehicle convoy rolled out of the Science Center, making their way to the cruise port. The first vehicle carried the makeshift bomb, the second the men and one other woman besides Carol; the third truck was a backup in case there were issues with the main two vehicles. All were old pickup trucks, but Crow told Henry the tribe's mechanic was a magician, and all the pickups ran perfectly.

Crow drove the first one, Henry and Jimmy beside him. Mark and Carol were in the second truck, with Sylvester driving. Mark sat in the rear bed. He realized that if he tried to sit inside the cab, only two people would have fit, so he told everyone he opted to sit outside in the air, saying he became motion sick if he rode inside.

Carol and the only other woman in the group sat in the cab with Sylvester. The woman's name was Leslie. Henry had learned this when he'd been introduced to the others in the attack party earlier that evening. She was stunning, with long black hair that hung down to her buttocks, and high cheekbones. She was excellent with a bow and arrow, and was considered a better marksman than most of the men with their crossbows. She also was attracted to Jimmy, who barely noticed. He loved Cindy, and only had eyes for her, since the day he'd first met her years ago, while working at her uncle's bar.

Jimmy cast a glance over his shoulder into the rear bed of the truck, where there were six barrels of diesel fuel mixed with ammonium nitrate. "Riding with that shit makes me nervous as hell, Henry."

Chuckling, Henry patted Jimmy's arm. "Relax, that stuff's safe as carrying dirt. It needs a detonator to become explosive once the nitrate is mixed with fuel. A stick or two of dynamite would have been perfect, but hopefully, this will do the job just as well." He held up the grenade.

"How'd you learn how to do this anyway?" Jimmy asked.

"I watched a lot of documentaries years ago. There was a bombing in 1995 in Oklahoma City. You remember that happening?"

Jimmy shook his head no. It was before his time. Being a kid then, he could have cared less about what was on the news or happening anywhere other than his own neighborhood.

"Well, this ex-army soldier parked a rented Ryder truck in front of a federal building in downtown Oklahoma City," Henry explained. "In the back was a homemade bomb of fertilizer, diesel fuel and a few other chemicals. He set the bomb with two, timed fuses. When it went off, it destroyed, and by destroyed I mean incinerated, dozens of cars, and damaged over three hundred buildings. The worst part was that a hundred and sixty-eight people died; nineteen children were part of that number. A lot of people were injured, too, of course. There was another bad one in '93, too. That happened at the World Trade Center in New York, in lower Manhattan. That bomb was different. It was some kind of nitrate-hydrogen mixture. The goal was to blow up the North Tower and have it collapse and take out the South one, but it failed. Still, seven people were killed."

"Jesus," Jimmy said, thinking about the bombings.

"Yeah, it's tough to think that even before we had deaders to deal with, people were still killing each other constantly." Henry grew quiet, and just stared out the window at the dark landscape, the headlights barely making a dent in the night.

"I guess the apocalypse kinda stopped all that shit, huh?" Jimmy remarked.

Crow had been listening quietly and he broke his silence. "Not from what I've witnessed. People are still killing people, just not in the same way they were before."

Still gazing out the windshield, Henry let out a soft gasp when a set of headlights appeared from around the bend in the road, on the opposite side of Route 95. From his earlier foray to the cruise port, he knew they were only about a mile or so away. "Someone's coming," Henry said, stopping any further conversation.

"No one uses this highway except the cannibals," Crow said. "Anyone in a twenty mile radius of the port knows it's dangerous around here."

"It has to be one of their scouting parties," Henry said. The approaching vehicle drove for another hundred feet, then it slowed and stopped.

Crow slowed to a stop as well, and parked halfway across the highway. Behind him, the other two vehicles braked and stopped. The other drivers had seen the headlights, too.

The two opposing parties were only about three hundred feet apart. In the darkness, only shadowy figures could be seen thanks to the headlights.

Henry climbed out of the pickup, walking a few feet so he was still in view of the truck's headlights. Across the highway divider of concrete Jersey barriers, the five cannies in the rear of their truck bed did the same. Henry counted the silhouettes. If there were five standing on the road, maybe there was another three in the cab. He doubted there were more than ten in total anyway.

The cannies gathered in a group as they stared at the three vehicle convoy, pointing and talking loudly. With the three engines of the pickups idling, it was impossible to hear what the cannies were saying.

"What do we do?" Crow called from the cab. "They're on the other side. We can't get to them from here."

"Hold on, I'm thinking," Henry said, but he didn't get long to do it. The headlights on the cannie vehicle suddenly turned off, and in the paltry gloom filtering down from the carpet of stars overhead, the figures on the road ran back and climbed into the rear bed; the truck spun around with a screech of tires and began driving back the way it had come, engine roaring as the driver floored the gas pedal.

"Shit, they're running!" Henry shouted, turning and dashing back to the pickup. Climbing in, he slapped the dashboard as he slammed the door closed. "We've got to catch them! If they make it back to the port and warn that tugboat they saw us, they'll be on the lookout for trouble, and everything we planned tonight'll be for nothing."

Crow slammed the transmission into Drive and accelerated after the cannies, waving his hand out the window for the other two trucks to follow. Henry wished like hell they'd had two-way radios to communicate, but it wasn't something Crow's people had stored in their supplies.

The cannie pickup was moving at a high rate of speed, easily hitting seventy. While not a dangerous speed in the old days, when highways were clear of debris, in a post-Holocaust world, driving that fast at night with nothing but headlights to illuminate the road was a recipe for disaster.

Crow did his best to catch up to the speeding pickup, but the full load in the rear bed was slowing him down. He glanced to his right to see Sylvester pulling up beside him, the two vehicles driving down the highway side by side. Henry prayed there wasn't some sort of obstruction in the road anywhere in front of them, or someone was going to get into a crash tonight.

Carol was waving at them frantically from the passenger seat. In her hand was her Olympic .22 target pistol. The overhead light in the cab was on, so Henry could see her clearly. She was pointing at the gun, then pointing before her out the windshield at the retreating cannies. Either she or Sylvester had also figured out that the cannies couldn't escape to tell what they'd seen. Henry figured Sylvester knew as much as Crow did about the area, and so had informed Carol of the situation.

"What the fuck is she trying to tell us?" Jimmy yelled as he looked at Carol waving and pointing.

"I'm not sure," Crow said. "Does she want to give you her gun?"

"No," Henry said. "I think she wants a shot at the cannies. She's good with that thing, or so she says." Henry reached up and turned on the light for the cab, illuminating him so Carol could see him clearly. He nodded yes to her, pointing and gesturing the same way, giving her a thumbs up, until Carol waved she understood.

Carol said something to Sylvester, and their vehicle surged forward, leaving Crow in the dust. With nothing in its rear bed other than a few people, there was much more horsepower for the driver to use.

"There's no way she's gonna hit anything, not from this side of the highway and in the dark," Jimmy said.

"Probably," Henry agreed, while turning off the overhead cab light so Crow didn't have to deal with the reflection on the windshield the light made, "but we have nothing to lose and we need to stop them!"

In no time, Carol's vehicle was in the distance, only its brake lights visible. The backup vehicle stayed behind Crow, not knowing what to do and not having alternate instructions.

Henry didn't see everything as to what happened next, but he was able to piece most of it together by the bits he saw.

Sylvester's vehicle was faster than the cannies, which was old and beat up and poorly maintained. It didn't take long for him to catch up to the fleeing vehicle.

With the wind whipping her hair around her head, Carol climbed out the passenger window, her butt sitting on the window frame. Leslie held onto her legs so Carol didn't fall out of the speeding pickup. Carol leveled her arms before her, not resting them on the roof of the cab, as it was constantly bucking, but hovering just above the metal.

Pausing for a fraction of a second, she fired once with the pistol. The .22 barely making noise over the rumbling engine and the wind, the caliber being so small. The cannie truck didn't swerve an inch, and Henry figured the shot had gone wide, not even coming close.

Carol wasn't deterred. Sighting again, she fired once more, this time someone in the rear bed of the truck crying out. No one fell off however.

Henry was still impressed. Shooting at a dark object, more than a hundred feet away, both target and her position moving simultaneously, and actually managing to hit something, well, it wasn't something he could have managed on his best day. Above the pickup, a green highway sign zipped by. In the reflecting paint of the sign, the headlights showed that the exit to the port was half a mile away.

"Get closer!" Carol yelled into the slip stream. "I need to try and hit the driver!"

"I'll try!" Sylvester shouted back. "This is crazy!" He floored the gas pedal, the truck surging forward yet again. The cannie truck was driving blind with no headlights, and it was nothing but a dark blur amongst the night shadows. Carol fired again, once more with no results.

But though she wasn't hitting anything, the cannies knew they were under fire, and the driver tried to coax even more speed from the battered engine. The driver was taking chances he never would have under normal conditions, and before Carol could get off another shot, what Henry had hoped wouldn't happen when his and Sylvester's trucks were parallel, happened to the cannie vehicle.

Though the side of Route 95 Henry was on was mostly clear of vehicles, evidently the opposite side wasn't. One second the cannies' darkened pickup was moving down the road, the next it struck something and rolled over. There was a shower of sparks as metal slid across asphalt. The passengers in the rear bed were thrown clear, each of the five bodies striking the road hard, to roll repeatedly until coming to a stop. The pickup also came to a stop, the passenger side of the vehicle touching the road, the two driver's side tires, front and rear still spinning.

Sylvester pulled over to the left shoulder of the highway, everyone getting out the vehicle.

Without hesitation, the men of Crow's tribe, along with Leslie, who practically climbed over Carol to escape the cab, all grabbed their weapons and dashed across the short ribbon of wild grass lining the shoulder. Jumping over the concrete barriers and sprinting to the crashed pickup, Carol was the only one who remained behind in the idling vehicle.

Crow slowed to a stop a little behind Sylvester's vehicle, the third pickup doing the same.

Jimmy saw the tribe crossing the highway and he fidgeted in his seat. "What are we waiting for? Are we going over there or what?" Jimmy asked, his shotgun in his hands, readjusted from where it had been resting between his legs.

"No need. Am I right, Crow?"

"Yes, Henry, my people can handle this without you two."

It didn't take long.

Under the stars, Henry watched Crow's people spread out, their knives and other melee weapons in their hands, the polished metal catching what little light there was. Weapons rose and fell over the prone bodies of the fallen cannies multiple times. Leslie used her bow on a cannie that crawled out of the cab of the wrecked pickup. He'd climbed up through the cab and then out the open driver's window, to then drop to the ground below, a higher height than normal due to the vehicle being on its side.

Hobbling with a bad leg, the man had tried to escape, but with lightning speed, Leslie put two arrows into his back. Henry assumed it was a man, but he may have been mistaken.

In less than three minutes the men and one woman of the raiding party were returning, hopping over the concrete barriers once more. Leslie was slightly behind the men, as she had to take an extra moment to retrieve her two arrows from the man she'd killed. She was still wiping the bloody tips on her pants to clean them when she rejoined the others. One advantage of using a bow or crossbow was that arrows and bolts could be retrieved and reused.

In the headlights of the pickup, Henry could see that the men's other weapons, such as blades and clubs, were also covered in blood.

"Fuck me," Jimmy said under his breath. Though he wasn't afraid to kill when threatened, the utter brutality of the Indian warriors was still daunting. "Remind me never to get on the bad side of your people, Crow."

Thomas Crow laughed, feeling the joviality that his men felt as they whooped and laughed while climbing back into the pickup. Sylvester flashed Crow a wide grin as Crow drove past him, once more getting into the lead position. Henry could see that Sylvester's face was covered in blood. Crow let out a loud whoop of his own, his people repeating it.

Henry cringed. It was all far too loud for him. Between Carol shooting, the cannie's vehicle crashing, and all the yelling and shouting, it would be amazing if the people on the tugboat or guards inside the terminal didn't know they were coming, despite them still being half a mile away.

Once everyone was loaded back into Sylvester's pickup truck, Crow begin to accelerate. Sylvester followed, the backup vehicle falling in at the rear once more, the lone driver solemn at not getting to join in on the slaughter.

"Okay, one problem down, a hundred more to go if we're not careful," Henry said. "Chances are, we just used up all our luck at one time."

Crow laughed, feeling good about the raid. "Take one problem at a time, my friend. One at a time."

There was a puddle under both women's tables, the urine long gone cold. Apparently, their captors didn't care if they soiled themselves, and with that realization, both women had no choice but to empty their bladders when it became too much for them. Cindy, her pants still down by her ankles, had an easier time of it, the urine sliding under her legs to patter onto the floor. Mary, still clothed from the waist down, had no choice but to wet herself. The feeling was terribly uncomfortable, but there was nothing she could do about it.

The possibility of escaping by their own ingenuity had quickly fallen flat. No matter what they did, their bonds were secure, and there was no way to extricate themselves.

They were sorely and truly stuck.

After two hours of trying to come up with anything, they'd given up for the moment.

"At least it's not cold in here," Cindy said, trying to keep the mood light, despite their horrible predicament. "With my ta-tas and hoo-hoo out in the open, I'd be freezing otherwise."

"Thank heaven for small miracles," Mary agreed, feeling a little exposed herself with her shirt pulled up, her breasts exposed to the night air.

The day had slowly turned to darkness outside the porthole, as did the room, and Mary wondered what time it was, but without a timepiece, there was no way to know for sure.

Eventually, the two women had drifted off into a restless, uncomfortable sleep, the exertions and stress of the day catching up to them.

An unknown time passed before the only door in the room creaked open and two men walked in, a lantern held in the first one's fist. They stumbled in loudly, snorting and laughing. The noise woke Mary and Cindy from their restless slumber. There was no way to truly sleep when a person was tied up like a hog waiting for the slaughter. Dozing would have been a more accurate description.

They looked up at the two figures entering, not saying anything. A makeshift lantern made from an old metal bucket, with holes cut on each side, was in the first one's hand, the face unknown to the women. He was small, barely over five feet-four, with a thin mustache and scraggly beard. He was Latino, with dark black hair and bushy eyebrows. His age was indiscriminate. He could be twenty or sixty under all the grime that covered any part of his skin exposed to air. He wore rags for clothing, a piece of rope holding up his pants. He was barefoot, as was the second figure entering behind him.

Both Mary and Cindy recognized the second man. It was George, evidently coming back for seconds, despite the warning Cindy had given him. The stench of alcohol preceded the men, and by the way they swayed on their feet, they were drunk.

"See, Pedro, what'd I tell you?" George slurred. "New meat, just arrived earlier today."

Pedro's mouth was hanging open, as he stared at the two, half-naked women lying before him.

"I warned you before what would happen if you touched either of us," Cindy said, her tone brooking no argument.

"I don't give a fuck what you do," George laughed with an evil grin. Being inebriated, he wasn't thinking clearly, thanks to a loss of inhibitions. At the moment, the only thing on his mind was being horny and wanting to get laid. Any consequences of his actions now weren't an issue. "I'll take my chances Big Mama doesn't believe you." He joined Pedro so that the two men were side by side, only a few feet from the prone women. "Which one first, buddy? Blonde or brunette?"

Pedro licked his lips as he studied Mary and Cindy, but the fact that Cindy's body was more exposed sealed the deal. He stepped closer and leered down at her. There was already a bulge in his pants.

"Good choice, Pedro, damn good choice," George said. "Tell you what, why don't you fuck her in the ass and I'll face-fuck her mouth." He moved over to Cindy's head, his groin only inches from her mouth.

"You try it, fucker and I'll bite it off," Cindy hissed.

George produced a small blade from a hidden pocket and placed it against Cindy's throat. "Try it, missy, and I'll carve you a new mouth and fuck that instead." He pressed the blade hard enough to elicit a thin rivulet of blood. It ran down the side of her neck to pool in her hair.

Pedro was undoing his trousers, while George did the same, only with one hand, the second having to hold the knife. Both men had their backs to Mary from the way they were situated around Cindy. Mary knew if she was going to save her friend from being raped, the time to do so was now.

Gathering all the strength she could summon, Mary began to pull as hard as she could on the left cord wrapped around her wrist, and when the pain became unbearable, she pulled some more.

Her lips peeled back in agony, a silent scream wanting to escape, but she held it in. Still, she continued to pull. Skin began to tear, exposing the muscle beneath, but still she pulled. Blood began to pool on the table by her head, but also over the cord securing her hand. With blood now lubricating her efforts, she renewed her effort.

Spots floated over her eyes from the pain, but still she forced herself to keep going. It felt as if her wrist was on fire, like someone had placed a hot poker against her flesh and was pressing as hard as they could.

It was now or nothing, she new.

George had his dick in his hand and was trying to get Cindy to part her lips and take him in her mouth, but the woman refused. George pressed the blade tighter to Cindy's neck, causing the small line of blood to grow slightly, but Cindy refused.

George was going to either have to back off or complete his threat. Pedro was stroking himself, trying to keep himself hard, but the alcohol in his system wasn't allowing him to stay stiff for long, it seemed. He was stroking energetically while he had a hand rubbing between Cindy's legs. He wouldn't need much longer until he was ready, inebriated or not.

Within the room, there was the soft sound of a dull crack, like a hiker stepping on a small branch. To George and Pedro, it wasn't detected, but to Mary, the sound of her thumb dislocating was like a stick of dynamite going off beside her head. A blinding flash of white light filled her vision and she thought she was going to pass out. It was only her iron determination that kept her conscious.

When her vision cleared, she saw that her left arm was now down by her side. She looked at her wrist and hand, covered in blood. There was an inch wide piece of flesh hanging from her wrist. Her stomach rolled over inside her, but she forced down anything that tried to come up.

Feeling queasy and like she would faint at any moment, she reached up to her right wrist and began to pull at the cord with her fingers. Her thumb was useless. She wasn't having much luck, but she realized there was a little more movement with her body now that one hand was free. She stretched her body and neck until she was close enough to begin gnawing on the cord with her teeth.

She wasn't under the assumption she could chew through the cord, not in the limited time she had at the moment. But all she needed to do was get the cord to loosen slightly, then hopefully, she could squeeze her hand through the loop. Her teeth went to work quickly, chewing and tearing into the cord. It was cotton rope, she discovered, her taste buds and the texture of the rope how she learned this.

In seconds she had chewed off a few of the threads that made up the rope; it was enough that they separated, and a few seconds more allowed her to do it again. She splashed blood onto the rope, agony flaring up through her damaged left wrist, then managed to slide two fingers of her left hand into the loop of her right.

Pulling hard outward with both her fingers, and yanking down her right arm, plus the blood adding enough slipperiness to the operation, the right hand popped out of the loop a hell of a lot easier than her left one did.

She wasted no time. Sitting up, with a glance over her shoulder to see that the two men were still occupied with Cindy, she began untying the cords holding her legs to the table, ignoring the spots flickering before her eyes. It was difficult to do this simple task, as she really only had one useable hand, the left hand being almost unusable. She knew once the adrenalin suffusing her system faded, she was going to be in more pain than she could ever imagine, with the exception of the time she'd been shot.

Lost in the pain of the moment, she barely remembered how she managed to untie the cords holding her legs, but one second she was pulling at the cords and knots desperately, and the next she was free.

Spinning on the table, she dropped her legs over the side and slid off. When her feet touched the floor, she almost collapsed. Slapping the table with her good hand, she fought to remain standing.

But her upright movement caught the attention of George, who had casually glanced Mary's way. His eyes went wide as dinner plates when he saw her standing up, and not secured to the table.

"What the fuck?" George shouted. He forgot about trying to stick his dick in Cindy's mouth, and stepped away from her, the blade retreating from her neck as well. His penis hung from his open fly, forgotten.

Pedro stopped what he was doing also, and hopped away from Cindy, while trying to get his pants up. His dick quickly deflated given the circumstances.

Mary gripped the side of the table and kicked straight up, her booted foot striking George in the chest. It didn't hurt the man but it caused him to stumble backwards, right into Pedro, who was shuffling around Cindy to grab Mary.

As the two men became tangled for a few seconds, Mary made her move to the workbench in the corner with the tools on it. She wanted to go for her .38, which was lying in a pile with her and Cindy's gear, but the bench was closer, and time was the one thing she was in short supply of.

She jumped more than ran across the room, scooping up the first item her good hand could grab: a large, fifteen inch crescent wrench crusted with dried blood.

Swinging around with the makeshift weapon, she raised it high in an arc, sensing more than knowing for sure that George was right behind her, about to stab her with his knife.

He didn't expect Mary to go on the attack, and he never saw the wrench, nor tried to avoid it, when it struck his lower jaw. The blow shredded his lower lip into ribbons, splintering his teeth into tiny pieces. His lower jaw cracked like an egg and became dislocated; it hung lose from its socket. On top of the destruction to his jaw, the impact of the wrench on his face sent him sprawling backwards, the blow so powerful it lifted him clear off the deck for a moment.

But Mary wasn't finished yet. As a dazed George went flying against the far wall, she lunged at him, swinging the wrench like a baseball bat, pulping his right eye into paste. Aqueous fluid dribbled down the man's right cheek. On the reverse swing, Mary connected with the moaning man's nose and forehead, pulverizing the nose and sending bone fragments into the lower half of his brain, which began the unstoppable process of his death.

"Son of a bitch! George!" Pedro shouted, seeing his friend's face turned into a bloody pulp of red meat and white shards of bone.

Mary spun on him, her face curled into a rictus of hate, her breasts swinging before her, her shirt still pulled up. Her brown hair flowed around her head, her chest splattered with George's blood. She looked like an Amazon warrior to Pedro, or a wraith come to kill him.

Still standing with his trousers down by his ankles, after he tried to recover his balance from George falling into him when Mary had first kicked his friend, Pedro realized how exposed he was. So instead of attacking Mary, he dropped his hands to his genitals to hide them from view and protect them, the beginnings of a plea for mercy on his lips.

Unlike many of the cannies, Pedro had never been a killer. He only joined up with the cannies, because at the time they'd found him and the group he'd been traveling with, they needed a few more recruits to shore up their numbers. The choice of dying and becoming their next meal or joining up with the cannies had never been much of a harsh decision. Especially when one of his traveling companions refused the offer of joining and had then been murdered before Pedro's eyes, his organs harvested, and his body sliced up for meat. The carcass was left for the animals of the forest.

"Please, lady, don't hurt m…" Pedro began before Mary cut him off.

"I really don't care," she spit, and swung the wrench as hard as she could at Pedro's midsection.

He tried to fend off the wrench, raising his hands to stop it. But the weight of the tool was far too much for his hands to deflect. Two fingers on one hand were broken, two others crushed to the point there would have been no surgery, even with a top doctor in the field, who could have saved the digits. The thumb on his left hand became dislocated, to hang from his hand like a wilted piece of lettuce.

Mary had been aiming for his midsection, but Pedro's flailing defense had caused the wrench to dip slightly, so instead of the bloody tool striking his torso, the wrench slapped dead on into his genitals.

Flesh was nothing compared to hardened steel. Pedro's scrotum sack was pulverized, leaving behind a sagging mess of gristle and tattered skin. With the cracking of bone filling the room, his entire pelvic girdle split open, sending him to his knees, his face holding a look of utter shock and pain.

With blood shooting from his destroyed balls, his mouth opened and closed like a landed fish as he struggled to comprehend the absolute agony suffusing his body.

Mary didn't wait for him to die. She adjusted the wrench in her grip and then brought it up like it was a golf club. The wrench connected below Pedro's chin, shattering the jaw and sending him flying backwards. He struck the wall and flopped face first onto the floor, his body twitching, legs kicking as he succumbed to the massive trauma his body was suffering.

A low gurgling sound pulled Mary from dealing with Pedro. George was lying on his back, bloody sputtering from his destroyed jaw. She moved closer to him, leaning over the prone body. She raised the wrench to bring it down on his head, planning on caving in his skull and ending his life once and for all, but just as she raised the wrench, the cannie stopped breathing, his head going slack, the remaining eye, which had been flicking back and forth in its socket, going still. Urine seeped out from his still exposed penis as he expired.

Lowering the wrench, she let out the heavy breath she hadn't known she was holding, and slumped against Cindy's table.

Only a few minutes had passed from when Mary had freed herself to the moment she was living in right now. It was all a blur, when she tried to recall each moment.

"Mary?" Cindy said softly. The room was dead quiet with both men dead. From somewhere on the ship men were laughing and shouting, but it was faint inside the room. "Mary?" Cindy repeated. "Are you all right?"

Mary looked down at Cindy, and Cindy watched as her eyes, which seemed unfocused, quickly came back into focus. Mary looked at Cindy, and the blonde knew that Mary was truly looking at her.

"Cindy," Mary said, not having more words to add.

"Ah, listen, girl, that was a hell of a thing you just pulled off, but can I ask you to do one more thing and cut me loose?"

Mary just looked at Cindy, not understanding, but then her face lit up and she stood taller. "What? Oh, hell, of course, what am I thinking?" Going over to George's corpse, she picked up his fallen knife which was near him. With her good hand she held the knife while shoving her shirt back down over her exposed breasts with the same hand. Then she got to work cutting Cindy's bonds.

"How the fuck did you get free?" Cindy asked after she was free as well. Sitting up, she took a few precious seconds to rub circulation back into her hands.

Mary raised her left hand, showing Cindy the torn skin and dislocated thumb.

"Oh Christ, that must hurt like hell."

Mary only shrugged. "Yes, a little." Her legs grew weak and she would have collapsed onto the floor if not for Cindy, who reached out and grabbed her, pulling her close. Cindy was still seated on the table, her legs also weak from lack of use, that being the only reason they both didn't go down together.

"Jesus, Mary, what's wrong?"

"Tired is all, I think whatever got me through that is wearing off now. God, I feel like I could sleep for a week."

Cindy carefully helped Mary to the table she was still on, then slid off it while letting Mary rest. Finally able to fix her clothes, she gratefully pulled up her pants and adjusted her shirt. It did wonders for her mood not to have her privates hanging out like she was at a nudist colony brunch.

"Just rest, Mary, I've got this now," she told her friend, Mary laying on her side, her injured hand jutting out so she wasn't pressing on it.

Cindy quickly went to the door, and pressed her ear against it. There was no noise on the opposite side, nothing to indicate anyone was aware of the violence that had occurred inside the room. The door was cold to her ear when she touched the door. Studying it more closely, she found it wasn't wood but made of metal. The frame wasn't like a doorframe in a house either. It was more like something found on a submarine, with a lip at the bottom that had to be stepped over. Pushing on the door, she felt no give at all. There would be no going through the door unless she used explosives, and that wasn't something she could get her hands on at the moment.

Next Cindy went to her gear piled in the corner of the room, along with Mary's. It was all there, which she found odd. Why hadn't the cannies taken the firearms for themselves? She thought back to when she and Mary, along with Mark, had been attacked and captured. No one had carried guns then. Maybe that was the reason why they hadn't cared to take and use the M16 and .38 revolver the women had been carrying.

Cindy glanced at the two dead men. Well, she wasn't going to be questioning them on the reason anytime soon. After getting all their stuff together and placing everything on Mary's table, she went to Mary and passed the women her .38.

Mary opened her eyes from where she'd been dozing and laughed upon seeing the revolver. "Now I get it. It would have been nice if I could have used it on those two." She pointed to the bodies.

"You did terrific," Cindy said with a smile. "You were like Xena the way you took those two assholes out."

Mary sat up, the few minutes of rest doing her a world of good. She checked her gun to make sure it was loaded, then slid off the table. She got lightheaded for barely a second, then was fine.

Cindy filled Mary in on the condition of the door.

"So we can't shoot the lock and try and make an escape?"

Cindy shook her head. "I'm afraid not."

"Then what do we do now? When Big Mama or her people come and find these two dead, I doubt they'll welcome us into their hearts with open arms."

"No, I doubt they will, too." Cindy tried not to think about Big Mama and what she would do to Mary and herself. It wouldn't be pleasurable, that was for sure. She hefted the M16 before her, and inspected the weapon, ensuring it was in perfect working condition with a full clip ready to go. "Mary, we may not get out of this alive, but at least we can take a shitload of the fuckers down with us. Make 'em pay for capturing us."

"Maybe I shouldn't have done what I did. Maybe we should have let them have their way with us. At least that way we would have given Henry and Jimmy more time to rescue us."

"No damn way, Mary. I'd rather die than let those pieces of shit fuck me." She spit at the corpses, a disgusted look on her face. "I owe you one hell of a thank you, you know."

Mary smiled. "It was nothing."

Cindy only nodded, then went and dragged the two bodies so they were in front of the door. After she finished, she went to the tool bench and picked up anything that wasn't flat, and also spread the items on the floor, just past where the bodies were. When anyone came in, if they weren't looking where they were going, they could easily trip over the corpses and the tools. The half-ass obstacle course might just be the edge they needed to kill whoever entered next, and make their escape, killing anyone else who got in their way of leaving the ship.

The lantern Pedro had brought in flickered and sputtered in the corner.

"I think we're going to lose our light," Mary said.

"That's okay, we won't need it in a minute." She took their gear off the second table, then moved the table into the middle of the room. As gently as she could so as not to make noise, she tipped it onto its side so it faced the door.

Mary quickly figured out what Cindy had in mind. She slid off the table she sat on and joined Cindy behind the toppled table. Cindy went to their gear and dragged it behind the table with them, then opened her pack and took a clean shirt from it, then gestured to Mary. "Here, give me that hand. Hopefully this'll be good enough until we can get you real medical attention."

Mary didn't respond, not wanting to be negative about the chances of that really happening. So she simply replied, "Thank you," while Cindy wrapped the wrist and thumb, and then slid the loose material into the wrap so that it wouldn't unwrap easily.

"There, all set." Cindy picked up her rifle and stared at the locked door. Mary turned, her .38 in her right hand, and did the same.

Five minutes later, as the two women knelt on the floor, behind the table, the lantern finally sputtered and went out, leaving the room in complete darkness, not even the porthole letting in any light.

"Cindy, if I ask you to do something, would you promise not to think any less of me?"

"I'd never do that. What is it?"

Mary reached out her good hand and touched Cindy's arm, so that even in the darkness Cindy would know where Mary was, how her body was situated.

"Would you mind holding me?" Her voice hesitated at the end, her iron self control finally cracking after the burst of violence she'd let loose. "I could really use a hug."

"Of course, honey, come here," Cindy said, needing a hug as well, only she hadn't had the strength to ask, not wanting Mary to think any less of her. Though never shy to show emotion, both women took pride in being as hard and cold as the men they traveled with when needed. To show no mercy if that was what the situation called for.

The two embraced, not as friends, but as sisters, two women who didn't know what the future held for them. But whatever came next, they were united.

Sitting alone in the darkness, the ship creaking around them, they waited in silence.

Waiting for the door to open and the battle to come.

Chapter 21

There was a three man crew on the tugboat, one to steer the tug, one to shovel coal, and the last to guard the boat, and be a lookout for returning scouting parties arriving on the pier.

It was past midnight, when the guard, drowsy from lack of sleep, looked up when he heard a cry of suffering from shore. He lacked binoculars, but he wasn't so far away that his naked eyes couldn't make out the form of what was obviously a woman, despite the gloom of night, and only a pallid glow bathing the water and port in luminance.

The figure had staggered out from between a pile of empty crates and fallen to the ground, sobbing loudly, the sound carrying across the water easily.

What piqued his curiosity the most was that the woman was half naked, her full breasts visible before she collapsed. Licking his lips, he went to the wheelhouse and stuck his head inside, getting the attention of the man who operated the tug.

"Hey, there's a slut on the pier. Bitch is half naked. I think she got attacked or raped or some shit. It's worth a look, even if it's just to have some fun with her ourselves."

"No shit?"

"I'm not lyin', you asshole, look for yourself. You can make out her body laying there." He pointed, the operator following with his gaze, until his eyes went wide. There was someone on the port, only a few yards from where they moored the tugboat.

"Do you think it's one of us?"

The guard scoffed. "Fuck no. The scouting party that left a while ago had no women in it." He leered at his fellow cannie. "Might be good for a fuck, if nothin' else."

The operator gazed off at the still body. "She might be dead, you know."

The guard shrugged. "Dead, half dead, still alive. As long as she's still warm it works for me."

"You're a pig, Clyde, you know that?" the operator said.

Clyde laughed. "Maybe, Bob, maybe, but I'm a pig who's gonna get his dick wet tonight."

Bob shoved him out of the wheelhouse. "Tell Leon to stoke the boiler and let's go have a look-see."

Excited that Bob was on board, Clyde turned and made his way to Leon, who was grabbing a few winks while he wasn't needed. The boiler was always hot, but when the tugboat was idle, he got a break until it was time to start shoveling coal inside the boiler again. It was a shit job but at least he was outside, not in the bowels of the cruise ship's kitchens, chopping up body parts for food.

The tugboat began moving a short time later, Leon shoveling coal in as fast as he could. Once Bob had informed him of what awaited on the dock, he was as enthusiastic as the others. He was looking forward to getting laid.

It took only a few minutes for the tugboat to reach the dock, which was the reason why it was only a few hundred yards off shore. Pulling in a little too fast, Clyde had to put the engine into reverse or risk the bow striking one of the struts to the dock. He had to maneuver so that the tug was even with a ladder attached to the side of the pier, which was a good ten feet higher than the small tugboat.

As soon as the ropes were tossed onto cleats, stopping the tugboat from further movement, and after Clyde shut down the engine, the three men were already racing up the ladder. Clyde was first, followed by Bob, and Leon, who'd had to make sure the boiler was okay. Leon was dead last, much to his chagrin.

Clyde's head was the first to pop up at the side of the dock, as the man climbed up and onto the asphalt pier. He quickly scurried away from the ladder to let Bob and Leon join him. There was no consideration to help his friends climb up the ladder. If he was first, that meant he would get first dibs on the woman.

Clyde licked his lips at the sight of the feminine form sitting before him, no more than thirty yards away. He didn't know for sure, but perhaps, upon hearing the tugboat's engine, the woman had managed to raise herself up, her arms outstretched to the side, hands flat on the ground to support her.

Even in the darkness, Clyde could see she was attractive, her breasts full and round, a little fat around the waist but to him that just meant there was more there to take his exertions out on. The more stuffin' the better the fuckin', he liked to say. Though covered in blood, her nipples were still prominent, her skin a silky white in the starlight.

From behind, Clyde heard Bob slither off the ladder and onto the pier.

Clyde barely looked, his eyes only for the woman. He pulled a small blade from his waist. It was mostly used for trimming lines on the tugboat, but it had seen its fair share of killing over the years.

He began walking towards the woman, who had her head hanging low.

Clyde was almost skipping, he was so pleased with their find. They would take the woman back on the tug, where it would return to its position out on the water, but instead of a boring shift until morning, there would be a lot of fucking and sucking, all thanks to the sobbing woman before him. Where she came from was irrelevant. She was here now and soon, she would regret stumbling onto the pier. When the three men were finally finished with her, they'd give her to Big Mama, who would hopefully reward them for bringing in fresh meat on their own.

Clyde was no more than fifteen feet from the woman, who looked as if she was sobbing, the way her shoulders were twitching, but when he got within ten feet of her, the woman's head popped up, her eyes locking with Clyde's.

The man's eyes went wide when he saw her face, knowing instantly that something wasn't right.

Instead of a tear-filled face, filled with sorrow and pain, fear and worry, the woman was actually smiling. The blonde hair that draped around the grinning face was the farthest thing from the visage of a terrified woman.

Clyde paused his stride, Bob almost walking into him. Bob hadn't seen much of the woman, Clyde blocking his view. He was about to snap a threat at Clyde to get the fuck out of the way, when there was a soft sound, like someone jamming a spike into a pumpkin. Bob didn't know what it was, the odd noise seeming to come from Clyde. He wondered if the man had just farted, one of the big ones he liked to let off after a large meal, when Clyde seemed to stumble on his feet.

Bob stepped up to his friend, grabbing his left arm and spinning him around. "Clyde, you all right?"

Clyde's body turned easily, as if Bob was handling a man devoid of his own control, like a drunk who'd let someone lead him wherever they wanted to. Bob didn't understand what was happening, but the second he turned Clyde around, he knew why it was so.

There was a crossbow bolt jutting from Clyde's right eye, only about two inches of the bolt visible. The rest was imbedded in the man's brain. A thin rivulet of diluted blood seeped down his cheek like a continuous tear.

Clyde was already dead; he just didn't know it yet.

"Holy shit!" Bob screamed, too startled to think of doing anything else but being shocked. When his mouth opened wide in a shout, a second crossbow bolt impaled itself within the opening, the tip of the bolt sliding through his upper palate before penetrating his brain.

Bob stumbled a few feet backwards, resembling a drunk who'd lost his equilibrium. His heels tripped over an uneven piece of pavement and he fell backwards, his head striking the ground hard. But Bob was beyond caring. Sputtering blood that seeped around the bolt and into his throat, he was going to drown on his own blood, long before the tip of the bolt did its final damage. But one way or another, Bob was joining Clyde on the last train west in a matter of seconds.

Leon, coming up the ladder last, had been delayed an extra half minute thanks to his shirt catching on a rusty rung. The time it had taken him to free himself and resume climbing, was the only reason he was still breathing without anything protruding from his body.

That changed the second Leon's head popped up from the side of the pier like a gopher coming out of its hole. He barely got a look at his two prone friends, before two crossbow bolts hit him in the face. One struck an inch below his right eye, the second one slammed into the center of his forehead. Neither bolt went fully into the man's head, thanks to the skull bone stopping them, but more than an inch slid into the skin and beyond before stopping.

Leon's head snapped back from the dual impacts, and his eyes tried to roll up into his head and focus on the two bolts jutting from his face simultaneously. He failed miserably and ended up letting go of the ladder and falling back onto the deck of the tugboat. He landed on a large looping of mooring rope, where he remained still. He was alive but in shock.

Up on the pier, more than half a dozen figures appeared from the darkness, skulking out from around crates and debris at the edge of the port. Henry, Jimmy and Crow were together, followed by the rest of the raiding party.

"That was some good shooting, Crow," Henry said. "Your people sure know what they're doing."

"I told you we could do it," Crow replied. "Just like my people took out the two guards in the terminal earlier." Crow had sent three of his best marksman to deal with the sentries inside the darkened terminal. Using crossbows, they had found and killed both guards without incident. No more were discovered.

Carol stood up, accepting the shirt Henry handed her, along with a small towel to wipe her face. Covered in rabbit blood taken from the Science Center farm, she didn't bother trying to clean her chest, but quickly slid into the shirt to cover herself. Henry averted his eyes while she dressed, but he'd still seen plenty, now and before, when she'd first disrobed and gone off to play damsel in distress. It only reaffirmed that she was an attractive woman, her breasts full and firm, despite her being past her youth. He ignored the dull ache in his heart as he thought of Sue. This sure as hell wasn't the time to be melancholy.

Mark joined the group as they gathered around Carol, while others went to the tugboat, and two of Crow's people went to check on Clyde and Bob. That didn't take long. Both men had their throats cut. Whether they were still alive or not wasn't an issue. They were truly dead after the slicing.

When Henry saw the bodies getting their throats cut, he cursed. "No, damn it, don't kill them. We need one to talk, to tell us where Cindy and Mary are on that ship."

Both men stood over the corpses with dripping blades, looking back at Henry and Crow. They didn't speak, not apologetic in the slightest.

"Sorry, Henry, my men are itching to kill, I'm afraid. This has been a long time coming."

"Well, it's done now, no reason to talk about spilled milk once it's on the floor. You can't put it back into the carton."

"Sure," Jimmy said, "but you can get on your knees and lick it up."

"Not helping, Jimmy," Henry snapped and began moving towards the ladder leading down to the tugboat. "Let's go. Longer we're on the dock, the better chance we have of being discovered."

As the group made their way to the tugboat, the bodies of Clyde and Bob were dragged out of view and dumped behind a cargo crate. Their blood was still glistening on the asphalt but it couldn't be helped.

Arriving at the ladder, Henry looked down to see there were two of Crow's people already onboard. Leslie and Sylvester were in the bow with blades in their hands, at the foot of the ladder. They stood over Leon, who was lying immobile, but with his eyes open, reflecting the starlight as it bounced off the water. His eyes blinked, telling Henry he was still alive.

"Don't kill that man, we need him alive," Henry yelled softly, if that was even possible. He knew voices carried across the water, and the cruise ship was directly across from the tug, despite being a quarter mile away.

Henry climbed down to the tug's deck, some others in the group following right behind him. Once everyone was on the tugboat, it was crowded, so Crow had some of the men go to the stern to wait for orders and inspect the boiler. One man waited above on the pier, keeping watch and waiting for the signal to bring the pickup truck with the ammonium nitrate bomb.

"I'll check out the controls," Carol said, and moved off.

"Okay," Henry replied then glanced over at Mark, who was standing quietly. "Your wife can really do this?"

Mark nodded. "She should be able to. Her dad was a tugboat operator out of New York, and he used to take her to work with him on weekends, when the boss wasn't around. Said she picked up a lot just by watching, and he liked to teach her and let her drive when they weren't pulling anything. It was real daddy/daughter stuff. She said she always loved it."

"Hell, Mark, your wife is full of surprises," Henry said. "You got a hell of a woman there."

Mark beamed with pride. "Believe me, Henry, I know I'm a lucky guy. She's way above my pay grade."

Henry nodded, the conversation over. There were more important matters to attend to. "Crow, let's get that pickup truck over here so we can load the barrels onto the tug."

Crow nodded and spoke to one of his men standing close by. The man went to the ladder, where he whistled two quick blasts. A head peered over the edge of the pier, looking down. Hushed words were exchanged and the man's head receded.

A few minutes later, the low growl of the pickup's engine could be heard. Its headlights remained off, so as not to alert anyone watching on the cruise ship.

As soon as the truck reached the edge of the pier, the men got busy off-loading the barrels, using ropes and a hastily erected pulley system. Henry didn't like how long it would take to load the barrels, but there was nothing that could be done about it. Without the homemade bomb, there would be no rescue. Crow's people had never dared a raid on the cruise ship due to their being no way to see a way to victory. The cruise ship was a warren, a maze so large his people would be swallowed whole until they were surrounded and slaughtered—or worse, used for food. The cannies knew the ship well, it being their home. It would have been a fool's errand to even attempt such a thing. But Henry's bomb would be the catalyst to allow them to attack and hopefully, root out the nest of human meat eaters in the chaos the bomb would create.

Henry stood over Leon, leering down at the man, who gazed up at Henry through pain-filled eyes.

"Secure his hands," Henry ordered, two of Crow's people obeying without question. Leon let out a yell when his arms were pinned to the rope coil beneath him.

Henry knelt down so that he was less than six inches from Leon, the two crossbow bolts in Leon's face only a few inches from Henry's. He wanted the man to hear him clearly, and with all the noise going on as the barrels were loaded, he didn't want to have to raise his voice.

"Two women were taken captive earlier today. I want to know where they're being held on that ship." He gestured with his chin to the cruise ship.

"Fuck you, meat," Leon hissed.

"Oh, you think so?" Henry moved his body so he was hovering over Leon completely. He placed a knee on the man's chest and reached out with his right hand, thumb extended, and making sure to avoid the bolt below the man's right eye, he placed his thumb on Leon's eye, then pushed as hard as he could.

Leon tried to scream, but Henry clamped his left palm over his mouth. The thumb dug in deep, crushing the orb into a pinkish paste that seeped out around Henry's digit. Leon's remaining eye rolled right up into his head, showing only pure white in the remaining eye. He struggled beneath Henry, but with his arms secured by Crow's people, and his head pressed tight to the rope under it by Henry's palm, all he could do was lay there and take the abuse forced upon him.

The initial scream of agony slowly subsided into a mewling noise. Henry, satisfied there wouldn't be a new outburst, released Leon's mouth, then stepped back. His thumb dripped a clear liquid, and bits of cornea were stuck to his thumb as well. He shook his hand to clear off most of it, then wiped his hand on Leon's filthy shirt, which wasn't too clean to begin with. His left hand was covered in spittle so Henry wiped it on his pants, not wanting to touch Leon again if he didn't have to.

Henry leaned in close once more. "Okay, I hope I've made my point. Where are the two women prisoners taken to the ship earlier today?"

Whimpering like a lost dog, Leon said nothing.

Henry moved even closer, his thumb hovering over Leon's remaining eye. "I'd say I could do this all night, but you only have one more eye left."

Leon squeezed his lips together, his countenance defiant.

Henry looked up at Jimmy and the others, gathered around them. Some had looks of disgust, but none said anything in argument, nor did they disagree. It needed to be done, and quickly. If this was the best way to get the information needed, so be it.

"Okay if that's the way you want it, be a blind man." He brought his hand up once more, the thumb hovering over Leon's eye.

To Leon, that thumb, only an inch from his eye, looked huge, massive as a planet, and it was about to come down and blind him for life. He didn't know the status of his health at the moment, the two crossbow bolts weren't something he was completely aware of. After the initial impacts, the pain was negligible, and there was almost no blood, the bolts stopping any bleeding. Only a few droplets had seeped out from around the bolts.

Leon's defiance caved, and his body, once tense, slumped into the ropes in defeat. He didn't want to be blind. He knew that was a death sentence. His own people wouldn't care for him, and would toss him into the larder the first time they realized he was blind and useless. He could try and escape the cannies if Henry let him go, but how long would he last alone and blind? Not long.

He had no options, and he wasn't about to give his life for Big Mama. The fat bitch could suck his dick as far as he was concerned. Besides, he didn't have any idea where the two bitches brought to the ship that day were being held. He was just a lowly tugboat crewman. He wasn't privy to things like that.

He told Henry as much, chattering about all he knew, but unfortunately for him, none of it helped Henry.

"So you have no idea where the women might be?"

"I told you I don't, I swear," Leon said. "I told ya all I know."

Henry frowned deeply, his face grim. "Then I don't need you anymore." He looked at the two men holding Leon's arms. "Do what you want to him, he's useless to me."

Henry turned and walked away, his direction the wheelhouse. Jimmy followed close behind.

"Wait, I told you all I know. I thought you weren't going to kill me if I talked?" Leon called out, his voice trembling in terror.

"I never said any such thing," Henry said over his shoulder. "Besides, you didn't tell me anything that mattered."

Leon attempted further protest, but was cut off when his throat was sliced ear to ear by one of the men holding his arms. Leon's remaining eye went wide and he sputtered and coughed as dark blood jutted from his neck. While still alive, but bleeding out, his body was dragged to the rail and dumped over the side. What happened to him after that was unknown; no one cared enough to continue watching.

Henry reached the wheelhouse at the same time the engine started up, a low rumbling filling the tugboat.

"You did it," Henry said with a smile.

"I sure as hell did. It's not like the one my daddy taught me on but I think I can figure it out," Carol replied proudly, though a bit of doubt was there also. "Someone needs to stoke the boiler. Toss coal into it so we can get up enough steam to move."

"Jimmy, can you deal with that?" Henry asked.

"Sure." Jimmy spun around, slid down the bridge ladder like a pro, and went to tell Crow what was required.

It wasn't long before coal was being shoveled into the boiler by two men, and Carol was steering the tugboat away from the pier, the mooring lines removed, a slow chugging coming from the modified steam engine.

The cruise ship was looming larger with each passing second.

Chapter 22

Hunkered down in the stern of the tugboat, along with the others in the attack party, Henry checked his wristwatch. The tugboat was halfway to its destination, the cruise ship getting bigger with each breath he took. Behind the tug, connected by a rope, a small rubber boat bounced over the waves churned up by the tug's propeller. The smaller boat had been packed along with the supplies taken from the Science Center for the raid, after being looted from a Sporting Goods store.

"It's almost two-thirty," Henry said to Crow, askance of him. "This shouldn't have taken so long."

Crow said nothing, and if he shrugged or gave some other silent response, Henry wouldn't have been able to see it, given the darkness.

"I hope Cindy and Mary are okay," Jimmy said from Henry's other side.

"I hope so, too. They're as tough as they come. If there's a way for them to stay safe, I know they'll find it."

"A lot of the people with us volunteered because they have debts to pay tonight," Crow stated. He was smoking, but made sure to keep the glowing tip of the cigarette hidden from view. Each exhale he made after taking a hit was invisible, the smoke lost in the wind current of the night.

"Oh?" Henry said.

"Yes, many that have had family taken, killed, and who knows what else." He sighed. "I try not to think about that last part."

"I'm sorry to hear that. But we're here now, and tonight they can repay some of those debts."

"Yes. I must warn you, Henry, my people will not show mercy. They have come here for one reason and one reason only. To kill every cannibal they find on that ship."

Henry thought about how the two tugboat crewman had been slaughtered without hesitation. He moved as close to Crow as he could, so that the Indian warrior could see Henry's face, though mostly still wreathed in shadow. "I wouldn't have it any other way." There was no more time for conversation. The tugboat had reached the cruise ship. Carol was at the cruise ship's bow and was following its hull, until, the boat reached mid-ship, where the opening close to the waterline was located. She was halfway there when the tugboat began to lurch to the left, away from the cruise ship and into open water.

"What the fuck's going on?" Jimmy said in a soft voice.

Henry had to admit the young man had summed up his thoughts as well. "I don't know. Jimmy, go to the bridge and see what's happening."

Jimmy was off like a rocket, covering the small area on the deck until he was climbing up the ladder to the bridge like a monkey. In the wheelhouse, Carol was hitting switches and cursing up a storm.

"Carol, Henry wants to know what the fuck is wrong. We're going the wrong way."

"Don't you think I know that?" Carol yelled. "The damn steering's gone, I can't control her!"

"Then what are we supposed to do?"

Carol was fighting the controls. "Look, I still have control over one of the rudders. I'm going to make a loop and try and get back. But you're just going to have to jump onto that ship as I pass it. I don't have enough control to make any kind of docking maneuver."

"Then do that. I'll tell the others." Jimmy spun to leave.

Mark called after him. "She's doing her best, you know."

Jimmy stopped at the ladder, and when he turned to slide down it, he called to Mark, "I don't give a shit. She just better get us to that fucking ship, and then you need to get ready to set off that bomb. Without that distraction, we're all screwed."

"I know my job, Jimmy, I'll see it happens," Mark replied. He instinctively patted the grenade in his jacket pocket, given to him by Henry earlier in the night. It was his job to pull the pin and toss it inside one of the barrels, before jumping off the tugboat along with Carol. The small rubber raft being pulled behind the tug was for them to escape. Henry and the others would figure out their own way off the cruise ship when it was time to leave it. One option was hopefully finding life jackets and jumping over the side, then swimming to shore.

Jimmy was back beside Henry in seconds after leaving the bridge, and he filled him in, along with Crow.

"Then we'll just have to make do with jumping," Henry said. "Tell your people the change in plans," he told Crow. "We're almost there."

Crow did as requested and soon everyone was up and ready to go. The opening in the ship's hull was coming back into view as Carol limped the tugboat in a loop, and began coming at the opening from the opposite direction. But she was fighting the rudder the entire time, and the tug began to scrape and bump off the cruise ship's hull. This had attracted the attention of whoever had been on the cruise ship inside the opening. There were multiple heads sticking out of the fifteen foot hole in the hull, watching and pointing as the tug jerkily made its way to them.

When the bow of the tug was no more than twenty feet away, Henry jumped up and yelled, "Now!"

Jimmy by his side, along with Crow's people, began to fire at the people inside the opening. Henry wasn't worried about the report from his Glock alerting the crew. The time for stealth was over. They needed to either kill or make anyone inside that ship duck for cover, so that his people could jump over safely.

Henry shot one head peeking out almost dead center in the face, the body pitching out the opening and into the water. The tugboat's bow bumped into the fallen body a second later, and it slid against the hull to be lost from view. Jimmy fired his shotgun, hitting another cannie in the torso, sending the man flying backwards to be lost from sight. Any remaining heads or bodies in view that were unharmed, were peppered with arrows and bolts from Crow's people.

"Everyone, get ready to jump!" Henry shouted and climbed onto the rail, then leaped for the cruise ship. He landed hard and awkwardly, rolling and coming up in a crouch beside a corpse. Jimmy landed almost flat on his face, but only his pride was bruised, and he rolled to the side as well, stopping when he pushed up against a bloody body. Crow came next, light on his feet and landing on the ship's deck easily. Leslie and Sylvester followed. But then the tugboat jerked to the right horribly, sending the others in the party tumbling to the deck of the tugboat or falling overboard. Some rose quickly from the deck and jumped to the cruise ship, but the tugboat was out of reach and they landed in the water. Their heads popped up a moment later and they swam to the opening.

Crow, seeing his people in the water, grabbed a fishing net and rolled it out of the opening. It would make a decent ladder for his people.

Henry looked at Jimmy, who returned his gaze. "You ready to do this?"

"Fuck yeah, old man, let's go save Cindy and Mary."

Alerted by the gunfire, three cannies came running down a passageway and into the room Henry and the others were in, their backs to open water. Henry and Jimmy mowed the three cannies down without mercy, then began to move deeper into the ship. They turned left into the passageway to go forward, but Crow and his people went aft, searching for targets to satiate their vengeance.

"We need to grab someone to interrogate and find out where the girls are," Henry said, pausing to read a door as he passed it. It had numbers on it, and so did others around him. He was on a deck that would have once been used for crew living quarters. The first number on all the doors was a three. It wasn't hard to figure out he must be on Deck 3.

"Hey, Henry, Crow and the others aren't behind us," Jimmy explained.

Henry turned and looked past Jimmy to see that the passageway was empty. "It doesn't matter. If we're right and the cannies don't have guns, we should be able to deal with anything that comes. Just watch our flank."

"Done."

The two men moved down the passageway, deeper into the ship. When they came upon an opening on one side, they stepped out into a room with elevators on the left and a stairwell on the right. A flickering lantern hung near the center elevator, allowing a pale gloom to fill the area.

Two cannies came charging down the stairs, axes in their hands. Henry, being first into the elevator banks, shot both of them. The cannies went down with a 9mm round in each of their chests, tumbling over the stairs until they stopped a few feet from him. Neither of the cannies moved, so they were ignored.

"Should we go up or down?" Henry asked Jimmy.

"How the fuck should I know?" He pointed to the two bodies. "What happened to getting a live one?"

"Next one will have to suffice. Come on, it won't be long before that bomb on the tug goes off and all hell breaks loose on this ship." Henry led the way up the stairs.

The next level was empty of enemies, another lantern illuminating the landing. He chose the passageway to his right, darting for the opening. He almost ran straight into another cannie, a short, stocky woman with cropped hair and makeup so outlandish it was more like clown makeup than for everyday use.

"Who the hell are you?" she shouted, not recognizing Henry, or Jimmy, who was standing behind him.

"We're the entertainment for this cruise," Henry said calmly.

The woman blinked at that, not understanding. Before she could do or say anything else, Henry used the butt of his Glock to knock her down, connecting hard with her left temple. She dropped to the faded commercial carpeting like her strings had been cut. Henry grabbed her arms, gesturing to Jimmy to do the same with her legs.

"Here's that live one you were asking about." He looked around him, seeing multiple doors hanging open, up and down the passageway. Inside each doorway it was dark; he didn't know if anyone was within. He doubted it. All the commotion going on, any able bodied hands would be doing something other than relaxing in their cabins.

He picked a door and began tugging the unconscious woman as he moved, Jimmy following his lead. Lanterns were spaced every twenty feet, their flames low, just bright enough to navigate the passageway.

"Where are we going?" Jimmy asked.

"In here. This woman is gonna tell us everything we need to know."

"And if she doesn't?"

Henry didn't reply, but the look on his face in the gloom of the passageway said if that was the case, it wouldn't bode well for the female cannie.

Carol was fighting the controls of the tugboat as she peered out the scratched windshield. The tug was more than sixty feet away from the cruise ship, but she was slowly managing her way back to it.

"Mark, I think I have it under control, but not by much. Go get ready to set off the bomb. We'll meet at the stern and the rubber raft."

"Are you sure? Maybe I should stay here a while longer," Mark said, worry all over his face.

"No, I'll be fine. I promise. Just go. Henry and the others are counting on us."

"Okay, but be careful."

"You too, dear." Carol swung the tugboat around as the boiler gave up its last bit of energy. The man who'd been stoking it was long gone, having joined the raiding party.

It was as she moved closer, no more than thirty feet away and closing, that something from above caught her eye.

Three decks above her, on what was the ship's Promenade, a walking path that circled the entire ship, multiple people were gathered, all looking and pointing at the tugboat. But worst off all, there was some kind of fire pit between them.

Carol couldn't decipher what was going on, so she continued her progress toward the cruise ship. Mark, meanwhile, had reached the stern, directly forward of the makeshift boiler, where the barrels filled with liquid explosive had been stored. The covers of the barrels the ammonium nitrate and diesel fuel were placed in were off, so that the grenade could be dropped into one of them, thus setting off that barrel and the rest consecutively. Just as the grenade pin was pulled and dropped into the barrel, Mark and Carol would jump off the tugboat and into the rubber raft, and float away. It was all a gamble, but then no other viable plan had come to anyone. And Carol wanted to do it, Mark also. They were becoming part of the team, and they wanted to do what they could to save Mary and Cindy. As she peered upwards, Carol saw heavy activity around the fire pit. She didn't know what was going on but a sixth sense told her it wasn't good. Leaning out of the wheelhouse, she called out to Mark, "There's something going on up there. I think I should try and turn around."

Mark glanced upwards and his eyes went wide when a large bucket of flames tumbled end over end down onto the tugboat, just as the tug reached the ship's hull once more. The tugboat was twenty feet back from the curve of the bow. It bumped into the cruise ship's hull, making a large dent, and stopped cold, sending Carol flying forwards into the windshield. She banged her head and left a crack in the tempered glass, but otherwise was fine. Below, in the stern, Mark went flying, the barrels of liquid bombs spilling everywhere, completely covering the deck.

Splashing in the diesel fuel, he kept his mouth and eyes closed, not wanting to get any in there, knowing it could cause serious damage. So with his eyes clamped shut, he didn't see the bucket of fire land on the tugboat's deck and quickly begin to spread, followed almost immediately by another.

Intense heat surrounded him, and he had no choice but to open his eyes. Shaking his head to clear as much of the fuel mixture on his face as he could, he parted his eyelids to find he was in Hell.

All around him the flames erupted, as a third barrel of fire dropped onto the deck. The cannies had a simple way to repel boarders it seemed. All they had to do was dump enough burning oil or tar—Mark wasn't sure which—onto an attacking boat until it was either destroyed or retreated.

He heard Carol calling his name, and he craned his neck around to see her trying to reach him; a wall of fire stopped her. "No, forget about me!" he shouted. "Jump, get off the boat!"

She couldn't hear him through the roar of the inferno the tugboat was becoming, so she continued to try and reach him. Hugging the rail, she inched past the licking flames, her back so hot she thought she would die. A few places on her clothing began to burn and she patted the flames out, burning her palms in the process. Still, she fought to reach Mark. Her forehead was bleeding from when she struck the glass windshield, blood dripping down the crown of her nose to drip off her face.

"No, go back, get off the ship!" Mark yelled, as the fiery blaze reached his legs and he began to catch fire. Covered from head to toe in diesel fuel, it was only seconds before his entire body was alight. He splashed and squirmed in the nitrate-laden diesel fuel, his shrieks loud enough to override the roaring of the flames.

He kept hold of the HE grenade, the pin still secured inside it. He screamed in agony as he burned to death, the grenade rolling out of his hand to lie on the deck in a puddle of fuel.

Carol finally managed to reach him, and she grabbed a fire blanket from where it lay off to the side, not soaked with fuel yet, and tried to put out the flames burning her husband alive.

Mark looked up at her but he couldn't see her anymore. His eyes were milky white, having boiled in his skull. He couldn't speak, his lungs full of smoke, and scorched after sucking in the flames. He was already dead, only his body wasn't accepting its fate yet.

Carol refused to stop, still trying to extinguish the fire roasting her husband alive. Her arms were charred, her skin flaking off, but still she fought to save Mark, ignoring the flames that were already surrounding her as well, her clothing catching again.

The fire was a full-fledged conflagration, the entire deck of the tugboat awash with orange, yellow and red flames. Finally, the heat was enough to ignite the thick layer of diesel fuel/ammonium nitrate mixture coating the deck alight, just as if Mark had used the grenade. For all anyone knew, by itself, the grenade might not have been enough of a catalyst anyway, but it was the only idea Henry or anyone else had come up with. But the raging fire was more than sufficient, equal to a hundred blasting caps.

When the mixture exploded, it not only set off the grenade too, but the boiler as well, the pressure that had been building inside it releasing in one massive explosion.

The tugboat disappeared inside a glorious fireball that lit up the water and the port as if it was daytime. Mark and Carol were vaporized in an instant, which was a mercy to them. Instead of burning to death, they simply ceased to exist, as if God himself had snapped his fingers together.

A giant cloud of flames enveloped the tugboat and a large portion of the cruise ship. The explosion was so massive that the entire cruise ship was forced over onto its opposite side, where its railings came close to caressing the water, before its natural buoyancy allowed it to snap back up to right itself. It rolled back the way it had been then continued, as if a giant child had been playing in the tub, and had slapped his hand near the ship to create a wave. Where the cannies had stood on the Promenade, dumping fire onto the tugboat, they were gone as well, either blown off the ship or killed in the blast. When the smoke eventually dissipated, there was a giant hole just forward of amidships large enough to drive an eighteen wheeler through the hull easily— five decks high and across, and penetrating almost into half the ship.

Immediately, the cruise ship began taking on water, and once it stopped lurching from side to side, it listed forward slightly, the bow drinking in all the water the ocean could give it.

Chapter 23

Minutes before the tugboat exploded, Mary and Cindy were waiting in their darkened room for what might come next. The lantern had sputtered out more than two hours ago. It was hard to know exactly how much time had elapsed, with no way to keep time.

They sat silently, huddled behind the table, wondering when they would have to fight for their lives. The answer after hours of waiting finally came when the familiar *click, thump, click, thump* floated into the room via the passageway.

"You ready?" Cindy asked Mary.

"As best as I can, given the circumstances." She hefted her .38, prepared to use it on whoever came through the door first. She hoped it was Big Mama. The fat cannie bitch wouldn't know what hit her if Mary had her say.

"We don't let them capture us again. We do this or die trying," Cindy stated.

"Agreed." Mary shifted beside Cindy, nervous for what would come in seconds.

There was a jangling at the door as the lock was undone, then the door began to swing open.

Wan light spilled into the room from the corridor. Two figures, walking in single file, stepped over the lip at the bottom of the door, and promptly fell face first after tripping over the corpses of the very dead George and Pedro.

Swearing and angry, they rose to their feet quickly, only to be shot down as Cindy and Mary fired from behind the toppled table.

"What the fuck?" Big Mama shrieked and pulled back from the door. "How the hell are those bitches free?"

Neither Mary nor Cindy knew who she was talking to, but both figured there were others in the corridor with her.

"Well, don't just stand there looking stupid, get the fuck in there and take them down!"

"But Big Mama," a man protested feebly. "They got hold of their guns."

"So what? Take them away from them!" There was a pause, then, "Do it now or I'll kill you myself and toss you into the cook pot!"

Feet stomped on the deck, and a second later, more bodies charged into the room. Mary and Cindy began to shoot, the men charging at them standing no chance. The attackers never got a chance to trip over the scattered bodies or tools littering the floor, but were shot the instant they entered the room. Their bodies danced a jig in death as bullet after bullet riddled their torsos. Cindy started at one man's groin and slowly worked her way up, stitching him from crotch to neck. He toppled over, dead before he hit the floor.

Silence reigned in the small room for a moment, the smell of cordite suffusing the air, along with the odor of blood and shit, thanks to George and Pedro, who had voided their bowels hours ago upon their deaths.

The doorway was clear, no one before it, a dim light from a lantern the only illumination. Mary and Cindy looked at each other in the gloom, wondering what was going to happen next.

They had a good defensive position where they were, but they couldn't defend it forever. Big Mama could keep sending her subjects at them, like cannon fodder on a battlefield. Eventually the defending women would run out of bullets, to then be at the fat cannie queen's mercy, which wasn't much from what they had already experienced. Both women would eat a bullet before they were taken alive.

"I need to reload," Mary said when there was a lull in the attack.

"Go for it," Cindy replied. She knew Mary needed extra time with her bad hand. After hours of nonuse, the hand was stiff and it hurt Mary to even try to use it.

Seconds passed, the tension so strong both women thought they might go mad with waiting. Cindy was about to suggest they charge the door and try to escape, when a large bulk filled the doorway, blocking out what little light had been filtering in from the passageway.

Big Mama was paying them a visit, personally.

"Too easy," Cindy said, standing up and leveling her M16 at the fat queen of the cannies. Mary stood as well, but held her fire as she finished reloading her .38 with rounds found in her pack. Cindy had already popped in a fresh magazine, prepared for the next attack.

"You think that gun scares me, you little bitch?" Big Mama said to Cindy, not moving from the doorway, her crutches tucked under her armpits. Her nostrils flared in anger and she snorted like a bull.

"It should, it's gonna kill you in about two seconds." Cindy hissed the words.

"I'm not afraid of your fucking popguns. That's why I didn't care if they were in this room or not." She laughed, a grating noise that sounded more like a pig grunting. "That's why I left them in here with you. I liked the idea of you seeing them just out of reach, but not able to get to 'em. It's my way of breaking a sex slave's spirit."

"It didn't work this time," Mary said, closing the cylinder on her .38, now filled with fresh rounds.

"Yeah, I can see that. Not that it matters." She took a step into the room, fearless of the two guns leveled at her. Mary had to wonder if the woman was crazy or stupid. The former seemed to be the best bet. While she could have retreated and gathered more of her crew to stop the two women, instead she had entered the room alone, unarmed.

It was utter madness.

"Enough talk," Cindy said, already squeezing the trigger on her rifle. "Time to die."

Down below, at the waterline, the tugboat ignited into a blazing bomb that took out a large section of the cruise ship.

One moment Cindy was about to shoot the cannie queen dead, the next the world was upside down and she was shooting the ceiling as her finger reflexively squeezed the M16's trigger.

The floor went sideways, tipping all three women over and sending everyone sprawling across the deck. Dead bodies, tools and the cannie queen, all got mixed up with Cindy and Mary, who found themselves lying prone on the deck.

Mary shouted in pain, her bad hand becoming crushed under her, the pressure of her body on the wrist excruciating. She saw stars and lost her breath.

Water splashed into the room via the porthole as the ship slapped the water, the wall now the floor, and the floor turning into a wall, along with the ceiling. The table they'd been hiding behind flipped over and almost landed on Mary and Cindy; it was only dumb luck that it didn't.

It seemed like the ship was horizontal forever, but in seconds it was bouncing back to right itself, then flopping over the opposite way, only the angle wasn't as strong as the first roll. Everything in the room, living or dead, was thrown to the opposite side of the room, until the leaning stopped and the ship slowly went back upright. This time it wasn't as bad, and both Mary and Cindy used the time to gather their wits. Their guns were gone, lost in the cavalcade of churning items on the floor.

"What the hell just happened?" Cindy yelled.

"I don't know? Were we hit by a torpedo?" Mary replied.

As the two women regained their footing, they stood up, inspecting the room and the pile of corpses scattered everywhere. It was like a young girl's room, once done with her dolls, had tossed them every which way when she'd finished playing with them for the day.

"What now?" Mary asked. The lantern in the corridor was still lit, and its flickering flame let in barely enough light to see by.

"We get the fuck out of here, that's what," Cindy said. Both women were about to do just that, and leave the room and the carnage within it, when the large pile of bodies in the corner, swept there by the movements of the ship, began to shift and move, undulating as if something was burrowing within the pile.

Once more, Cindy and Mary locked gazes, not understanding what they were seeing, that is until with a roar like a locomotive, the bodies on the top of the pile seemed to fly off, as if a geyser had erupted.

The bodies went in all directions, landing in soft heaps when they struck the deck. Cindy and Mary had to duck or risk being hit by flailing corpses.

In the center of the pile of bodies, Big Mama stood upright, covered in blood, her muumuu soaked completely through in clotting crimson.

"You've got to be kidding me," Cindy said as she took a step backwards.

"Come here, you little bitch," Big Mama hissed, her eyes glaring at Cindy. "I'm gonna rip your arms and legs off and suck out the marrow while you watch."

Big Mama took a step forward, kicking a corpse out of her path to do so. Her crutches were gone, lost amid the pile of bodies and items strewn everywhere. But she didn't need them for what she wanted to do. Adrenaline was saturating her body, giving her the power to walk unabated. Standing to her full height, and not hunched over with her crutches, she easily topped six feet four inches.

In the small environment of the room, she was like a goliath, her head scraping the ceiling.

Cindy backed up some more, not liking where this was going. Big Mama charged like an angry rhino, her feet stomping the deck so that the vibration could be felt, even over the shudders the ship was already making after being blasted by the bomb.

Big Mama came for Cindy like a runaway freight train, her speed surprising Cindy considering the woman's bulk. Her eyes locked onto the blonde and never deviated. Mary was forgotten for the moment. Cindy had nowhere to go, so she prepared to punch Big Mama when the time came. Which was only a second away.

She reached Cindy and grabbed her by the neck, slamming her against the wall and squeezing. Cindy managed to get off one punch but all it did was strike fat. Then Cindy had both hands to her neck, trying to release the vise-like grip that was crushing the life out of her.

"Die, bitch," Big Mama hissed, spittle flying from her lips. Cindy's feet dangled a foot off the floor, and she kicked weakly, a toddler in the arms of a football player.

There was no question that Cindy was going to die. As white lights flashed across her vision, she knew this was the end. There was no escaping this behemoth of a woman. Only death would end the attack.

Cindy tried to kick out with her legs, but all she did was strike rolls of fat, the padding too thick to make Big Mama even flinch.

Cindy's face began to turn red, then purple as the oxygen was cut off from her brain. The only good thing about it all, to Mary's eyes, was that Big Mama was trying to strangle Cindy, rather than just snap her neck, which the cannie queen could have easily done. The large woman wanted Cindy to suffer.

But Mary wasn't idle on the sidelines when Big Mama launched herself at Cindy. The moment Cindy was plastered to the wall like an ornament, Mary had raced to the opposite side of the room to figure out what she could do to save her friend.

It came in the form of one of Big Mama's crutches, which was lying under a body, only the handle end visible. Mary didn't hesitate. She jumped over the detritus on the floor, scooped up the crutch and ran at Big Mama, swinging the crutch low at her legs, right at the back of the knee. She ignored the agony her bad hand was sending to her nerve receptors, her mind focused on saving Cindy.

The crutch had no weight to it but none was needed. Hitting the right leg directly behind the knee, the leg folded in on itself, a reflexive action. It was something she used to do with her friends when she was a child, sneaking up on one of them and tapping that spot so that their leg would give out. Of course, being kids, they rarely fell, but caught their balance quickly with their other leg, as the tapped one righted itself.

Not so for Big Mama, who had four hundred pounds balanced on two stubby legs. When the crutch connected, the leg didn't so much as fold, but simply collapsed, just as if she'd knocked out one piece of a structure held up by only two I-beams.

Big Mama found herself toppling like an aged tree in the forest. Cindy was forgotten, and was released to drop to the floor, gasping for breath, while the fat woman wind-milled her arms, trying to keep her balance. But it wasn't even a possibility. The massive body dropped straight to the deck on her back, the same leg Mary had tapped snapping in half when Big Mama's full weight fell onto it. The large woman howled in pain and rolled back and forth on the floor. She wanted to reach down and cradle her broken leg but she couldn't manage it. Doing something like a sit-up would have been as unattainable as trying to fly.

Cindy lay on the deck in a heap of arms and legs, gasping and doing her best to suck in oxygen. Even the stench of unwashed bodies and gore did nothing to make Cindy feel she wasn't taking in the sweetest air of her life. She moved to a sitting position, her back against the wall.

Cindy slowly opened her eyes, to see Big Mama rolling over so that she was on her stomach. She did it much like a turtle would, having to sway back and forth until there was enough energy to roll. Once done, Big Mama crawled towards Cindy, who pressed her back harder against the wall, as if she could simply sink into the metal to escape the crawling menace coming for her.

Mary swung the crutch again, this time at Big Mama's head. The large woman reached out with a thick arm and blocked it, before grabbing the end and yanking it to her. Mary, not letting go, was thrown forward to fall on top of Big Mama.

"Ha, I got you now!" She began wrestling with Mary, who fought back, kicking and punching. Only big Mama being on her stomach caused her not to fully grab Mary.

Big Mama went to her knees, the pain of her snapped leg forgotten in her fury. She was running completely on adrenaline now. She perilously hovered over Mary, a grizzly bear towering over its prey.

Mary was on her butt, and she tried to scooch away, but Big Mama reached out and grabbed her right ankle with a meaty hand.

"Going somewhere, sweetie pie? I don't think so. I guess you die before Blondie."

Big Mama yanked at Mary's leg, making her slide across the floor easily. Another meaty hand clamped onto Mary's left ankle, so that her legs were held down, as if Mary was about to start doing sit-ups, and Big Mama was assisting her. Mary tried to punch Big Mama's head, but the blows were ineffectual.

Big Mama removed a hand from an ankle and clamped it down on Mary's knee, then pulled her closer. Mary gagged from the stench of the unwashed woman, forcing herself not to vomit. She slapped the floor with her hands, trying to stop her momentum, but Big Mama just yanked some more, Mary almost completely going under the large woman. It was as if Big Mama was the Blob, absorbing Mary into her body.

Mary's left wrist seeped blood from the wound, covering her arm in red. She ignored it. She ignored everything around her. Only Big Mama existed in her terror-filled world. This large woman was going to kill her, and there was nothing she could do to stop it.

Big Mama's face was alight in the violence of the moment, her eyes locked with Mary's. But then Mary saw something change in Big Mama's deep set orbs.

Suddenly, there was a look of consternation, and Mary felt the vises clamped on her legs loosen slightly. Not enough to break free, but still, less pressure.

A heartbeat later the hands released completely, and Mary rolled and kicked her way clear of the obese woman. Coming up to lay on her side when she was free, Mary looked back to see the reason Big Mama had halted her attack.

Cindy was now repaying Mary for saving her, not that either of them needed to do such a thing. They were a team, and blood sisters, and that was the only reason to help one another.

Cindy was on Big Mama's back, riding the fat woman like a bronco. Cindy had taken a piece of cord once used to secure the women to the tables, and had wrapped it around Big Mama's neck like a garrote.

The folds of flab encircling the thick neck made it much more difficult, however, and Big Mama reared up and tried to grab Cindy, who kept turning her body so that the cannie queen couldn't reach her.

Huffing and puffing, Big Mama tried to get to her feet, but forgot about her shattered leg. She toppled to the deck, flat on her stomach. But she tried to roll, Cindy not letting go for anything. The cannie queen's face turned beet red as spittle flew from her lips. Slapping both hands to the deck, she pushed herself back to a kneeling position, and then swung her body against the wall. Cindy was crushed between the wall and the large woman's bulk, and she screamed from the pressure, but she refused to let go.

Big Mama reared back and tried again, slamming her back against the wall once more. But this time the force of the impact wasn't as hard. She was weakening from oxygen being cut off from her brain.

Cindy renewed her attack, pulling even harder on the cord. It cut into her hands where it was wrapped around them, but she didn't stop. She wouldn't relent until the fat woman was defeated. This was going to end here and now, and when it was over, one of them would be dead, either Cindy or Big Mama.

Mary tried to rise but slipped on blood coating the deck. Gathering herself, she stood up, trying to think what to do next. Her eyes searched for a weapon amongst the corpses. Multiple items were seen, and as her mind raced on which one to grab, she glanced at the two women to see there would be no need to intervene.

Big Mama was once more on the floor, her arms out before her. She slapped the deck multiple times in futility. The eyes slowly opened and closed, the mouth as well, spittle and bloody drool sliding from the corner of her thick lips. The head began to sag despite Cindy's tension.

The cannie queen's entire body seemed to lose form, like a deflated balloon. The limbs, twitching before, went limp, the body slumped to the deck, and the eyes stopped moving but remained open. A stream of urine appeared from under the body to pool on the deck.

Cindy didn't stop, she continued to squeeze with the cord; it bit so deep into the flabby neck it was invisible.

"Cindy, I think she's dead. You can stop."

Cindy didn't hear Mary, her focus solely on killing the cannie queen.

"Cindy!" Mary shouted. "Stop! She's dead!"

Cindy snapped out of her fugue state, looking around at Mary, then down at Big Mama's prone corpse.

"She's dead. You can stop," Mary repeated, softer this time.

Cindy glanced down at the body, seeing the head not moving, the chubby fingers still; she let go, leaning back on the body. She said nothing. Mary could see her friend's neck was covered in bruises. Black and blue; it must have hurt to swallow. But Cindy was breathing normally, so nothing appeared irreparably damaged.

She stood up from the fat corpse, sighing in relief. The reign of Big Mama was over, the queen was dead.

Boot steps sounded in the passageway and both women looked at one another, knowing there was no time to celebrate their victory over the cannie queen. Cindy climbed off the corpse and with Mary, the two women began searching for their weapons.

But they both already knew it would be too late, as the boot steps were almost upon them. Turning to face their new foes, the women stood side by side in the center of the room. Covered in blood after rolling around on the floor, they resembled ghouls more than human females.

The doorway was wreathed in darkness when the first figure entered, followed by a second one. It was dark in the room, only the lantern in the passageway giving off illumination, but both women knew immediately who stood before them. After years of traveling together, the silhouettes of Henry and Jimmy were easy to discern.

"Henry?" Mary said hopefully.

"Jimmy?" Cindy added.

"We found you," Henry said, relief flooding his voice. "Thank God."

Jimmy darted around Henry to embrace Cindy. He ignored her bloody clothes and face and kissed her happily. "Babe, holy shit, I was so worried."

"I'm fine, Jimmy, really." Cindy returned his embrace, the two kissing quickly.

Henry went to Mary, the two hugging. Mary closed her eyes and folded into his arms, relishing the feeling of security, even if for only an instant.

Henry released her, his eyes scanning the room, seeing all the bodies on the floor. "I should have known you guys wouldn't need help."

"As if there was any doubt?" Mary joked and stepped back from him. There was another explosion and the ship lurched subtly.

Henry's gaze stopped on Big Mama's corpse, the size alone making it stand out amongst the rest of the bodies. "Who's that?"

Mary stepped to the side and gestured to Big Mama. "That, Henry, is the self-proclaimed cannie queen of this ship."

"Huh, doesn't look like much in the way of royalty to me," he replied.

"How did you find us?" Cindy asked the two men.

Jimmy showed her a wide smile. "We asked for help and this time they were more agreeable."

Both women didn't understand, but neither did they really care. They'd been through hell, and wanted off the ship immediately.

Henry nodded to Jimmy, the two sharing a secret joke. The female cannie they captured earlier had been a lot more willing to share information on the whereabouts of the girls. After Henry cut off one of her fingers, the cannie had caved easily, sharing all she knew.

Henry had almost regretted shooting and killing her after getting what he wanted and leaving the body in the cabin. But he'd made a pact a long time ago. The only good cannie, was a dead one. He had shown the woman mercy by shooting her, however, and wasting a bullet to give that mercy. As she'd begged Jimmy to spare her, Henry had stepped up behind her, seated and tied to a chair, and shot her point blank in the back of the head. She'd never seen it coming. A harsh mercy in a harsher world.

The entire ship rocked to the side, a groaning of stressed metal frames filling the room. From somewhere on the ship, an explosion could be heard.

"What the hell is going on?" Cindy asked. "What was that explosion?"

"A distraction," Henry explained. "One I think worked better than I thought." He grabbed Mary's good arm, seeing the bloody left one. His eyes asked the question and Mary shook her head. "I'm fine. I just need a new bandage."

That was good enough for him, at least for now. Later, if they managed to get off the cruise ship alive, they could fill each other in on the past day's activities.

The ship lurched forward and to starboard, pieces of the ceiling falling inward.

"Wait, our guns are in here!" Cindy shouted and began searching for them, shoving bodies out of the way. "They're here somewhere. We lost them in that first explosion."

The four companions got to work, and with four eyes searching, it took less than half a minute to find their gear and weapons. Everything was covered in blood and gore and would need a thorough cleaning later.

"Okay, so if we're done here, can we leave now?" Henry asked politely, as if they were packing for a trip, and not hastily preparing to leave a sinking ship.

There were no objections, and with Jimmy leading, they stepped out into the passageway.

Three cannies were waiting for them, one with a fire axe and two with blades. They charged at Jimmy and the others. Jimmy leveled his shotgun and shot the first cannie in the legs, cutting the man off at the knees with the charge of double-ought buckshot. He fell forward, his legs disintegrating in the blast; his feet were severed, lying on the deck. Flopping to the floor, the man screamed in agony, his eyes as wide as dinner plates.

The second cannie got it in the stomach. It blew him backwards to land on the deck with a hole big enough to put his fist through. Intestines sagged out of the hole as the man lay gut shot, shrieking in agony.

The third cannie decided retreat was the better part of valor. He spun on his heels and took off back the way he'd come. Jimmy raised the shotgun to shoot the man in the back, but Henry stopped him.

"Let him go. We're not here to kill all of them. Crow's people can deal with that. Our job now is to get off this ship."

The cruise ship lurched yet again, a fifteen degree angle to port. Staggering down the passageway like a couple of drunks, it took only a minute to reach the elevator banks and the stairs.

"Which way?" Jimmy asked. But no sooner did he ask than water rushed into the stairwell from below, the entire lower levels flooded.

"Do you really have to ask?" Henry said as he passed Jimmy and ran up the stairs two at a time, while dragging Mary by her good hand.

"Well, no, not anymore," Jimmy responded and followed Henry, Cindy right behind him.

They climbed two more levels until reaching Deck 7, which upon stepping onto the landing, elevators and stairs opposite one another, like on every other level, instead of the darkness of passageways for cabins, there were glass doors leading onto the Promenade walkway. The flames burning on the water and the ship on fire itself illuminated the night, so that an orange glow could be seen past the glass doors. Henry ran right for one, pushing it open and coming out onto the deck.

He was on the far side of the tugboat explosion, and other than the ship's terrible list, all seemed fine. A few cannies ran past them, Henry raising his Glock in defense, but no one seemed interested in the companions.

The cannies kept right on running, to where was unknown.

"Looks like our distraction worked out pretty well," Henry said.

"A little too well, if you ask me," Mary said, grabbing the railing so she didn't go over the side. "What did you do? Set of a nuclear bomb?"

"Later, when we're off this ship." He was trying to figure out what to do next, when one of Crow's people came running down the walkway. It was Sylvester.

"Henry," the man said, "it's good I found you. Crow and the rest of us are in the aft part of the ship. We're lowering one of the lifeboats into the water. You want a lift?"

"Of course," Henry replied. "Lead the way."

The ship listed another five degrees, everyone adjusting their stride.

"That seemed awful coincidental, Henry," Mary said. "Did you have a way off this thing?"

Henry shrugged. "No, not really. I was kind of leaving that up to chance."

"Oh really?"

"Sure. I figured we could grab some life jackets if we could find some, jump off and swim for it, or maybe figure out some other way."

"I don't think there are any vests on this ship, Henry," Mary said. "We were told swimming to escape wasn't an option."

"Then I would have come up with something else," he said defensively.

Cindy laughed. "Way to half ass a plan, Henry. You're getting lazy in your old age."

He gave her a sideways smirk. "Yeah, maybe. So next time, why don't I give it another day or two to figure out something better." He met gazes with her as they moved down the ship. "You won't mind waiting a little longer for help, will you?"

Cindy laughed some more. "Oh, I don't know. I think Mary and myself were doing pretty well without you men around."

"Ain't that the truth," Jimmy said proudly. "You two kicked some serious ass back there, from the looks of it."

"We sure as hell did," Cindy said, Mary and her sharing a knowing grin.

There was a hive of activity before them, and from the way Sylvester acted, Henry knew this was Crow's people. In the gloom of the night, the lifeboat had been lowered into the water, and each of the raiding party was now climbing down a rope onto the roof of the boat. It held fifty people, so was more than enough room for everyone.

Bags and crates were also being lowered. Crow came up to Henry, the two shaking hands.

"Henry, good to see you're still alive."

"And you too, Crow."

Crow looked past him to Mary and Cindy. "This must be the two ladies you risked everything for. Hello, my name is Thomas Crow."

Both Mary and Cindy introduced themselves.

Crow looked over his shoulder to see there were only two more of his people left on deck, the rest were in the lifeboat. "I think its time we left this ship. It's going down, you know. That was one hell of a bomb you fabricated."

"I guess I don't know my own strength," Henry said and gestured to the bags and crates being lowered. "What's all that?"

"Things we scavenged while on the hunt for the cannibals. No reason not to take anything of value." He grinned. "Hell, some of what we recovered was our own stuff, stolen from us months ago."

Without further discussion, each of them went down the rope. Mary was lowered the same way the bags and crates were let down, with a rope fastened under her arms, looping around her chest like a belt. Her wounded hand made it impossible for her to climb down on her own.

Crow was the last one off the sinking ship. He yelled to the others to push off, and with makeshift paddles made from shuffleboard poles and some dinner trays, they began rowing away from the cruise ship. The oars were terribly fabricated, mostly made with tape and luck. The rowers made almost no progress across the water. But they were off the ship and eventually would make it to shore or return to the port in some fashion thanks to a gentle current.

The lifeboat made excruciatingly slow progress around the cruise ship. Once the side the explosion was on could be seen, everyone gasped. From on the vessel, there had been no way to see the damage the bomb had made, but now, as they floated slowly away, they were able to take it all in.

The bow of the cruise ship was almost completely submerged, and was tilting more to the port side with each passing second. Cannies were jumping off the ship by the dozens, the ones that Crow and his people hadn't killed, that is.

Henry looked at Crow, who shrugged. "We wanted to kill more of them but once we figured out the ship was sinking, we decided it was time to abandon ship. Besides, without their queen or their ship as a base, I doubt they'll regroup. And if they do, we'll deal with them then. With less numbers, we should be able to wipe them out easily."

"I hope it all works out for you," Henry said as he watched through one of the openings in the lifeboat. It had a roof and was a lot like riding in a bus, with seats lined up in rows and on both sides, with an opening on port and starboard that could be closed if the boat was in rough waters.

Half an hour later, the lifeboat was halfway to the pier, the rowers doing their valiant best, but having great difficulty. Most of the fiery debris floating in the water had been extinguished, but there was still enough burning flotsam to make the night a little brighter.

During that time, Henry had filled Mary and Cindy in on more of his original plan, how Mark and Carol had helped with the tugboat and homemade bomb, and how Henry and Jimmy had worried terribly about the two women.

The cruise ship had rolled onto its side and was settling on the ocean floor. A large portion would remain visible it seemed, the depth of the channel not deep enough to swallow it whole. The channel had been dredged enough for the ship to come and go from the cruise terminal, but not become fully submerged in that location. A frothy mess surrounded the ship; anything not strapped down floated around it, and thousands upon thousands of gallons of water were sucked into the ship.

A few cannies had tried to swim to the lifeboat, begging to be taken aboard. They didn't know it wasn't their own people controlling the boat. Crow's people had slaughtered them mercilessly in the water, to leave the bodies floating around the boat in a greater number with each foolish victim that pleaded for help. There would be no quarter given to any cannie that asked for it.

Mary was the one who noticed something first. "Where are Mark and Carol? You said they were on the tugboat."

Both Jimmy and Henry looked out over the water, where there was nothing but debris floating around the cruise ship. One looked at the other in thought. "Do you think they blew up with the boat?" Jimmy asked.

"I don't know," Henry said, concern in his voice. He'd come to like Carol and Mark. "Hopefully they made it off okay in that rubber raft we gave them, and even now they're waiting for us at the pickup trucks."

There was a loud gushing of water, like when a whale would spew water from its blowhole, and around the cruise ship, the water began to settle down. The ship had finally completed its submergence, the entire belly now filled with ocean water and the corpses of any who didn't escape. A fitting tomb for the inhuman monsters that had dwelled within its hull.

Henry finally stopped watching the destroyed cruise ship and took a seat in the lifeboat, Mary by his side. Her head was on his shoulder, her eyes closed. It wasn't long before she drifted into a restless sleep, finally feeling safe enough to do so. Jimmy and Cindy were sitting together as well, their arms around one another, talking softly. Henry watched Jimmy for a few seconds, the way he talked to Cindy. There was a maturity in him that Henry rarely saw. He felt an intense sense of pride for the younger man right then. Jimmy was a hell of a warrior and a damn good friend, a far cry from when they'd first met years ago. Now, Henry couldn't imagine traveling around the devastated country without him.

Another half hour later, the lifeboat finally bumped into the pier, and with the oars, it was moved to the ladder, the same one the tugboat had used hours earlier.

One by one, everyone left the lifeboat and offloaded what Crow had looted from the ship. Crow's people had retrieved the pickups from where they'd been stashed and soon, the vehicles were being loaded with salvaged cargo, and everyone was climbing onboard the trucks to return home. Henry noticed that someone else he knew was missing, and he asked Crow about it.

"Leslie didn't make it," Crow said flatly. "She got stabbed by a cannibal minutes after we were on board. It was in the heart; there was no saving her." He gazed out onto the water in thought, at the half-sunken cruise ship lying silently on its side. "That's her tomb now."

"I'm sorry to hear that. She was a hell of a fighter, and a beautiful woman."

Crow nodded. "Leslie was my cousin." He sighed. "I'll miss her terribly, but she died a warrior's death. I know that sounds cheesy coming from a Native American, but in some things we still follow the old ways."

"I think it's beautiful," Mary said, standing beside Henry. She was still covered in blood, only her face a little cleaner, after using some seawater to wash. Cindy had done the same.

Crow explained that other than a few of his people being wounded, but nothing life threatening, Leslie had been the only casualty.

With the entire raiding party loaded into the pickups, and with a surge of engines, the three trucks drove away from the edge of the pier, their headlights cutting through the night.

Crow was driving the lead pickup truck again, Mary in the center of the bench seat, and Henry in the passenger seat, his right arm resting out the open window. Jimmy and Cindy were in the rear bed, now mostly-empty without all the barrels and other gear used in the raid. The new scavenged items were in the second and third pickups, along with the rest of the raiding party. With Leslie gone, and Mark and Carol presumed missing, there was more than enough room for Jimmy and Cindy to be alone in the rear bed of Crow's pickup.

As Henry rode away from the port, his hair blowing in the wind, he leaned forward in his seat a little so he could see out the passenger side mirror. He watched the cruise ship for as long as he could, until the truck turned a corner to go around the empty terminal, the ship lost from sight forever.

Chapter 24

After arriving back at the Science Center around four in the morning, the companions went straight to bed, exhausted. Only Mary delayed her slumber, first needing to have her wounded wrist looked after. Crow's mother was a talented healer, and with the ample supplies the tribe had on hand, Mary's wrist was cleaned and redressed. Mother had to give Mary a dozen stitches, to ensure the wrist healed properly. Then her thumb was reset. Antibiotics were also something they had, to ensure Mary's wound didn't become infected, something that could be a death sentence in a world without functioning hospitals.

Henry rose late in the afternoon, around three. After using the bathroom, he went looking to eat; he was starving. The plan would be to remain in the center overnight, and the next day the companions would leave, to where was yet unknown. With a full day of rest under their belt, they would be ready for anything.

Returning to the redoubt wasn't an option, not with the security droid waiting. Crow had already offered the group one of the tribe's pickup trucks to take with them. That would probably be what would happen. He hadn't decided yet, not wanting to think about the future, and just glad that for the moment, all the people he cared about were safe.

On his way to the cafeteria, where he hoped to find some food, he passed a large room where Crow and a few others were working, inventorying the items salvaged from the cruise ship. Henry joined them, curious as well. Though his stomach was growling, he figured it could wait a few more minutes before it was fed.

Crow looked up from the worktable he was concentrating on when he saw Henry step in, a half-smoked cigarette hanging from his lips. "Hello, Henry, how are you feeling?"

"Rested, thanks." Henry jutted his chin at the table. "What's going on here?"

"Oh, we're doing a detailed inventory of what we brought back from the ship. We found so much it'll take a few days to go through it all."

On another table next to Crow's, Sylvester was dumping out a bag filled to the top with stuff. Weapons and first aid kits, along with tools and silverware, all poured out onto the table.

"We can melt the silverware down," Sylvester explained as he picked up some of the spoons and forks. "Then we can make what we need."

Henry nodded in approval, his eyes roving over the pile of stuff. Then he paused, something catching his attention. Moving over to the table, he looked at Sylvester and reached out to pick something up. The look said, 'Do you mind?'

Sylvester shrugged that he didn't care.

Henry picked up a large ammunition round, one he recognized immediately. It was a 66mm, armor piercing round used in a LAW, and it looked fully intact.

"What'd you find?" Crow asked, seeing Henry holding the giant round of ammo.

"Something I can use, if it's okay."

"Sure, whatever you want is yours, Henry. I know we helped you out saving your women, but you did us a great service as well."

"Thank you. This changes everything for me and my team, if I'm right."

"Glad to help." Crow went back to inventorying the supplies and Henry turned and left, carrying the round in his hand. He wondered where the cannies had found such a thing but then, they had been scavengers as much as meat eaters of humans. Probably, one of them had found it on a salvage raid, and had taken it back to the cruise ship with whatever else had been scavenged that day.

But now Henry had it, and he knew exactly what to do with it.

The following morning saw the companions outside the Science Center, well rested and ready to begin their travels. Their clothing had been laundered and dried near a fire.

All their weapons had been cleaned and oiled and their supplies of food were restocked, thanks to Crow's people. Jerky and dried goods were just a few of the food stores they now carried in their packs. The only thing not restocked was ammunition, but they still had a decent supply to get them where they were going next, and then, they would deal with the issue when it came up.

The pickup truck Crow had given them was the same one Henry and Jimmy had used to recce the port. The faded red paint job seemed to absorb the sunshine, its glossy finish long gone.

Jimmy and Cindy decided to sit in the rear bed again, and the two were talking quietly together. They had been inseparable since meeting up again on the cruise ship. Mary was sitting inside the cab, in the passenger seat this time, her arm resting on the doorframe of the open window. With her window open, and only being a few feet away from where Henry and Crow stood talking, she heard them easily.

"Thanks for everything," Henry said, as he and Crow clasped hands. "I'm glad we met." Crow was alone sending off the companions. The others in the tribe weren't very interested in Henry or his friends. Though the tribe was more than friendly, in the end, Henry and his crew wasn't part of the family, and so when they finally left, no one really cared they were leaving. If anything, they were pleased that the strangers were no longer amongst them.

"That goes for me as well, Henry," Crow agreed. "Best of luck on your future travels. Are you sure about not needing the truck after you drive through that burned-out town? As I said, you may keep it for good, to go wherever you need to."

"No, that's as far as we'll need it. So you know where it'll be in a day, right? Keys will be under the driver's mat. I'll park it behind the only building still standing." It was also the building Mark and Carol had been found in, when Mark was shooting at them. No one had ever seen the couple again; they never turned up after being left on the tugboat to detonate the bomb. Henry assumed they had died during the raid, but how exactly was unknown, and something he would probably never discover.

"Yes, I understand. In a day I'll send some of my people to retrieve it. Still, it seems odd."

"Maybe, but that's all I'm gonna say about it. Just be glad you'll get your truck back." Henry turned and walked around the pickup, and climbed into the driver's seat. Turning the key in the ignition, the engine roared to life.

"Be well, my friends. May we meet again," Crow said as he waved at the companions.

Henry smiled, then shifted the truck into Drive and began to roll down the driveway. Jimmy and Cindy were now facing Crow and both waved to him as well.

Crow stood there, waving and smiling, until Henry reached the bottom of the driveway. The vehicle took a right and was lost from sight. Crow stood alone for another full minute. He gazed up at the blue sky, breathed a sigh of happiness, and went back inside the Science Center. Was it him or did the air smell just a little fresher. Or was it just the knowledge that the cannie ship had been destroyed, and for now, his people were safe.

Driving down Route 95, Mary smiled as the wind blew her hair. "If we're leaving this truck in that burned-out town, I take it we're going back to the redoubt?"

Henry nodded. "You guessed right."

"Despite the security droid waiting for us?"

"You bet, but first I need to make a pit stop to solve that little problem."

"Where?"

"That gun store we checked out before."

"But it was empty, nothing left you said," she commented.

"True, but there was one thing there that was useless before, but should come in mighty handy now." He patted the 66mm round on the seat between them.

The ramp of the redoubt leading to the outside world was dark, no light at all penetrating the blast door. With no movement within, the motion operated overhead lights had clicked off. Utter silence reigned on the ramp, and inside the rest of the redoubt. Nothing living stirred, and on the ramp, the security droid waited, powered down, only a small red light blinking on its chest as it conserved power.

It was prepared to wait for years for the intruders to return if it had to, but as the blast door began to open and recede into the ground, the droid found that its wait had come to an end far earlier than expected.

Powering up, its weapons also began to hum. The M-60 cannon on its left arm began to spin in anticipation of engaging the enemy, and the tip on its right arm began to glow yellow before turning to purple. All systems were operational; it was ready for battle. The moment the blast door had fully retracted into the ground, the security droid rolled slightly forward, but then stopped.

The opening at the top of the ramp was devoid of enemies. There was no target to shoot. Its processors tried to figure out this dilemma as it scanned the opening over and over, until a more desired result occurred.

Its mechanical reflexes were almost taken off guard when suddenly, a figure stepped out from the side of the door opening, to stand directly in the center of the ramp. The droid processed this information instantly, and brought its weapons to bear on the intruder.

But Henry was just a little faster on the trigger, as he had already been squeezing the trigger on the LAW anti-tank tube while he stepped out into the open, exposing himself. In the close confines of the ramp, it took him barely half a second to sight the tube on the sec droid and fire. Even as the 66mm anti-tank round erupted from the tube, Henry was already discarding the empty launch tube and ducking back out of sight of the sec droid, the flame of ignition shooting out the back of the tube just before he dropped it. Having tangled with the droid already, he knew what it was capable of. A good thing for him, too. As he ducked and rolled back out of the opening, a beam of heat sizzled past where he'd been standing an instant before. That was the only shot the sec droid managed, however. As it prepared to begin rolling forward to engage the enemy at the top of the ramp, the LAW shell connected with it, mid torso.

The sec droid was tough, as Henry and his friends had learned the hard way. It could handle grenades and most rounds of ammunition. But it wasn't tough enough to handle an anti tank, armor-piercing shell, with a muzzle velocity of 475 feet per second.

When the round struck the droid and detonated, the entire ramp was enveloped in smoke and flames from the explosion. As the companions stood off to the side of the blast door, they had to pull back even more when a wave of heat shot out the opening, along with a few dozen pieces of shrapnel that was once the sec droid.

When the explosion seemed to be over, Jimmy wanted to go investigate but Henry stopped him cold.

"Not yet, give it a little more time."

Jimmy showed an annoyed face, but he did as he was told.

Henry waited for a full five minutes, then he slowly stuck his head around the doorframe. There was a part of him that expected his head to disappear when a laser bolt hit him and exploded his head. But nothing happened. He moved out into the opening cautiously, and when he was confident it was safe, he waved the others to join him.

Standing at the top of the ramp, they could see scorch marks on the walls, ceiling and floor. The overhead lights for half the ramp were out, destroyed in the blast.

Walking carefully into the redoubt and down the ramp, Henry crept over to where the sec droid had been before he'd fired the LAW. The droid was still there, only now its upper half was completely gone. About a foot of the droid still remained, wires sparked and hissed, but it was truly destroyed. He was still mighty impressed that there was something left. The droid had been built to take a beating, that was for damn sure. He wondered if anything other than the 66mm round would have been enough to stop it.

Waving the others to follow, he called out to Jimmy. "Go ahead and grab our gear and close the blast door. We're safe. It's dead."

Jimmy did as instructed, and with Cindy's help, he carried their gear until he rejoined Henry. Mary wasn't allowed to carry anything, not with her hand healing. No one wanted to risk her stitches popping, either, so she was on light duty for the time being.

Jimmy, looking down at the destroyed droid, couldn't resist kicking it. More wires hissed and sparked, and Jimmy unslung his shotgun, unsure it was really dead.

"Relax, Jimmy, there's nothing left that can hurt us." Henry picked up his gear from where Cindy had placed it near him, nodding thanks to her. "Let's go check out the matter transfer room. See if it's still working."

"And if it's not?" Cindy asked.

"Then we still have the pickup truck. We can go back and take it and go wherever we want."

The matter transfer room was a mess after the battle with the security droid, but many consoles were still active, lights flickering as the machines processed data.

Henry looked to Mary, who had become the defacto scientist for the matter transfer system after previously reading some of the manuals. "So, what do you think? Will it still work?"

Mary shook her head, unsure. "There's no way to know, really. Maybe the set up knows to reroute if some connections are severed. But then maybe not. We could use it and end up having our molecules scattered across the planet, never to materialize again."

Jimmy rolled his eyes. "Oh, that sounds wonderful. Let's try that."

"Very funny, Jimmy," Mary said. "Look, guys, there's no way to know unless we try it. That's all I can say on the matter. But given all the safeguards built into it, I highly doubt it'll work unless it knows it's safe to do so."

Henry considered Mary's words, then looked over at the dais, where it was harmlessly waiting in the corner of the room. Finally, he made up his mind. Walking over to the dais, he leaned down and grabbed his Anorak from where he'd dropped it two days earlier. He stepped up onto the dais, placed his gear beside him, and sat down with his back to the wall.

"I guess there's no time like the present to see if it's in working condition or not. You guys with me?"

By the way Henry asked and looked at them, each of the companions knew this wasn't an order. He was asking them to come with him voluntarily. If any of them had a problem with his decision, they could voice it now and possibly kibosh the whole thing.

It was Jimmy who spoke up first, while taking Cindy's hand in his. "What do you say, babe? Wanna go for a spin around the universe one more time?"

She smiled at his words. "Sure, why not? After all, we've faced zombies, crazy generals, cannibals and a rogue priest. Why not fly around the world by having our bodies dissected and then put back together. Given how our lives have gone, it seems perfectly plausible."

Still holding hands, the couple joined Henry on the dais, sitting down across from him. They made sure to pick up their winter jackets, also, and toss them onto the floor of the dais.

That left Mary, standing alone on the control room floor. All eyes were on her.

She stood silently for a full minute, the others just watching her, not pressuring her in the slightest. Finally, she flashed a smile of her own, reached out, and pressed the buttons that should, if it was working correctly, engage the matter transfer system. "Screw it, let's do this." She hopped up onto the dais, snagging her cold weather jacket off the floor where it had been dropped alongside Henry's, and sat next to Jimmy and Cindy, her pack beside her.

Henry said nothing to the three people before him. There was nothing more to say. He was pleased they were with him.

A full minute went by but nothing happened. Then another minute.

Henry was beginning to feel foolish. After all he'd done to get them back here, and the damn machine wouldn't work. He could see the same thought in each of the others' faces, though they were hesitant to voice it.

When another full minute passed and nothing happened, Henry was about to give up, and prepared to tell the others as much, when a familiar ozone smell tickled his nose.

Small flashes of lightning began flickering over their heads, and fog began to form on the dais as the matter transfer system began going though the first cycle of its operation.

"Oh fuck me," Jimmy said softly. "It's gonna work after all."

"Maybe it needed a few extra minutes to synchronize all the damaged circuits?" Mary surmised.

No one responded; there was no reason to.

Everyone closed their eyes, psyching themselves up for what would come next.

Before Henry did the same, he gazed at each of his friends one more time, without them looking back. He let a thin smile play over his lips as he watched them, eyes closed, waiting.

Jimmy was muttering something, a prayer perhaps. That was funny; Jimmy wasn't normally a religious person. He was gripping Cindy's hand in hers, his knuckles white. If he was squeezing her hand too hard, she didn't show her discomfort.

He looked at Mary next. Her hair hung across her face, partially obscuring it, her eyes squeezed closed so tightly it looked as if she was waiting to get slapped, and not knowing when it was going to come. She looked beautiful. Her bandaged hand was sitting on her lap, carefully placed so that she hoped it wouldn't be hurt when she lost consciousness.

He took in his new family before him, the people he loved the most in this ravaged world, and he smiled even wider. Being with these people was the best thing to ever happen to him, and though there had been some truly bad times, looking back at all the adventures he'd had, all the dangers they had overcome as a team, there had also been some extremely good times, and he wouldn't have changed anything, even if he had the chance.

He could feel the familiar sensation of the matter transfer system tugging on his mind as it cycled up to full power.

Knowing it was best to relax and close his eyes, he did so, pressing his back firmly against the chamber wall, his friends having done the same.

His last thought before he was swallowed into a dark void was of Sue, and that wherever she was, her soul at least, he hoped it was in a better place than where he was.